MARTIAN KNIGHTS™
& Other Tales

Stephen D. Sullivan

Walkabout Publishing • 2011

www.stephendsullivan.com

Walkabout Publishing
S.D. Studios
P.O. Box 151
Kansasville, WI 53139

Cover art and design by Stephen D. Sullivan.

Special thanks to Kifflie Scott & E. Readicker-Henderson

The Blue Kingdoms is a trademark of Stephen D. Sullivan & Jean Rabe.
Martian Knights, Frost Harrow, Crimson, and other fictional characters & settings herein are trademarks of Stephen D. Sullivan.

2nd Edition — February 2011

To Jean Rabe —
My dear friend and Blue Kingdoms collaborator, without whom I
might never have published a short story. Thanks for everything.

"Martian Knights" was originally published in shortened form in *Sol's Children* by DAW.

"Renaissance Fear" was originally published in *Renaissance Faire* by DAW.

"House of Mirrors" was originally published in *Carnival* by Lone Wolf Publications.

"Into the Fire" was originally published in *Circus* by Lone Wolf Publications.

Contents

Introduction — The Long and Short of It

I'm not a prolific writer of short stories.

Like most writers, I have more ideas than I know what to do with, but the ideas that pop into my head tend to stretch out toward book length. In fact, there was a time when I would have told you that I didn't know how to write short stories. Every time I tried to write one, it ended up being more of a brief novella than an actual short story. Novels? Those were easy for me. Short stories? Hard! Eventually, I figured out why.

As a novelist, outlining is the "trip planner" of my work; it's the map that lets me make a journey of many thousands of words and still have some control over where I end up. I outline extensively and then I stick to the outline. The strategy works very well for me—as nearly thirty published novels (and counting) will attest. But using that same strategy for short stories usually results in very *long* "short" stories—like "Martian Knights: Buried Secrets."

Martian Knights was the story that drove the point home for me. Carefully outlined, MK became so long that I actually had to trim a thousand words from it for publication. As written (and as it appears here, for the first time) it was just too long for the anthology I'd written it for. Oops.

I'd seen the same thing happen with my other attempts at short projects. *Luck o' the Irish* (also available from Walkabout Publishing) was supposed to run 12,000 words or so. It ended up being closer to 20,000.

Clearly I needed to adopt a different strategy if I was to avoid turning all my short stories into novels. At a meeting of the Alliterates (the famed writing group founded by J. Robert King), I hit on the secret: Don't plan, don't outline, just write.

Adopting that strategy not only allowed me to attempt my "Year of Fear" project (soon to be published as *A Season of Fear:*

100 Nights of Fright from Walkabout Publishing), but also helped me express my feelings in story form during the 9/11 tragedy.

After the attacks, I wrote as an outlet for my emotions about what had happened. If I'd had to plan those stories (presented here for the first time), I would have gone crazy.

Just write. Find an idea, find a place to start, and go. Don't worry about where you're headed or how long the trip will be. Maybe jot down a few lines—a turning point and the end, maybe. Or maybe don't.

Just sit down and start typing.

Later, there can be editing, but the trick at the start is to just go.

For me, that's the way to do shorts. It works well, it's less stressful, and the stories actually end up short—most of the time.

Sometimes I end up where I expected; sometimes I don't.

Sometimes it's fun, sometimes it's moving, sometimes it's scary.

Reading the stories in this collection, I hope you'll feel all those emotions and more.

Drop me a line and let me know.

And, remember, keep it short.

Enjoy.

—Steve Sullivan, July 2007

www.stephendsullivan.com

MARTIAN KNIGHTS
Buried Secrets

"Percival's bones! It looks like you've got half of the Hellas Planitia in here, Morris! I've never seen so much damn sand." Sigourney Saxon crinkled her nose and glowered at the old scrounger. She thrust one gloved hand into the turbine of the hover-car and pulled out a fistful of grainy red dust. She cast the grit away from the dune where she was working. A summer breeze caught the powder and swirled it into the thin Martian air.

Morris shrugged and rubbed the graying stubble on his chin. "I don't know how it coulda happened, Sy," he said.

"I know how it happened," Wolfgang McDonald said, the edges of his black mustache drooping with annoyance. "You forgot to put the dust shield on last night, Morris. Your sand filters have holes in them, too." Wolf adjusted his grip on the open-topped car, and the servos in his power armor whirred. With very little effort, he held the vehicle at chest level so Sigourney could crawl around and work underneath it. The car swayed slightly, and red sand poured out of the grille and settled around Wolf's feet. "Are you gonna be much longer, Sy? This armor's made for combat, not lifting."

Sy stuck a wrench into the car's innards. "Not too much longer, Hawkeye," she said, smiling playfully at her bond-male. "Besides, how much combat have you seen since the war ended? Lifting this piece of junk is easier than towing it back to Jacob's Well and then renting garage space—cheaper, too."

Wolf grunted at his bond-fem and nodded his agreement. "Shitty way to treat a fine piece of armor, though." He adjusted his grip on the car again.

"You'll get over it," Sy said. "And I'll lube your armor later if you strain a servo or something." She smiled at Wolf again, and this time he smiled back.

Morris tugged on the collar of the parka he was wearing over his battered P-suit. "You're the best mektek in the south colonies, Sy. I always said that."

"We'll see if you think so after you get my bill," she replied. "Fetch the blower out of my kit, would you? Wolf'll drop the car if I ask him to."

Morris found the tool and handed it to her. Sigourney began to blow sand out of the hover-car's turbines. "You got lube leaking in here, too," she said. "It's mixing with the sand and mucking everything all to hell. You're damn lucky you broke down near our squat."

The old scrounger dug the toe of his P-suit into the red dust. "You were on my way—to this job, I mean," he said. "This is a good car, though. Quality stuff. Shaftco—pre-war."

"It doesn't matter who made it if you leave the dust shield off at night," Sy said. She stopped working a moment and regarded the older man.

If the hover-car had seen better days, so had its owner. Four sols' growth covered Morris' round chin. His eyes were watery and bloodshot. He seemed taller and thinner than he had when last she'd seen him. Perhaps he wasn't spending enough time in habs with normal human gravity. His P-suit looked battered and worn, fraying at the joints. He wore a parka over the top of it, suggesting that the garment's enviro-system wasn't working properly. The suit's dome was conspicuously absent. Morris' weathered face stood exposed to the thin Martian atmosphere. The chilly afternoon breeze tousled his sparse gray hair. Sigourney wondered if her friend were "going native."

"Where's your helmet, Morris?" she asked, turning back to her work. She finished with the blower and stuck a wrench into hover-car's undercarriage again.

"Dome's cracked," Morris said.

"You can say that again," Wolf quipped.

Sy ignored him. "You'll get it fixed before you go out on this job, right?" she said to Morris.

"Um, I'm short on hydrocredits right now," the old scrounger said, forcing a smile onto his leathery face.

"Great," Wolf grumbled. "How's he gonna pay *us*, then? Morris, you are one sorry S.O.B."

"Hey," Morris said, flushing all the way to the top of his balding head, "I'll have plenty of creds soon. I'm working with Gared Jacob on this deal. I'll be able to pay off what I owe him, *plus* what I owe you, and still have enough left to flop for a while. Gared's got more money than God."

Wolf and Sigourney glanced at each other and frowned. "You hang out with Jacob long enough, Morris, and you'll get yourself killed," Sy said. She turned to her bond-mate. "You can let this old beater down now, Wolf. I've done all I can." She backed out from under the hover-car, shook the sand from her gloves, and propped her hands on her hips.

Her bond-male grunted slightly and set the car down onto the sand. The servos in his armor whirred and clicked as they resumed their normal duties. He was a handsome devil, Wolfgang McDonald: tall and dark-haired with a rugged face and a long black moustache. Sy took a moment to imagine the muscular frame inside the armor. The thought made her body tingle.

Feeling a bit warm, she adjusted the trim of her skinsuit and turned down the environmental controls at her belt. She brushed the dust off her legs, her arms, and her chest, and pulled her gloves tight once more. She leaned her hands against the fender of the car and arched her back, stretching. The breeze tugged gently at the ebony locks of her bobbed hair, and prickled some color into her smooth cheeks. She winked slyly at Wolf and he winked back at her.

"So, what is this job you're doing for Jacob?" Wolf asked Morris.

Morris ran one dusty glove through his thinning hair. "Jacob's got some deal going with Pig Town. Needs some old tek to trade with them," he said.

"Old tek?" Wolf asked.

"*Cybotek*," Sy said, frowning as she leaned into the car's open cockpit. "That explains the illegal chip sensor Morris has patched into his panel here."

Morris ran protectively around the car to where Sy was standing. "You got no business fiddling about in there!"

"Just making sure you don't end up stranded out in the dunes somewhere," Sy said, poking around the interior some more. "You can't afford another service call."

Wolf snorted. "He can't even afford this one."

Sy leaned over the top of the door and flipped switches. "Well, your MPS is working, but your scanner's blown. The main E-cells need replacing; I wouldn't trust them for a long trip. Your turbines aren't recharging them real well. You might want me to check the electricals next time you're in. Com system looks pretty messed up, too."

"The audio works," Morris said, frowning. "That's all I need."

"Morris," Wolf said sympathetically, "you need the scanner, too. What if a storm blows up while you're in the dunes? You won't have any warning."

The older man crossed his arms over his thin chest. "I've been a salvage engineer since before you were hab-broken. I think I know how to spot weather."

"What about this helmet, then?" Sy said, fishing the cracked dome out of the car's back seat. "Are you intending to pop oxi-pills for this whole trip?"

Morris dug the scuffed toe of his boot into the dust. "I've done it before. I'll be okay."

"You'll be lucky if you don't get oxygen poisoning," Wolf said. "You know the pills are only meant for short-term use. They're no replacement for a helmet, just like a parka is no sub for a working P-suit. You were in the cavalry; you know that."

"I don't see either of you wearin' helmets," Morris said.

Wolf scowled at him. "You put in an emergency service call. We got out here as quickly as we could. Oxi-pills are made for this kind of trip. The expedition you're planning, though. . . !"

The scrounger's face grew red again, but this time with anger. "Look," he said, "I called you buttinskis to do a job—not to run my life."

Sy gently rested her long fingers on the older man's shoulders. "We're just trying to look out for you, Morris," she said.

He shook Sy's hands off and climbed into the hover-car's cockpit without looking at her. "Well, don't," he snapped. "Send your bill to my flop and I'll pay it when I get back." He punched the starter and the car's turbines whirred to life. The battered vehicle lifted off of the red ocean of sand.

Sy and Wolf stepped away from the backwash as Morris skimmed away, his car quickly gaining altitude in the thin Martian air. The pair glanced apprehensively at each other.

Wolf shrugged. "Well," he said, "it's *his* funeral."

Sy frowned. "I hope not. I kinda like the old coot."

Together, they watched the car disappear into the dusty atmosphere. Then they boarded their open-topped mini-transport, parked on the next dune over, and headed for home.

*

Abel Morris scowled and cursed himself for being such a hothead. He punched the master course into the car's control panel and a tiny nav map came up on the windscreen. He pulled the hood of his parka up tight around his face and adjusted his wind goggles. The environment controls on his battered P-suit weren't up to snuff, and the extra parka helped stave off the chill. He wished the terraforming of Mars had been completed before

The Collapse on Earth. Even at the height of summer, Mars was still damn cold.

He flipped the scanner switch once, twice, three times, and then banged on the box with his fist. Sure enough, it was fried. Why did Sy always have to be right?

Morris cursed again and checked the heads-up map display. The old battlefield shone with a big green "X." Morris had marked the spot on the navicomp last night, just before forgetting to clip the front dust cover onto the car. The location he'd marked was in the middle of the desert; no settlements anywhere near it. The closest things to the site were an abandoned Martian archeological dig, and—many kliks beyond that—a decommissioned power plant. Probably there were some squatter settlements and maybe a stray native Martian or two around as well. Morris didn't expect either of those to hamper his search, though.

The battlefield had been picked over since the Cybowar, of course, picked over many times. But most of those searching were amateurs; Morris was a pro. Plus, he had an advantage that previous scavengers didn't—the illegal chip sensor he'd gotten from Gared Jacob. The sensor could spot most cybotek from a klik away. The old scrounger chuckled to himself: an illegal sensor to find illegal chips.

Cybotek was even more illegal than the sensor, of course, but what did Morris care? He was working for Gared Jacob, and Jacob made his own rules. Gared was descended from the founder of Jacob's Well and kept the settlement under his thumb just as easily as his forefathers had. If the cityboss wanted cybotek, he'd get it—whether Morris helped him or not. Morris figured he might as well cash in on the deal.

The battle of Podkayne's Dune had been one of the last gasps of the Cybowar. In it, the Colonial Power Cavalry had finally crushed the troops of the cybo General Toth. The cost in CPC lives and material had been great, though. The wreckage of machines, cybos, and humans littered the field until the sands reclaimed it. Even now, nine years later, people avoided the place. The native Martians said it was haunted, but Morris didn't believe in ghosts; he believed in hydrocredits.

He turned the wheel until the car's course angled straight for the 'X' on the map. Then he leaned back in the seat and admired the landscape. Rusty dunes stretched away in every direction, wind rippling their surfaces and filling the air with tawny dust. To the northwest, the distant crags of the Hellisponte Montes loomed out of the afternoon haze. Closer by, a pod of floaters drifted lazily through the air, the breeze tugging on their huge, baglike bodies. The enormous translucent creatures waved their long tendrils, siphoning their invisible food from the atmosphere.

Morris wondered what the creatures had fed upon before the terraformers brought the microspores to Mars. He shook his head. It didn't matter what they'd eaten before; now the floaters ate the small, oxygen-producing microbes. Maybe that was why Mars hadn't become more like Earth; the floaters were keeping the atmosphere in its present state.

He cursed himself for thinking about science puzzles instead of on the job at hand. The creatures were beautiful, though, with the pale, distant sun shining through their translucent purplish membranes. The afternoon light caught the edges of the floaters' bodies, and their outlines shone like silver. Despite himself, Morris watched the graceful, shimmering herd for the better part of an hour as his car angled toward Podkayne's Dune.

Morris had just begun to doze off when a noise disturbed his reverie: a howling whine, similar to the hover-car's turbine engines, but much louder. The old scrounger blinked twice, forcing his weary eyes to focus. He wiped the dust off his goggles with the back of his gloved hand.

Ahead of him loomed a monstrous twister, cutting through the dunes like the finger of Ares himself. Dust billowed up around the monstrous reddish cyclone, blotting out the landscape below. The force of the winds sucked the placid floaters into the funnel of the storm. The creatures collapsed into umbrella-like shapes to ride out the tempest; they'd survive, little the worse for wear. Morris knew he wouldn't be that lucky.

Cursing his broken scanner, he twisted the steering column and banked away from the huge tornado. Out the corner of his eye, he saw the buried shapes of the ancient Martian town less than a klik away. He aimed the nose of the hover-car for that small pile of rubble, knowing he'd never make it. The twister reached out one dusty arm and swept Morris and his car up into the whirlwind.

The roaring in his ears reminded the aging scrounger of waking up in a turbomill after a three day bender. The wind threatened to rip him out of his seat, despite his restraining belts. Morris clutched the car's steering column with all his might, trying to maintain some control. It was hopeless.

The air around him swirled, thick with rusty sand and ochre dust. Morris clamped his mouth tight in an effort to keep the biting grains from smothering him. He wished he'd been wearing his cracked helmet.

A shudder ran though him as something large hit the hover-car. Morris caught a glimpse of flailing tentacles and a huge, bulbous body. A floater; he'd hit a floater. The engines suddenly died, and the car nosed down into the maelstrom. Morris pulled on the steering column to no avail. The wind ripped a terrified scream from his parched and blasted lips.

The hover-car spun in a dizzying circle, the wind tossing it like a child's toy. The tornado buffeted Morris, bruising his body and straining nearly all his muscles. Something bumped, and then thumped, and then the car spun in and the autocushions deployed. Morris' world went black.

*

Morris awoke coughing sand from his lungs. He leaned over the side of the hover-car and threw up. The deflated autocushions covered his lap like a giant plastic balloon with all the air run out. He noticed a smear of red on one, reached up to his weathered scalp, and quickly discovered the source of the blood. It was a nasty scratch, but not too deep.

"You're one lucky S.O.B." Morris said aloud to himself. He threw the switch to deflate the autocushions, and the soiled bags crept slowly back into their deployment hatches, jamming about three-quarters of the way in. Morris cursed. He reached around, undid his restraining belts, and hopped out of the car.

The nose of the hover-car was almost completely buried in sand and rubble. Dust from the storm's passing still saturated the air around Morris and the stranded vehicle. The old scrounger coughed and tried vainly to wave the grit away from his face. Peering into the gloom, Morris saw that he'd not only crashed into a sand dune, he'd also hit a wall of the half-buried Martian ruins.

A big block of stone sat squarely on the car's hood, making a nice dent in the battered steel. Even without the rock, the car didn't look so good. The sleek metal of the hover-car's nose was crumpled like an accordion. At the back, one of the turbofans hung by a few scarred wires.

Morris swore again. No way he'd be driving away from this. Images of credits flying out of his moneybelt filled his head. He walked around the half-buried car and kicked the side panels. Then he hopped back in and pulled out the radiophone. He brushed the dust off the handset and punched up Sigourney Saxon's' number.

Her machine answered, and Morris left a message—hoping that she and Wolf would extend his credit far enough to tow him back to Jacob's Well. Images of winged credits flying away to never-never-land danced through his groggy brain again. Then something else caught his attention: a light blinking near his control panel.

The chip sensor!

The chip sensor was registering a cybochip somewhere nearby. Morris stood up, tangling his legs in the half-retracted autocushions. His eyes strained, peering into the dusty darkness. Around him, the Martian ruins rose like tombstones in the twilight. Right in front of the car, between two of the ancient buildings, he noticed a gap in one of the monolithic Martian walls.

His eyes strayed from the hole in the wall to the rock resting on the car's hood. It looked about the right size and shape. He pulled the chip sensor from its harness and swept the area. Sure enough, the signal emanated most strongly from the hole. He dropped the sensor and let it dangle on its long, springy cord. He'd have to leave it behind; it needed the car's E-cells to power it anyway.

Sweat beaded on Morris' dusty forehead. He untangled his legs and stepped into the sand once more, his head swirling with possibilities. This buried Martian town had been well-picked over before the Cybowar—stripped of anything valuable the natives had left behind. He doubted that many people had visited the ruins since the war ended. Why come here? Only a few stray colonists, like Wolf McDonald, had any interest in archaeology. And there were many more-impressive Martian sites to study.

No. Probably no one ever visited these ruins anymore. Something hidden here after the war might still remain undiscovered. Morris licked his rough, parched lips. Hardly daring to hope, he walked forward. He pulled the glowlight from the belt of his battered P-suit and shone it into the hole. The pale green radiance illuminated a wide chamber on the other side of the broken wall.

Cautiously, Morris stepped through the opening. The room beyond the hole was as wide as three heavy hover-tanks and twice that deep. A dusting of red sand covered the stone-paved floor.

There was a doorway on the far side of the chamber, but something shiny and black blocked his view. The realization of the obstruction's identity sent his heart racing.

Two light cybotanks, their spidery legs splayed around them as if they might strike at any moment, stood blocking the far passage. Sweat broke out on Morris' balding pate. He stood stock still, fear gripping his aching muscles. Only after several long minutes did he realize that the tanks were dead—out of energy. Perhaps their organic brains had perished long ago. Why had they come here, though? And why had they sealed themselves within this rocky tomb?

Suddenly, a strong desire to see what lay beyond the cybotanks welled up in Morris' breast. He ran across the room, almost stumbling on the sand-strewn flagstones. Carefully, he picked his way around the tanks' sharp spines and through the opening beyond. Just past the threshold of the ancient corridor, lay a body.

Morris held his breath and his eyes went wide. He'd never seen a cybo like this before. It was dead, there could be no doubt about that. From its chest down, it was mostly a skeleton. But the right side of the body from the waist up—the arms, the spinal cord, nearly all of the head—plus the clawed feet, were entirely mechanical.

The old scrounger frowned and let out a long whistle. Most cybos had just a few body parts replaced; legs, perhaps for speed, or arms for combat, or a cybo implant in the head to enhance neurological functions. This thing seemed to be nearly half machine. The thought of it made Morris shudder, but the workmanship was exquisite: vintage Shaftco, probably manufactured just before the company's destruction at the end of the war.

A vision came to Morris, the image of hydrocredits pouring down on his head in a nearly endless stream. These cybos were a treasure almost beyond price! With them, he could pay off all his debts to Gared Jacob and still have enough left to live like a prince for the rest of his life.

The only trick was figuring out how to get his prizes back to Jacob's Well. For a moment, he regretted having called Wolf and Sy. Now he'd have to think of a way to keep the discovery from them. But it would be dark soon, and that might help.

He could pull the smaller cybo out of the ruins and hide it in the trunk of his car. He'd have to conceal the cybotanks where they were. Using the tarp from his trunk, he could block off the hole in the wall. If he covered the tarp with sand and a few rocks for camouflage, Sy and Wolf *might* miss the hole in the darkness. Yes. It could work.

Morris smiled, pulled back the hood of his parka, and wiped the sweat from his brow. He stepped up to the cybo's body and kicked the dusty bones away from the machineworks. Then he knelt down and picked up the gleaming metal skeleton. Long, wire-like strands of servos connected the thing's spine to its clawed "boots." That meant he could carry it all in one trip.

He put one of the cold arms over his shoulder and hefted the weight of the machine onto his back. It dangled down behind him like a cape, its feet scraping against the stone floor. "Just like carrying wounded during the war," Morris muttered.

The thing jangled like coins as he walked. Visions of swimming pools and showers filled the scrounger's mind. And women—bevies of beautiful women, lounging on the patio by his pool. And shade palms blocking out the distant sun.

Lost in his reverie, Morris hardly noticed the clacking of the metal as he pushed past the dead tanks with his precious burden. He never felt the spinal cord of the dead cybo brushing up against his P-suit's belt power pack.

Suddenly, a red haze of pain flooded the old scrounger's senses. Morris gasped and staggered forward, falling to his knees—almost losing his grip on his burden. Why did his back hurt so? Why was it hard to think?

He glanced over his shoulder into the glaring green eyes of the cybo. The eyes blinked away the dust covering them. Morris tried to scream, but the blood bubbling out of his mouth smothered the cry.

*

The morning sunlight reflected through the high windows and caught the water as it fell, turning the precious liquid the color of gold.

Artificial rain cascaded down from the arched ceiling and over Sigourney Saxon's smooth, well-muscled body. The warmth and wetness made her skin tingle. She scrubbed herself carefully, lingering over every wonderful sensation, and then washed her hair.

The smell of soap and shampoo thrilled her. And the water . . . the fresh, mineral tang of the liquid! It was almost too much to bear. She let the spray run into her mouth, over her teeth and tongue, and then squirted the water out between her lips.

Warm light filtered through the fronds of the plants growing at the chamber's edges and dappled the rainroom in shades of living green. Everything seemed so wonderful in this place, so alive. How thrilling this opulent liquid; how fleeting the luxurious sensations. Sy wanted to stay here forever.

"Sy . . . ."

Far away, someone called her name, but she couldn't place the voice.

"Sy, wake up."

Wolf. The voice belonged to Wolfgang McDonald. Was he hiding in the foliage? Sy smiled at the thought.

With a soft sigh, she opened her eyes.

The gentle thrum of the turbine generators filled the caravan. The hiss of the recyclers as they turned waste back into potable water and dry fertilizer tickled her ears.

"I was dreaming," she said sleepily.

"What about?" Wolf asked.

"Rain."

Standing next to their air mattress, he sighed.

Sigourney Saxon sighed as well. No rain. Never any rain here. All rain on Mars was an illusion. Maybe someday—if the terraforming was ever complete—she'd hear a real rain shower, but not now. Only the rich could afford rain, and then only in their private habs. How foolish: Martian colonists simulating the ecosystem of a dead, burnt-out Earth. How foolish of her to desire such a thing. Sy wondered if, somewhere deep within their hidden underground caverns, the native Martians had rain.

"Do you miss the life you had before the war?" he asked. "Do you regret giving up the wealth and power to come live with an old cavalryman?"

She shook her head. "Never," she said. "I was just a girl then. Now I'm a woman." She took a deep breath of the filtered air. "Sometimes, though, I wish for rain."

He nodded, and sat down on the bed beside her.

"What about you?" she asked. "Do you miss the cavalry—the camaraderie, the excitement of battle?"

"The cramped quarters, the smell of machine lube, the sound of gunfire. . . ?" he added with a laugh.

She smiled, still clinging to the last pleasant remnants of sleep. "You've got all those things here, too," she noted.

"But I've got a better roommate." He leaned down and kissed her. She kissed back. After a while, they parted.

"You're enough excitement for any old soldier," he said.

She smiled and sat up. "Why'd you wake me? I thought this was a rest day."

"Our autorob took a call from Morris last evening," Wolf said. "He's crashed out in the old ruins, near Podkayne's Dune."

Sy rubbed the sleep from her eyes. "Shit. What time is it? Is Morris okay?"

"He sounded fine on the recording," he said.

"Shit. We shouldn't have had the machine on. We should have gone out when he called."

Wolf shook his head and smiled sympathetically at her. "With the storm, we couldn't have gone out last night anyway. Besides, even Morris can't expect two service calls in one day."

Sy frowned slightly and nodded. She flexed her muscles and stretched. Her left arm tingled and she took a moment to massage her shoulder.

"Arm bothering you?" he asked.

"I just slept on it funny," she said.

He nodded.

She let out a long breath. "Well," she said, "we warned Morris. I'm not going to punish myself for taking a little R&R after bailing him out yesterday. I hope he's learned his lesson, though."

Wolf smiled. "I doubt it," he said. "Morris always has some excuse when he cocks up. 'My shoddy maintenance record had nothing to do with it!' he'll probably say."

Sigourney stood and pulled on the top of her skinsuit. "Well, let's get dressed and rescue his sorry ass. You fire up the mini; I'll take the sled. Morris and I can ride back together while you tow that heap he calls a hover-car. Assuming he needs a tow."

"After what I saw of his car yesterday, I wouldn't doubt it," Wolf said. "But I'll pack your toolbox, just in case it's something *small* this time."

*

Sigourney Saxon throttled back and skimmed the hover-sled low over the sand, angling for the half-buried Martian ruins. Wolfgang McDonald swooped in behind her, showing off the driving skills that had done him proud during his stint in the Colonial Power Cavalry. Sy smiled, despite her worries about Morris. Seeing Wolf at work always thrilled her. He spent too much of his time assisting her on repair missions; riding free over the dunes in his power armor was where he really belonged. No matter what he said, he was still a soldier at heart.

She blew him a kiss over the vox in her helmet. Wolf chuckled in return. "Getting lonely out there, darlin'?" his warm voice asked. "Not cold in that skinsuit, are you?"

"Rather the opposite," she said, knowing he couldn't see her smile. "Everything okay in your armor?"

"I think I'm ready for some heavy lifting," Wolf replied. "Knowing Morris, he'll probably need it."

"Let's hope not. See any sign of him?"

"Nope. His emergency transponder's gone dead, too."

"That's odd."

"Yeah," Wolf said. "But the message he sent had an MPS reading attached. He should be just behind that native building ahead."

"Roger," Sy replied, adjusting her heading appropriately.

"Don't call me 'Roger,'" Wolf jibed. "I feel like you're talking to another man."

Sigourney chuckled and coasted to a stop on the ridge of a dune near the MPS coordinates. Wolf brought the mini down to rest gently beside her. He checked the sensor readout in his suit. "Looks like he might be in that building," Wolf said, pointing.

Sy nodded and started to hike down the dune toward the ruined Martian plaza. As she took the first step, though, a huge, flabby tentacle rose up to meet her.

The lithe mechanic sprang to one side, hit the sand in a roll, and landed in a crouch, her left hand instinctively reaching for the lectro-blade strapped inside her boot. Wolf's autogun leapt into his hand, his reflexes automatically tracking the menace.

"Hold it!" Sy said. "It's just a grounded floater—one of the filter feeders. Not carnivorous. No danger to us."

Wolf's brown eyes studied the creature for a moment. "What's it doing here?" he asked.

Sy skidded down the dune beside the huge, flabby beast. "It's wounded," she said. "Looks like a hover-car hit it."

"Morris," said Wolf.

"Probably," she replied. "I think I see his beater up ahead. C' mon. Nothing we can do for the floater. It'll either get airborne again or become food for something else." She headed for the ruins.

"Too bad," said Wolf, admiring the floater's translucent body. "Let's hope that Morris fared better." He shambled down the hill behind her, leaving the huge wounded animal flapping on the side of the dune. The pair-bonded couple soon found their friend's car at the edge of the ruins.

Inside her domed helmet, Sy frowned. "What the hell happened here?" she said, her gray eyes flashing over the wreckage of the hover-car.

"No floater did this, that's for sure," Wolf added.

Sy nodded, suppressing a shiver that ran up her spine. She leaned over the side of the car and inspected the damage. "Last night's storm didn't do this either," she said. "The car's been stripped. The E-cells are gone, along with most of the electronic equipment. That explains why his emergency transponder's not working."

"Why would Morris strip his own car?" Wolf asked. Then he paused a moment, nodded grimly, and said, "Oh. He probably didn't."

"That's what worries me," Sy said. "Any reports of bandits or dune pirates in this area?"

Wolf punched up a display inside his helmet. "Nothing within twenty-five kliks for the last thirty Sols or more," he said.

Sy shrugged. "That doesn't rule them out, of course," she said, but . . . what's this?" She turned from the car toward the broken wall nearby.

"Looks like a hole in the wall," Wolf said, deadpan.

She shot him a playful scowl through her dome's faceplate, and the two of them walked toward the ragged opening. "Maybe Morris took shelter inside," she said.

"Let's hope," Wolf answered, falling into step behind her. They ducked through the hole and into the broad stone chamber beyond.

Sigourney gasped and clenched her teeth tight to fight a wave of nausea. "I think we found Morris," she said.

"What's left of him," Wolf agreed.

Blood stained the rough flagstones of the wide room, leading in a gory trail from the middle of the chamber to near the opening where they stood. Strewn along the way was an assortment of body parts: fingers, toes, two arms, and part of the old scrounger's head.

"'Cudas, you think? Or a dune shrike?" Wolf asked.

Sy shook her head. "'Cudas wouldn't leave so much behind. Neither would a shrike. Besides, that big floater outside hasn't been eaten. Martian animals would never pass up a floater for stringy meat like Morris."

"What then?"

Sy shook her head. "I don't know. What worries me, though, is . . . Where's the *rest* of him?"

Wolfgang and Sigourney glanced warily each other. "Check the far side of the chamber," she said. "I'm going to look out near the speeder, in case we missed something."

He nodded. "Roger."

"Roger dodger," she countered and then stepped outside. When she returned to the big room, Wolf met her by the opening.

"I didn't find anything," he said. "There's a passage at the far end, but it's collapsed just a couple of feet beyond the entrance. Some scratches on the stone floor, but that's it. The only tracks I got on IR belonged to Morris. The strange thing is, they look like they leave the building."

"I think Morris *did* leave the building," Sy said. "At least, *part* of him did."

26

"What do you mean?" Wolf asked, worry playing across his handsome face.

"I found some tracks by the car," she said. "I didn't notice them before, because it never occurred to me to look. I'm guessing that what made those tracks is probably the same spidery limbs that made the scratches you saw."

Wolf blanched. "Shit! Not. . . ."

Sy nodded. "Cybos."

"Percival's bones," Wolf whispered. "I thought we'd gotten them all in the war."

Sigourney laughed ironically. "You know better than that, Wolf—even if that's what Gared Jacob and the other citybosses want everyone to think. There are still a few dangerous ones lurking around. Enough to kill old Morris, I guess."

"Podkayne's Dune isn't far from here," Wolf said. "It was one of the last Cybowar battlefields. Maybe that's where cityboss Jacob was sending Morris to scrounge. If you want cybo parts, that'd be a good place to start."

"Makes sense," she replied. "With that illegal chip sensor Gared Jacob gave him, Morris might have found some cybo pieces that others missed."

"Pieces, yes. But—after all these years—how could he have found something that murdered him?"

"We won't know that until we find his killer," Sy said. "C' mon. I spotted the chip sensor unit hanging by its cord in Morris' car. The thing that dusted Morris must not have known what it was. We can hook the unit into the mini and find the bastard that did this."

Wolf nodded. "Roger."

"And Wolf. . ."

"Yeah?"

"We better break out the heavy weapons."

*

Sigourney's sled and Wolf's mini-transport rose into the dusty air. The dunes and the ruined Martian town rapidly fell away below them. Out of the corner of her eye, Sy spotted a pack of sandcudas circling the grounded floater. She shook her head; no time to worry about wounded animals. A living cybo warrior meant big trouble for every colonist on Mars.

It hadn't taken her long to adapt Morris' sensor chip into the mini-transport's console; she'd even beefed up the range a bit. They'd have to follow the cybo's tracks as best they could until they got within the scanner's range, though. Fortunately, the sand storm that grounded them last night would have kept the cybo in the ruins as well. It was on foot and couldn't have that much of a lead on them.

The afternoon sun arced high in the pale pinkish-blue sky. In the distance, a dust devil danced lightly across the dunes. A pod of jellyfish-like floaters drifted near the storm's edges, sucking in the nutrients the whirlwind stirred up. "Check the dust funnel," Sy said into her vox.

"I see it," Wolf replied. "No indication it'll become a full twister."

"Thank God. This is going to be tricky enough without any weather."

"Don't worry," Wolf said, "I've followed colder trails in my day. Don't know how I missed the tracks in the first place."

"You're no cybo; you had other things on your mind," Sy answered. "So did I."

"What do you think, then—a light cybotank?"

Sy pulled her hover-sled into the mini's slipstream to conserve power. "I figure," she said. "We'll do a quick recon and then, if we're right, call Gared Jacob. His security team can mop up this mess. He and the city can afford the cleaning bill."

"Think Gared will go for it?"

She shrugged, knowing Wolf would see her in the mini's rearview scanner. "He wanted cybotek," she said. "Looks like he's got it—in spades."

"I'm not too keen on Jacob getting his hands on whatever this thing turns out to be," Wolf said.

"Me, neither," she replied. "But I figure he'll have to pound it to hell to kill it. Probably won't be able to salvage much—if anything—after it's dead."

In the open cockpit of the mini, Wolf nodded. "Hang on," he said. "The chip sensor's picking up something. Okay, I've got a lock. Stay close, we're going in." He kicked the throttle of the mini and it shot forward; she sped after him.

Minutes later, they spotted a small black dot atop a far dune. "Can your helmet binocs make that out?" Sy called over the vox.

"Just a mass of metal legs from here, I . . . wait a minute . . . Shit! I think there's more than one."

Sy cursed. "That'd make sense; walking in each other's tracks is standard cybo procedure."

"Makes it worse for us, though," Wolf said.

"Not if it's Gared Jacob's problem," she replied. "We'll get close enough to verify the formation, then call in the big boy's private army."

"Roger."

"Don't call me Roger," she said, smiling. "It makes me feel unlady-like."

"Roger dodger," he replied.

As they approached the small shapes, Sy pulled her sled alongside the mini-transport, to get a better look at the creatures they were pursuing. Ahead of them, two light cybotanks crawled purposefully over the dunes, their spidery metal legs churning up the ochre dust.

"Where do you think they're headed?" Wolf asked.

"Probably carrying out whatever mission they had before they deactivated," Sy said. She did some quick calculations in her head. "Isn't the old power plant in this direction?"

"Yeah," Wolf replied. "But it was decommissioned ages ago."

"But these cybos don't know that," she said. "They're still fighting the battle of Podkayne's Dune. Shit! Look out!"

One of the cybotanks suddenly swung its main gun in their direction and fired. The energy pulse seared the thin atmosphere between the two vehicles as Sy and Wolf peeled off in opposite directions. As they maneuvered, the air filled with small arms fire.

"What the hell is this?" Wolf called. "We should be out of their tracking range."

"Apparently not," Sy called back. "Keep your head down and let's get out of here." As she said it, though, a blast from the second tank's gun seared the rear turbine on her sled. "Shit! I'm hit!"

"How bad?" Worry tinged Wolf's voice.

"Just the car's turbine," she replied. "But I can't stay airborne."

"I'll cover you and follow you down," Wolf said. He pulled out his autogun and fired it over the mini's windscreen at the cybos. The dunes near the tanks erupted into a cloud of dust.

Sigourney twisted the controls of the sled, trying to keep its flight path steady. The ground rushed up to meet her and the nose of the sled buried itself in the rough sand. The hover-sled's autocushions deployed, protecting Sy from most of the impact.

She unbuckled her harness and pulled herself off the damaged vehicle, quickly taking cover behind a larger dune. Moments later, Wolf landed beside her. "Are you okay?" he called.

"I've been better," she said, brushing the dust from her skinsuit. "The sled's been better, too. Are they coming for us?"

Wolf checked the scanner in his helmet. "No, thank God. They're still on their mission to frag the power plant. I put out some decoy smoke before landing; they probably think we're fragged."

"Either that or they think we're no threat to them," she said.

"If they think that, they're dead wrong," Wolf replied. A grim smile played across his face.

"Don't be so sure," Sy said. "I spotted something as I was going down . . . One of those tanks has a rider."

"What?"

"Yeah," she continued, "I saw him melded into the thing's cockpit. I think it was General Toth."

"Toth? Are you sure?"

"I'm pretty familiar with Shaftco and their more infamous creations," she said.

He nodded. "But isn't Toth dead? I thought he'd been killed at Podkayne's Dune."

"Some cybos are harder to kill than others," Sy replied, frowning. "I heard a rumor that Toth had his human memories burned into cybochips. If that's true, he—or some element of him—might have survived the death of his human parts during the war."

"Shit. And he's used Morris for raw materials to rebuild himself."

Sigourney nodded grimly. "Looks that way. Morris' body and the E-cells and parts from his hover-car."

"Well, like you said earlier, this is Jacob's problem now. I'll get him on the box." He went back to the mini and worked the radiophone for a few minutes before returning.

"Jacob's not buying it," Wolf said, turning up his palms in disbelief.

"You told him they'd killed Morris? You told him they're heading for the old power plant?"

Wolf nodded. "I told him, or rather, *her*. Kali White, his security chief, intercepted the call. She wouldn't let me speak to Jacob directly."

"Did you mention that Toth will go looking for fresh targets when he finds out the power plant is dead? Did you tell her that he'll probably come for Jacob's Well next? It's the closest place for replacement parts—and fresh meat."

"I mentioned all that. Kali thinks this is some kind of stunt—a trick to get her to expend valuable resources. Or maybe some way for us—or Morris—to get a free ride back to town. That's what she said, anyway."

"The arrogant bitch," Sy grumbled. "I'd spit if I didn't have this dome on."

Wolf laughed. "So, what do we do? Tow the sled back for repairs and let Jacob stew in his own juices when the cybos come calling?"

A momentary grin tugged at the corners of Sy's mouth, then turned into a frown. "Shit. We can't do that, no matter how much I'd like to. No telling what trouble Toth could cause if we don't stop him. I wouldn't mind him killing White and Jacob, but a lot of innocent people will get hurt with Toth on the loose."

"I guess we'll just have to kick his metal ass, then," Wolf said. "Just like my old days in the Colonial Power Cavalry. We'll need a plan, though. I've only got a half-dozen or so guns in the mini. Those tanks will cut us into fillets if we face them out in the open."

"I've got an idea," Sy said. "Let's see if any of my weapons got damaged in the crash. We'll have to come back for the sled later. Otherwise, Toth'll beat us to our objective."

"And our objective is. . . ?"

Sy smiled. "The old power station."

*

The wreckage of the old power station loomed out of the red sand like broken teeth. Most of the workings and metal had been taken for salvage long ago, but the hulking Marscrete walls still remained—bleached pale by the passage of time.

Sigourney Saxon sat atop one of the old turbomill generator towers and scanned the horizon. A fully-loaded autogun rested on the roof at her side, and she'd powered up the wrist and ankle units that turned her skinsuit into custom, ultralite power armor. The hum of the armor made her skin tingle. She called up her helmet's binocs and trained them on a dust cloud to the northwest.

"Wolf," she said into her vox, "I see them. Are you all set up?"

"Yeah. They're registering on my scanner, too."

"We'd better fire a few volleys at them before they get too close," Sy said. "Make them think that this is still a working installation."

"Roger dodger," Wolf said. "I'll move to the front of the complex and take some potshots, just to keep them interested."

Sy watched as her bond-mate moved across the dunes between her and the enemy. With his power armor active, he bounded lightly across the red sand like a huge Martian hopper. Wolf positioned himself behind a large drift hill and scrambled up the side. He used the periscope on his armor to target the cybos and then popped over the top of the hill and fired.

The slugs screamed across the dunes, impacting the metal shells of the cybo machines but doing little damage. Wolf ducked down and moved to another hillock as the cybos returned fire.

"That's got them going," he said over the vox.

"So long as they don't get you," Sy said.

"Darlin', I've been at this a lot longer than you have," Wolf said.

"Sorry, Hawkeye," she replied. "I'll shut up and let you do your job."

"Don't worry," he said. "I'll lure them into our ambush just as pretty as you please." He popped up over another dune and fired again, retreating before the sand exploded with deadly cybo counterfire.

"They're buying it," Sy said. "The tanks are splitting up to blanket your side of the complex in a crossfire. Toth's dismounted and is coming in on his own. Make sure he doesn't catch you napping; it looks like he's armed to the teeth."

"Those would be Morris' teeth," Wolf's voice said over the vox.

Sy's mouth drew into a thin line. "Yeah."

The dune where Wolf had crouched shattered under the cybos' next volley, but he had already moved on. The cybotanks fanned out on either side of him, trying to pin Wolf down. Toth ignored the former cavalryman, striding toward the complex on his half-human legs, deadly purpose shining in his metallic green eyes.

Wolf ducked under the fire of the advancing machines. "Think they've figured out there's only one of me yet?" he asked over the vox.

"I doubt it," she said. "They're firing slugs, saving the plasma cannons for taking out the complex's power generators."

"If they're relying on the E-cells from Morris' hover-car to power those cannons, they may not have much energy," Wolf said.

"Let's hope," she replied. "I don't know how long we could stand up under that kind of barrage."

Suddenly, Toth spotted Wolf moving through the dunes. At the cybo general's silent command, the machines swiveled their guns toward Sy's bond-mate. Sigourney felt, more than heard, the tanks' main guns charging for a lethal blast.

"Wolf, they've seen you!" she yelled. "Get out of there!" As she spoke, she punched a button on her wristband. At her signal, two pre-placed gunchers swung on their tripods and fired grenades at the cybotanks.

An involuntary cheer broke from Sigourney's lips as the explosives hit home. The tanks rocked and reeled for a moment, and Wolf leapt out of their target lock. The cybos shook off the effects of the grenades and began to track the former power soldier once more.

"Thanks, darlin'," Wolf called to Sy. Two servo-assisted leaps took him behind the battered Marscrete walls of the power complex. White-hot tracers cut a swath through the late afternoon air as Toth fired at Wolf. Wolf dodged the last few slugs and then sprinted into the complex, moving toward a defensible position they'd scouted earlier.

As Toth fired at Wolf, Sy's remotes ripped another volley at the cybotanks. The tanks sputtered and hissed. Small pieces of metal flew off their armored carapaces, but they still didn't fall. Acting as one, they trained their guns on Sy's automated emplacements and blasted the gunchers to smithereens.

"Ouch," Sy said. "That's a few hydrocredits up in smoke."

Wolf's confident voice came over the vox, "Better a few guns than you and me. We can always make more money."

"Personally," she replied, "I intend to bill Gared Jacob for every round we use and every piece of ordnance that gets fragged."

Wolf laughed, but then stopped suddenly. "Hold on," he said. "Those tanks are entering the complex. Gotta run. Take care of Toth for me, will you?"

"Roger, Hawkeye," Sy said. She watched as Wolf bounded through the complex, heading to intercept the nearest cybo. With luck, he could draw it into the trap they'd planned. Her heart fluttered for a moment at the thought of her bond-male fighting the hellish monster alone. Then she steeled herself for the job at hand. Raising her autogun, she clicked it into guncher mode and trained it on Toth as he approached the power plant's main entrance.

The binocs in her helmet gave her a good view of the cybo general's half-human face. Her jaw tightened as she recognized the stubble of Morris' beard peeking out between the general's metal "enhancements."

She only hesitated a moment, but it was enough. Toth spotted the laser sight on her gun, and he leapt to one side just as she squeezed the trigger. Her grenade exploded five meters from Toth as he landed. Dust and rocks showered down on the cybo, but Sy knew she hadn't come close to killing him. She cursed and fired again.

Toth dived out of the way once more, sheltering behind a crumbling wall. A small cannon sprouted from his arm when he reappeared. He fired a plasma blast toward Sigourney's position.

The burst hit Sy's tower and shattered the weathered Marscrete. The steel reinforcements within the structure groaned and then bent as the tower toppled toward the ground. Sy let go of her autogun and leapt.

Her fingers found purchase on the rough surface of the next tower over. Her body hit hard, and the air rushed out of her lungs. The strap holding the autogun around her shoulders snapped and the gun clattered to the rubble-strewn ground below. She clung to the wall for a moment, like a human fly, and caught her breath.

"Sy! Are you all right?" Wolf's voice blared over the vox.

"Too busy to talk right now," she said. As she spoke, Toth shattered her new perch with another plasma round. She jumped again, this time angling for an old catwalk support. The ultralite's servos kicked in, propelling her across the vast space easily. The catwalk itself was gone, salvaged long ago, but she landed lightly atop the pylon, grabbed hold, and quickly shimmied toward the ground.

Toth bellowed with rage.

"You run like a Cavalry trooper, little bug!" he called in a voice eerily like Morris'.

As she hit the sand, Sy pressed the speaker button on her skinsuit. "And you fight like a rusty machine!" she called back.

Wolf's voice came over the vox. "Sy, don't talk to him; kill him!"

"What do you think I'm *trying* to do?" she snapped back. "Just keep those tanks off my ass!"

"Roger. Will do. Love you."

"Love you, too. Now shut up, so I can concentrate." Sweat beaded on her forehead and ran down to her lips. She pulled the small stinger from her hip and switched off the safety. With her other hand, she found the sole grenade hanging at her belt. She darted behind the wall and checked her helmet's tactical display.

Toth carefully picked his way through the decommissioned power plant; only a half-dozen pylons and a few meters of Marscrete separated him from her. She checked his coordinates one last time, stepped out, and lobbed a grenade in Toth's direction.

The general fired at Sigourney as she appeared. His tracers hummed past her, the polarity of her armor turning grazing shots into near misses. Not everything missed, though. A blast caught her left shoulder, burning in one side and out the other. Sy gasped with pain. Her grenade exploded a few meters short of the general.

Too late, Toth realized her plan. The detonation ripped through the pylons in front of him, sending them toppling onto the surprised general. Toth's automated weaponry swung up, firing a deadly barrage at the tons of Marscrete falling toward him.

Precious oxygen hissed out of Sy's ruptured skinsuit armor. She knew she could survive in the thin Martian air for a time, but there was no way she'd be able to fight without good air. Popping her helmet open, she pulled an oxi-pill from her wrist medi-kit and dropped it into her mouth. Ignoring the pain in her arm, she aimed her stinger to where she'd last seen Toth.

The displays in her helmet told her he was still there, amid the smoke and rubble. She couldn't tell whether he was alive. A moment later, though, the cybo warrior charged out of the dust cloud toward her.

Toth's cybo armor was battered, and many of his weapons had been destroyed. The sharp spines on his carapace still made him a formidable opponent, though. Sy knew he could crush her easily with his metal arms if he grabbed hold of her. "Bitch!" he rasped. "You'll die for that."

Sy fired a full stinger burst into the human part of Toth's face, hoping the drugged needles would slow him down. "You were going to kill me, anyway," she replied, leaping aside as he came at

37

her. The servos in her suit and Mars' low gravity allowed her to clear twenty meters with the jump.

Toth spun toward her and followed; the drug didn't seem to faze him at all. Sy was lucky, though; even with Toth's cybo enhancements, Morris' old P-suit was no match for her ultralite armor. Darting between the columns of the crumbling power plant, she easily kept ahead of her foe.

"Out of ammo so soon, soldier-borg?" she called back. "I'd have thought the great General Toth would be better equipped."

"No need to waste energy on meat like you," he replied, leaping after her. "I can kill you just as easily with my own hands!" He caromed off a wall unexpectedly and bounded right into Sy's path.

Toth thrust a spiny arm at Sy's head, but she ducked under the blow. She hammered her right fist into his human gut, putting all her strength behind the punch. She felt something pop within Abel Morris' old flesh.

The cybo spun through the dusty air and landed hard against a broken wall. A gun emerged from the general's metal forearm, and he fired at her. She dodged the first few shots, but the last got through her suit's deflection field and traced a long scrape down her right thigh.

Blood leaked from the wound, and her leg felt as though it were on fire, but she ignored it; she'd had worse. "Changed your mind about shooting me, Toth, or are you running out of options?" she asked.

As she landed, he pointed the gun at her again, but this time the chamber clicked empty.

"Too bad Morris didn't bring you any ammo," Sy said, a wry smile washing over her sweaty face.

"Do I know you, meat?" Toth's metallic voice rasped. His cybernetic eyes burned green in the gathering twilight.

"I doubt it," she replied. "You've been dead for most of my life. Unless you're remembering the memories of the man whose flesh you've stolen."

"Meat is meat," Toth replied. "I neither know nor care whose skin I wear. Though perhaps I'll take your hide once I've killed you."

"I don't think so," she said.

He sprang, razor-sharp spines bristling. She leapt backward, somersaulting into the air. As he passed beneath her, she dropped her stinger and drew the lectro-blade strapped inside her boot. She pressed the blade's power switch with her thumb.

Sigourney landed cat-like behind him, and in one swift move plunged the blade into the metal joint at the base of Toth's skull. The servos of her skinsuit whirred as she bore down, driving the electrified metal in as deeply as she could.

The cybo general shrieked as electricity arced through his armored frame. Toth wheeled, yanking the blade from Sy's hands. He turned on her, his machine eyes blazing. Sigourney took a step back, tripped, and landed hard on her tailbone. Fire sprang up in her wounded leg and arm, and spots danced before her eyes.

Toth staggered forward, his spines sparking, his mouth sputtering incoherent obscenities. Groping blindly, Sy found a medium-sized rock, the only weapon at hand. She tried to get enough traction to stand, but her legs merely kicked the sand out from under her.

The cybo general closed in, staggering. Sy threw the rock, but it bounced harmlessly off Toth's metal skull plates. Morris' tongue lolled out of Toth's mouth, like a snake looking for a victim. Sy imagined the slimy thing encircling her throat.

Toth took one step toward her, then another. His green eyes burned with hatred of all things human. His claws stabbed toward the dome of her helmet. She leaned back as far as she could. Toth's fingers fell just short of her face, and he collapsed in a heap at her feet. A great cloud of ochre dust welled up where his huge, machine-enhanced frame hit the sand. The cybo's metal limbs twitched briefly, and then he died for a second time. Sy's blade, still protruding from the back of his neck, sparked slightly.

Sigourney Saxon let out a long breath. Slowly, she forced her aching body to stand. Then she remembered.

"Wolf!" she called into her vox. "Wolf, Toth is dead. Where are you? Are you all right?"

In reply, a huge explosion shook the crumbling power plant. She looked up and saw the flash and dust, but no sign of Wolf.

Panic welled up in her gut. Had the battle with Toth jarred her vox circuits loose, or. . . ? She didn't dare think about it. Pausing only long enough to retrieve her blade, she bounded through the Marscrete ruins toward the site of the explosion.

When she got there, she found Wolf standing proudly between two burning cybotanks. Seeing her, he smiled.

"Our plan worked," he said. "I got them to fire on each other. Some cybos never learn. Thanks for keeping Toth distracted. I'd never have gotten them if he'd been directing the battle."

Sy ran to her bond-male and pounded her fist onto his armored chest. "You brute!" she said. "Why didn't you answer when I called?"

"Oh," he said, shrugging. "I turned the vox off after the last time we spoke. I didn't want to get you killed—or vice-versa."

"Take that helmet off, idiot," she said, doffing her own bubble.

He did the same and they kissed until his air ran out. He put his helmet back on. Then his face fell. "Uh-oh," Wolf said. "My scanner is showing incoming vehicles."

"God, not more cybos!"

His frown turned to a smile. "No," he said. "Jacob's private security force, I think, judging by the signals. Looks like they believed us after all."

"How long until they get here?" she asked.

"Ten, fifteen minutes. Why?"

"I need to make sure they don't find anything useful on General Toth."

"Better bandage that arm first," he said. "If Kali White catches you bleeding, it'll ruin your rep."

Sy forced a grin and glanced at her wounded shoulder.

"Guess I'd batter patch this up," she said.

*

Kali White wasn't pleased to find them there—but then, she was seldom pleased about anything. Jacob's security chief lectured the couple for a while, but in the end merely ran them off before scouring the old power station for pieces of the cybos that her boss could use.

Sy and Wolf picked up their mini-transport from where they'd hidden it in the dunes southwest of the plant. Then they drove back and picked up Sy's wrecked sled. By the time they reached home, the sky was dark and Phobos and Deimos were arcing high overhead. The moons shed their pale light on the red dunes outside the caravan.

Sigourney Saxon stripped off her skinsuit and collapsed onto the air mattress. The weight of the hab's grav plates tug at her tired bones; so much weight after hopping around outside all day.

Wolf collapsed into a chair near the caravan's kitchen and slowly removed his armor, one piece at a time. "You think there's anything else buried out in those ruins where Morris dug up Toth?" he asked.

"I don't know," Sy said. She closed her eyes and listened to the soft hum of the recyclers. "If we move our caravan there, though, no one else will have a chance to make trouble. We could keep other squatters away, as well as nosy touristas. And that big chamber in the ruins would make a fine garage, once it's cleaned up." She opened her eyes and gazed at him. "Our repair business could use a more permanent home. Plus, you could dig around the ruins a bit—indulge your archeological bent. It'd give you something to do while I work."

"Are you saying you don't want my help anymore?"

"Of course not. But I know you get bored with mektek sometimes. Admit it. You'd be happier poking around the ruins than lifting cars all day."

He smiled, "Okay, I'll cop to that. But, Jacob probably won't like us moving into the ruins. His family owns title to most of this sector."

"Screw him. Besides, he owes us one here—even if he won't admit it. We took some heavy losses protecting his ass today. And those cybo parts we left for him will get him the supplies he needs from Pig Town."

"Even though we stripped Toth's carcass of anything useful."

"Well, there's no sense letting Jacob get his hands on anything really dangerous. He's enough of a bastard as it is." She sat up, reached into her skinsuit's belt pouch, and pulled out a handful of cybo chips she'd salvaged from the evil general.

"What are you going to do with those?" Wolf asked.

She turned the tiny wafers over in her right hand. "Melt 'em down tomorrow, probably," she said. "Unless I can salvage something."

He nodded. "Makes sense. Look, about moving our squat to the ruins: do you think it's a good idea? It's further from the city than we usually camp. It might hurt your repair business."

"But it'd be a regular place," she replied, "somewhere to hang our armor. People would know where to find us if they need us."

"There's an upside and a downside to that," he said. "For instance, what if Jacob sends Kali and her goons out to see us about squatting on his land?"

"Then I'd love to kick her ass," Sy said, "Or Jacob's, if he's brave enough to show his powdered face."

Wolfgang smiled. "Me, too. I owe Gared Jacob one—for Morris." He sighed, kicked off his boots and sat down next to her on the bed. "More than one, actually. Until I can pay him back, I guess squatting on his land will have to do. How's your arm?"

Sy peeled back the burned skin and inspected the damage to her left shoulder. Clear lubricant leaked out of the wound and dripped down past her elbow. Inside the ragged hole, sparks arced between the exposed microwires. Toth's bullet had torn up the mechanisms pretty badly. Nanocircuits hummed, futilely trying to repair the injury. The servos of the arm's steel muscles whirred as she flexed the fingers of her left hand. She winced against the pain and said, "Nothing I can't fix." Sighing, she lay back on the bed once more. "Tomorrow."

"Let me tend to your human parts, then," Wolf said, rising and fetching a roll of bandages from the caravan's medi-kit.

"I was hoping you might," she replied sleepily.

"You know, Sy," he said, mopping the red blood from her leg and winding the clean white gauze around her thigh, "you are without a doubt the nicest cybo I've ever met."

"You're just saying that because I'm the only cybo you know who's never tried to kill you."

He laughed. "I wouldn't say *never*."

"Well," she said, smiling, "hardly ever."

Reaching up, Sigourney Saxon extinguished the overhead glowlights, and Martian night descended inside the caravan.

THE COILS OF THE PYTHON

At the start of the new millennium, we've discovered everything worth knowing. No one is afraid of the dark anymore. There are no unfathomable mysteries hidden within the world's ancient places. Reality is immutably governed by the laws of science and logic. God is dead and superstition has given up the ghost.

Yeah. Right.

Anyone who believes any of that is a complete asshole.

I'm not one of those people, though I'm not a wide-eyed believer, either. I'm the type of person who likes to poke her nose into places where it doesn't belong. Call me seeker, adventurer, or fool—it's up to you.

My name, though it doesn't matter to this story, is Fallon Shana O'Gale. My friends—those few who have stuck with me this long—call me "Shana."

My physical appearance is even less important to this tale than my name. For the record, though, I stand five feet seven and one-half inches tall. I weigh one-hundred and twenty-five pounds, more or less, and I've a passable if not stunning figure. My hair is the color of a bonfire at midnight and my eyes are green as emeralds. I like to wear comfortable clothes and am not at all interested in showing off my God-given assets—at least, not *most* of the time.

I suppose that my most endearing trait would be curiosity. At least, that's what *I* find most amusing in myself. Others have praised me for my intelligence, my wit, and even for my looks. Fortunately, I don't put much stock in what other people say.

If I listened to other people, I'd never have found myself in the ruins of the Temple of Apollo on that warm spring night.

Now, I suppose that some people would be glad to miss out on an experience filled with sheer, mind-numbing terror. I, on the other hand, savor new experiences—and I intend to keep on doing so until one of them kills me. Which, I expect, someday one will.

Kristos had told me as much that evening. Sweet, handsome, dense, Kristos. He'd been cautioning me ever since I dreamed up my latest plan. Sure, sneaking into the sacred precinct of Delphi under cover of night might seem foolish. But, of such things are great adventures made, and—as noted—I love adventure. If I wasn't deterred by Greek law, I certainly wasn't about to be dissuaded by one-hundred and sixty pounds of well-sculpted male muscle.

Kristos repeatedly warned me against going, but then he trailed me like a lonely puppy as I snuck up the ancient road toward the closed national park. Men are idiots that way. They'll follow the ditziest bit of fluff into Hell if they think they might "get some" out of it. In that respect, Kristos was no different than any of my previous traveling companions.

I came to Delphi for truth and enlightenment; he came to get laid. But he wasn't getting any from me on *that* particular night. I'm too wise in the ways of ancient religions to think that making whoopee on Holy Ground is at all amusing to the gods. More likely such an adventure would earn you a lightning bolt up your ass—or some other, far less imaginable fate.

So, no sparks flew between the two of us that night. Instead, Kristos tagged along as I first purified myself in the Kastalian Spring and then stealthily made the trek up the Sacred Way into the ruins of the temple itself.

The view from Delphi is spectacular in the day—and only a little less so at night. The cliffs of the Phaedriades rise up around the small plateau, silent Titans protecting the crumbling temples. Below, the lush valley of the Pleistos River winds its way to the Gulf of Corinth. Delphi is not a large place, just a few acres on the cliffside, but its ancient glory still looms large over the land and the people who live there.

In the light of the new moon, it was easy to imagine the country's original inhabitants walking through the ruins, attending their secret business.

Kristos might have been one of them. The stolid Greek features of his ancestors marked his handsome face, dark eyes, and black hair. He had a smile that would have done Eros proud and a body worthy of carving into a statue. His voice was warm and pleasant, almost musical.

I say he might have been one of them. *Might.* But he wasn't. In his attitudes, he was pure Generation X. Even raised half a world away from America, he still cultivated that devil-may-care "live for today" attitude that we Americans are so proud of. I suppose we have TV and movies to thank for that—if "thank" is the right word.

Still, Kristos was pleasant enough company, at least in the short term, and he looked right at home in the ruins. Until he opened his mouth, that is. I tried to make it clear to him that we should speak as little as possible tonight. He nodded his handsome head and complied—probably more from fear of alerting the monument's guards than anything else. I don't think he ever knew what I hoped to find in Delphi on that nearly moonless night, but I didn't expect him to understand.

In fact, I wasn't sure what I would find there myself. I've always been better at "seeking" than at "finding."

The two of us lay in the center of the temple ruins under the stars and the wan moon, speaking only in whispers, and sipping judiciously from a flask of ouzo I kept tucked in the belt of my jeans. The old stones felt hard and cold against our backs, which was one reason I'd brought the ouzo. Another was that I like it. Maybe it's the hard-drinking Irish in my background.

Watching the star-filled sky—nearly unchanged since the times of the ancient Greeks—it was easy to let the millennia slip away and imagine Delphi in its glory.

I have no recollection of dozing off, though I remember hearing Kristos' gentle snores beside me before I drifted away.

I know that I must have slept, for I distinctly remember waking up thinking I was in the midst of an earthquake. I've been in earthquakes before—I went to school in both California and Japan—and I know what they feel like. Earthquakes are *not* fun, despite the fact that Universal Studios thinks they're a good subject for a thrill ride.

In real life they're not so much thrilling as terrifying. The earth shudders and ripples like the ocean, or a great dragon turning over in its sleep. The soil beneath your feet becomes liquid and your stomach jumps up into your throat. In the best of circumstances, earthquakes are disquieting; in most instances, they make you want to wet yourself.

Delphi, of course, has been wracked by earthquakes since pre-history. Earthquakes have laid waste to the mighty temples built upon the sacred soil more than once. Priests and devotees always rebuilt the shrine until the Christian God drove out the last pagans around the fourth century A.D.

When the quake hit, I woke up, rolling to my feet, fully expecting to dodge falling rocks. I cursed the luck that had brought me on the ancient pilgrimage at just the wrong time.

What I *actually* found was Kristos still snoring gently beside me. I saw no signs of the earthquake or any aftershocks. The air in the ruins echoed quiet and somber. Only the voice of a distant owl disturbed the silence—ancient Athena calling to her lost brethren.

Then I noticed the fissure.

Scholars have speculated that fissures in the earth provided the Sybils of Delphi with *mephitic vapors*—some kind of hallucinatory gas that induced the prophetic trances that made the oracles famous. Pilgrims came from all over the world to hear the prophecies and advice of the Delphic oracle, or *Pythia*, as she was sometimes known.

Legends tell that Apollo won this spot for his temple by overthrowing the great Python, a huge snake-like monster that lived in Delphi. The Pythia was the creature's spokeswoman. The sun god killed the Python and claimed the monster's priestess for his own. From that day forward, the Pythia spoke with the fair god's inspiration and blessing. Present day skeptics insist the Oracles were merely high on drugs—or vapors.

In any case, though widely popular, the theory about trance-inducing vapors seeping from deep within the earth has never been proven. One reason for this is that no one has ever been able to locate the supposed fissure the mists came from.

On that night, though, beneath the twenty-first-century sky, I saw the fissure before me, winding into the deepest parts of the ruined temple.

The crevice stretched away from me and into the earth. It was narrow at its starting point—just a crack really—but it grew rapidly wider before the living stone swallowed it once more. Vague mists rose from the fissure and danced like nymphs between the temple's aged columns. My sleep-fogged mind wondered how no one had noticed the crevice before.

Then I remembered the earthquake—the one my faithful companion had blissfully slept through. Perhaps the quake had thrown open this crack, so long hidden from human sight.

Rising from my haunches, I walked forward to investigate. As I drew closer, I saw that the hole in the stone wasn't a fissure in the traditional sense. Instead it was as though the stone slowly sank into itself–like a door opening downward, or a path leading into the stygian depths. At the far end, the crack was big enough that a man—or a *woman*—might step inside.

It didn't take me long to make up my mind. I've traveled the world seeking forgotten pathways, both physical and spiritual. Before me lay a path that no person had trod for more than fifteen hundred years. I cast one backward glance at Kristos, where he lay slumbering in ignorant bliss. Then I put my foot on the path of Apollo and strode boldly into Gaia's bosom.

I had to duck my head when I neared the far end of the crack to avoid the overbearing rock. Beyond the threshold, the path continued, a passageway into black oblivion. For a moment, the darkness choked me and fear rose up like a snake in my gut—but I didn't back out. I lingered at the doorstep of the utter blackness, screwing up my nerve and wondering if I should go back and cut a branch to make a torch. As I hesitated, though, my eyes adjusted to the starless dark, and I realized that I could see what lay beyond the opening.

The inside of the crevice shone with a pale, blue luminescence—dimmer than the moonlight, but enough for me to continue. I took a deep breath and ducked inside.

I found myself in a winding tunnel, snaking deep into the earth. The walls of the passage were rough, though the sharp edges had been eroded away by water at some point in the distant past. The floor that I walked on was smoother still, though my boots occasionally caught on some small bumps. I peered ahead as far as I could, but the winding of the passage seldom allowed me more than a dozen yards visibility.

As I walked, the passage steadily widened. When I first entered it, there had been scarcely enough room for my shoulders. At the entrance, my fingertips—held cautiously in front of me and slightly to each side—lightly brushed the walls of the tunnel. Now, I could barely touch either wall with my outstretched hands.

I marveled again that no one had discovered this hidden passage before. I wondered if the earthquake had loosed some mechanism—a secret known only to the ancients—which had caused this serpentine avenue to open for the first time in millennia. In the dimness, I saw that the passageway showed traces of human workmanship. The walls grew smoother as they widened, and a pattern of blunt, diamond-shaped paving stones covered the floor.

The flagstones grew in size as the passage progressed. When I stopped a moment and leaned down to touch one, I was surprised to discover that it felt slightly warm—much warmer than the rocks I had slept on in the temple above.

The passageway changed again. It doubled back slightly and curved subtly upward. The walls widened no further, but they became even smoother. In the dim light which suffused them, I saw vague writings and traceries on their surface. I wished that I had spent more time studying ancient Greek alphabets before coming to Delphi. I longed to know what the forgotten words said.

I ran my fingertips over the characters, and my heart sank when they smudged under my touch. Had I just erased eons of history? Oddly, the residue the writing left on my fingertips was damp and vaguely sticky. I raised my hand to get a better look but, as I did so, I heard a strange noise echoing through the benighted tunnel. I forgot about the smudged words and listened.

Singing. No . . . *chanting*. I looked in the direction of the sound and saw a dim red light down the passage, just at the edge of my vision.

I sighed with relief and then chuckled as I realized I'd been holding my breath. *Not really so brave, are you, Shana*, I thought.

I'd almost believed that something wondrous had happened to me—that I'd found a forgotten path beneath the Temple of Apollo. Apparently, though, my trip into darkness and mystery had merely led me to some mountainside near the shrine—a grotto where local people sang to each other by the light of a bonfire. I felt disappointed that my great adventure had ended in such a mundane way.

Surely the folk at the other end of the passage knew of this "secret" traverse. Probably the tunnel was well known to the locals and only hidden from the prying eyes of tourists. While I felt privileged to know the secret, I no longer felt the thrill of discovery that had suffused me when I first entered the fissure.

Deciding to make the best of it, I strode boldly toward the end of the passage. After a final curve, the tunnel straightened and angled directly for the surface. I saw torches or braziers burning in front of me; the chanting grew louder. I wondered if I'd come upon some kind of local stage production for, beyond the firelight, I saw vast columns rising up in the darkness.

Well, if it were a play I was about to burst into, I decided to give the audience a surprise for their money. I sprinted the last few yards out of the pit and threw my arms wide, fully expecting a gasp of shock from a crowd of bemused onlookers.

This time, however, the shock was on me.

At the top of the ramp I *didn't* find the amphitheater I expected. I didn't find a surprised audience of half-drunken Greeks. Instead I found a lone woman sitting on a three-legged stool, her eyes closed, chanting in the firelight.

I wasn't in a theater; I was in a temple—the very duplicate, as near as I could tell, of the temple in which I'd lay down to sleep with Kristos earlier that evening.

But this temple didn't have fallen columns; its roof wasn't open to the night sky. This temple was built on strong, unmarked pillars of marble. It was lit, not by moonlight, but by braziers burning with laurel and olive branches. The temple I found myself in wasn't old—it was *new*.

My mind reeled, and, for a moment, I imagined myself still in the Greece I knew. I fancied that I had discovered an historical recreation near the great temple at Delphi—though I didn't remember one being mentioned in the guidebooks. Then the priestess sitting on the stool opened her black eyes and looked at me. When she spoke, all my illusions vanished.

It wasn't what she said that sent chills down my spine. Rather, it was the fact that as she spoke, I heard her not only with my ears, but also with my *mind*. To my ears, her words were unfamiliar, though they sounded vaguely Greek. My brain, though, understood her plainly enough.

"Welcome," she said, her clear, deep voice echoing in my head. "I have been expecting you."

"Where am I?" I asked, my words sounding strange and distant as they left my lips.

"You are at the navel of the world," she replied. In the firelight, her dark hair glistened as if it had been oiled. A smell of ripe olives pervaded the small chamber. We seemed to be alone, she and I. The flagstone path I had wandered up stretched past the woman and into the darkness.

"And you are. . . ?"

She fixed me with well-deep black eyes. "You know who I am, seeker. You have quested for me across the ages . . . as I have sought you."

I shook my head, refusing to acknowledge the truth screaming inside my soul. "Are you . . . Pythia?" I asked quietly, forcing the words from my suddenly parched throat.

"Yesss," she whispered. Her red lips savored the word; the way she thought it made my forehead throb.

"Where am I?" I asked again, my body tensing involuntarily. I tried to keep a shrill note from creeping into my voice, though I didn't entirely succeed.

"In the land of dreams and prophecy," said the priestess. "You have sought us; you have found us; you shall *stay* with us."

I untied the knot in my gut and tried to force up my bravery. "I came for enlightenment," I said, "not for a lifetime. If you're really Pythia, you should know that. Even a Psychic Friend could figure out *that* much." I hoped my feelings would follow the courage of my words. They didn't.

If the priestess understood my sarcasm, she didn't deign to respond. Instead, she said, "Our futures are seldom what we deem them to be." She stood from her seat and motioned to me. "Come," she said.

She held out her hand. I didn't take it, but I did follow. She led me from the temple's inner precinct to its outer court. I stood, wrapped in awe, on the steps of the restored Temple of Apollo.

Before me towered the god himself, his perfect body clad in ivory and gold. Apollo's statue glistened in the pale glow of the new moon, almost seeming to shine with a light of its own. Nearby rose the Altar of Chios, resplendent in its marble glory. Beyond that lay votive treasuries and minor temples, brilliantly constructed and stacked with golden offerings. Exquisite statues decorated the temple's silent courtyards. The Sacred Way wound past the frozen gods down the hillside to the entrance of the Holy Precinct.

Beyond moonlit Delphi stretched the valley of the Pleistos River; the Phaedriades towered on either shoulder, their mighty cliffs both protecting and dominating. The pristine countryside before me lay unmarked by the hand of modern man. No streetlights, or headlamps, or any artifice of the twenty-first century marred the landscape. The air smelled fresh and clean, scented by the soft sea breeze and the pungent aroma of olive trees in bloom. The soft cry of an owl echoed in the cloistering hills. In the distance, I heard the whisper of the sea.

I leaned heavily against a column at the temple's entrance, my heart pounding in my throat, my breath coming in ragged gasps. Somehow, as I walked that hidden path, I had journeyed back *through time* into the very heart of ancient Greece.

As if reading my thoughts, the priestess said, "Behold the glory of Delphi, seeker. You have come willingly and brought with you the gift that we desire most. The gift that, among all others, we *need*."

I roused myself from my stupor, fought down my panic, and asked, "What gift?"

"Return to the temple with me," she said, "and I shall show you."

I wanted to fight the suggestion, but some part of me found it irresistible. I felt dazed, limp, like a bird under a cobra's spell. I followed the Pythia back into the inner chamber of the temple. I saw now that the temple wasn't new—just *newer*. Even now, more than a millennium before I fell asleep, it was still very ancient.

My initial shock had blinded me to the small flaws in the exquisite design. Everything around me displayed centuries of prolonged, hard use. Yes, the temple was well maintained, but signs of its age crept through: cracks in the columns, worn stones on the floor, cobwebs in the high corners, and even a bird's nest or two tucked under the shadowed roof. The flood of tiny, nearly imperceptible faults lent a subtle air of menace to what had seemed so marvelous just moments before.

When we reached the inner chamber, the priestess took her seat once more. I saw now that it wasn't merely a three-legged stool she sat upon, it was *the tripod*—a combination throne and cauldron. From this sacred perch the Pythia laid forth her famous prophecies. The tripod itself was said to hold the bones of the long-dead Python—the serpent that great Apollo slew when he usurped the shrine from its heathen founders.

Before I could fully digest this new fact, the priestess spoke again. "The coils of Python wind through time itself, a serpent in the tree of knowledge, lending strength and wisdom to every branch it touches. We see all that is and all that will be to the last day of the world—even to our own end."

"Yes," I said quietly, remembering tales of the temple's destruction in the fourth century. "Even Delphi must fall."

"Like all peoples," she said, her voice purring in the semi-darkness, "we seek to delay our inevitable demise. In that we, too, are merely human. The sight of the Python is strong; we see that we have more to do before our end. Yet, the magic runs out of our world. The science and learning of the Greeks who worship us drive the enchantment out. We know that the end is nigh.

"But it must *not* come yet. This time and place still have need of our wisdom. Prayer, careful planning, and sacrifice postpone the day when the Oracle will fall deaf to the sacred whisperings. The sacrifices of my world, however, are no longer enough to sustain the Oracle.

"The blood found hereabouts is common. It runs thin; it will no longer suffice. So, we reach forward to the land of dreams and bring to us those with the power to delay the Oracle's downfall."

Here her eyes fixed on mine and I found myself growing more drowsy. "You are such a one, Shana O'Gale. You have come to feed the oracle's power. Your sacrifice brings wisdom for all mankind."

With this, she rose from her seat and laid a slender hand on my chest. She pushed me backwards gently onto a low altar near the pit. I tried to resist, tried to grab her hand, but my fingers had lost their will. My fingertips brushed against the Pythia's arm as lightly as a lover's caress. Then my arms fell limply to my side. The world spun—darkness and chaos beckoned.

The Pythia stepped away from the altar and threw a handful of laurel twigs upon a nearby brazier. The fire leapt up bright and red, the color of blood. The flames danced in her eyes and across her hair and her pale, simply clad form. She became the essence of primal power—as irresistible as nature itself.

My eyes languidly tracked her as she glided about the chamber, chanting softly and making preparations. I wrestled to raise my flaccid body from the altar, but I failed. Terror rose up and knotted my guts. I'd never felt so scared in my life. I wasn't sure what was coming, but I dreaded it.

And yet, another part of me *knew* that what was about to happen was *right*. My fate would be a *good* thing. What I was about to do here, under the priestess's guidance, might well save the world.

When the Pythia turned to me once more, she held a great, triple-curved dagger in her hands. The haft of the knife was carved in the likeness of a snake's head; the blade formed the serpent's sinuous body. The gold of the reptile's skin glowed red in the firelight; its emerald eyes shone green in the darkness.

"Arise, mighty Python," the priestess intoned to the black night. "Receive this, your sacrifice, that you may live another hour, or day, or century! Come to the worshipers who need you. Bring us your gifts, as you have since before the bright usurper stole your shrine!" Chanting words I could not understand, she raised the dagger high above her head, poised to strike it deep into my heart.

Then she paused, waiting.

The terror within me built to a thunderous cacophony. My heart pounded in my throat. My mind screamed, *Run! Run!* But my body refused to obey. Waiting to die made the fear unbearable. I longed for the thrust that would end it all. I couldn't imagine what the Pythia waited for. Scared as I was, though, I hadn't seen the worst of it—not yet.

Slowly, as I lay paralyzed, my ears perceived a vague rustling sound, like leaves blowing through the temple ruins. I felt the ground shudder, as it had before I first woke to this nightmare. Straining my eyes in the darkness, I saw a monstrous shape moving behind the Pythia, just beyond the glow of the braziers.

As I watched, the shape resolved itself into a gigantic serpent—the great Python of legend. The mottled blue-black snake wound around the chamber until its tail disappeared into the pit from which I had entered this far-away land.

Suddenly, I recognized the pattern on the paving stones of the passageway. They were *not* stones at all, but the diamond-shaped *scales* of the Python—the prophetic abomination that coiled through time itself, luring victims to its obscene lair.

I wish I could say that some supreme force of will wrested me from the spell of that awful serpent, but I was powerless. I lay prostrate to its terror, unable to move. The sights, the smells, the sounds of archaic Greece wrapped my body and held me petrified. All my years of training and study, all the mental and physical disciplines of the martial arts I'd learned, all the sights I'd seen in my travels, none of them were enough to break the fascination of the Python.

Fortunately, though, we O'Gales have always had more than our share of luck; I count myself glad to be numbered among that hoary Irish clan.

Pythia built her chant into a frenzy, and her great beast reared high into the cavernous chamber. As the monster's head neared the ceiling, the crest of its blue-black skull brushed the rafters.

A few small twigs and leaves fell, like a gentle rain, from the tall column's lintel to the marble floor. Suddenly, a great commotion arose near the Python's head, and a piercing cry filled the night-dark chamber. The Pythia looked up; her black eyes grew wide. She stopped chanting and threw her arms up in front of her face as a great owl swooped down from the rafters—its secret nesting place destroyed by Pythia's sacred monster.

The bird screeched and clawed at the woman, its talons leaving long, bright red trails on her pale forearms. The Pythia shrieked, but she held onto her dagger.

The owl's attack broke the spell that held me prostrate. I rolled off the altar, landing lightly on my boot-clad feet.

With a few swift cuts of her dagger, the Pythia fended off the bird. As the owl disappeared into the darkness, the priestess turned back to complete my sacrifice. But despite her prescience, the Pythia hadn't foreseen my sudden recovery.

I seized her knife hand and twisted. For all her gifts in prophecy and magic, the Pythia lacked combat skills. I, however, have trained with martial arts masters on four continents. The dagger flew from the priestess' hand and skittered across the room, stopping against the base of a pillar.

Before the Pythia could recover from her surprise, I struck her once in the forehead with the flat of my palm. I said a silent prayer of thanks to Athena, the owl-escorted warrior goddess, as the Sybil slumped to the floor, unconscious. I wasn't out of trouble yet, though.

Not nearly.

A huge hissing sound echoed above me, and I felt the moist, black breath of the Python on my bare neck. The creature struck, falling at me like a toppled column. Its jaws snapped with a sound like thunder. I dropped to the floor and rolled to one side, my fingers questing for the dagger or some other weapon.

The monster missed me; its toothy maw struck the sacred floor near the body of its priestess. The nearby altar shook. My hand found the dagger, but it seemed a frightfully inadequate defense. The creature raised its great head from the floor and fixed its baleful golden eyes upon me.

For a moment, my knees went weak.

Fortunately the O'Gale will asserted itself, and my resolve firmed in time to save me. As the creature struck again, I darted behind one of the pillars supporting the roof of the chamber. The body of the monster laid into the column, shaking the temple to its roots. The impact dazed the Python for a moment. While it recovered, I sprinted across the chamber and took up a position behind the Pythia's burning brazier.

Momentarily shielded from the monster by the flames, a bold plan formed in my mind. I needed to return to the pit to escape, I knew that. Unfortunately, the Python *itself* was the path from its past to my future—*it* was the mystic portal I needed to go home. I doubted that the monster would willingly let me stroll back down its scales to my own time.

Reaching into my belt, I retrieved the flask of ouzo that I'd shared with Kristos in the ruins earlier that evening, many ages ago and more than a millennium in the future. Roughly uncorking the bottle, I took as much of the alcohol into my mouth as I could. The great serpent poised to strike once again; I crouched down behind the burning brazier.

The monster lunged, jaws snapping, white foam spraying from its hideous maw. As it did, I spit the ouzo from my mouth in a fine spray, directly into the fire before me. The volatile alcohol burst into a fireball, catching the serpent full in the face.

The Python roared in pain as the flames blinded it; I seized my chance.

Sprinting past its flailing head and gnashing teeth, I jumped full onto the serpent's broad back and slid down the monster's body into the dark pit from which I'd come.

The ride down the Python's coils was like a cross between a roller-coaster and a bucking bronco. The monster flailed and writhed, but there was nothing it could do to stop me. The passageway was too narrow for the serpent to double back on itself. It tried, though, and for a terrifying moment, I thought it might catch me in his huge jaws.

At the last second, I ducked to avoid losing my scalp on the portal's threshold. The Python's head snapped shut behind me and I slid into the darkness.

For a while, it was all I could do to keep from being dashed to pieces against the walls of the tunnel. As I slid further, though, the monster's thrashing subsided and the path straightened out. When it did, I jumped to my feet and ran. Despite the closeness of the tunnel, I didn't dare look back; I feared what might be coming behind me.

I sprinted blindly in the near darkness. The tunnel around me shuddered, as with the first tremors of an earthquake. Ahead I saw a dim luminescence—a blue, wholesome radiance from moonlight and stars.

Then the roadway I ran on, the scales of the Python itself, began slipping out from beneath my feet. The serpent was coiling itself back into the dim past that I was trying to escape!

I nearly fell, and for a moment it was like running up the down escalator; I was moving fast but getting nowhere. The quaking and shuddering of the ground grew more powerful. My guts knotted up again. I knew I didn't have much time left. Soon, the fissure in *my* time would close, trapping me forever in the Python's Cimmerian kingdom.

I ran with every ounce of strength I possessed. Sweat poured from my body and my breath grew ragged. Fire surged up my legs, and some sadistic, invisible quack put a few tight sutures in my side.

I saw the crack ahead of me, the only exit, my one hope. It seemed impossibly narrow and desperately far away.

Suddenly, though, I surged through it and into the cool night air of my own time. Behind me, the tail of the Python slithered into the ground, pulling the crack closed behind it, leaving no trace of its passing.

I collapsed panting onto the stone floor of the ruined temple, more grateful to be alive than I can possibly explain. I rolled over onto my sweat-drenched back and gazed up at the stars of the familiar night sky. The twenty-first century constellations shone above me. They were dimmer than they had been in Pythia's time, but infinitely more warm. As I caught my breath, the first golden rays of dawn peeked over the Phaedriades.

Nearby, Kristos stirred and sat up. "Mmm," he grumbled, stretching the sleep from his handsome frame. "Morning." His lightly accented voice was as warm as the rising sun.

I sat up and nodded. "Morning." With one hand I wiped the damp red hair from my eyes.

Kristos seemed oblivious to the fact that I looked like I'd just run a marathon. "The strangest dreams I had," he said. "Guards chased us, but we kept running in circles. They did not catch us, but we could not get away from them either." He scratched the dark, curly hair on the top of his head and smiled his broad Greek smile. "This old place spooked me, I think. Best to leave here before my dreams come true."

I stood and nodded. "Sounds good."

Kristos clambered to his feet and stretched again, looking out over the sleeping valley to the sea far below. "You know," he said, "this place... it must have been *something* when it was new. I would have liked to have seen it, eh?"

I looked down at the triple-curved dagger, still clutched tightly in my hand. The eyes of the carved Python glinted green in the early morning light.

"You know," I said, taking a deep breath of the cool morning air, "I think I prefer these ruins just the way they are."

FOREVER CRIMSON

I lay in the flower-spotted field watching my lifeblood leak away and thought, *"Not again!"*

I'd enjoyed this life and was not ready to see it end.

The manticore had a different idea. It stood over me licking its blood-stained face and swishing its long scorpion tail back and forth like an angry cat.

I tried to reach for my sword, but the monster's poison had already worked its way down my limbs. I couldn't feel my fingertips. *At least,* I thought, *I'm dying alone.*

I hated when my little adventures got people killed. It's bad enough when I die myself; no sense causing anyone else's untimely demise. I guess that's why I'm a lifelong loner.

I made one last try for the sword, but it was no use. That feeling of serene warmth had already set in—the torpor of death. My body was not my own any longer; a feeling I'd grown used to in recent years.

I didn't have time to review my life—which was okay. It wasn' t really *my* life anyway, but I'd been glad to take part in it.

By the time the manticore finished preening and ripped my throat out, I hardly felt it.

*

My first thought as I woke up was: *Where am I?*

That's *usually* my first thought. I suppose I could use these initial waking moments to reflect on my past mistakes—but I've found that doing so is often a good way to get killed . . . again.

I opened my eyes and gazed at the sky of a different world. Sunset painted the clouds yellow and gold, but the stars hadn't yet come out. I saw two moons hanging in the firmament, one bluish white, the other green and red. I recognized them.

This was a world I was familiar with—Illion—one of the first worlds I'd lived and died on. I had good memories of this place. It was a pleasant world, far nicer than the dimension ruled by super-intelligent slime molds, or the planet where humans were slaves to giant maggots. And let's not even talk about the faerie realms. There's nothing more annoying than a place where everyone walks around with delusions of godhood. Nothing. No wonder faeries treat everyone else so badly; no wonder everyone I've ever met— aside from the faeries themselves—thinks that faeries are the biggest assholes in the known universes.

Illion was a world dominated largely by humans and their near-human kin—which was just fine with me. It had magic, but not an overabundance of it. It also had technology, but not enough to ruin the ecosystem. I'd spent several extended stays here. Most of that time had proved enjoyable.

I didn't dwell upon where in the multiverse I was for very long. Instead, I sat up and looked around. An autumn forest greeted my pale blue eyes: maples and oaks, turning gently from green to gold to brown; clean, crisp air; rich, moss-covered earth. I was alone. No one jumped out of the forest to kill me before I could get my bearings; no sounds of beating manticore wings disturbed the still air.

Everything seemed safe and normal. I exhaled, long and slowly, feeling my chest gently sink as the air seeped out of my lungs. I let my hand slip from the hilt of my sword; the hand had instinctively darted to the weapon as I sat up. I took one more look around for hidden dangers, and then I stood.

I brushed the ashes off of my clothing—I'm always ash-covered when I first awake. Everything seemed to be in its proper place: maroon tunic with chainmail beneath, black leather belt, black leggings, sword, brown suede boots with a flint knife tucked into the right cuff and an obsidian dagger secreted in the left.

I stretched, trying to shake off the odd sensations washing over me.

There's always a period of adjustment when I first wake. My new body is mostly me, but the weight and proportions are different. That's gotten me killed more than once. I drew my sword and made a few practice cuts in the air. The silver-traced steel felt good, right, in my hand. I sheathed the blade.

I used Illion's two moons to get my bearings; it would have been easier once the third moon rose, but I didn't feel like waiting around until after dark. A game trail led from the clearing in a direction that I deduced was southwest. I stretched once more to get the stiffness out of my newly minted limbs and then walked down the trail.

Twenty minutes later I came to a road running north and south. I saw nothing to the north, just a rambling dirt lane wandering golden autumn hills. A slight grey haze hung over the hills to the south. A town, probably—fires, food. My stomach rumbled. I set off in that direction.

I hadn't walked long when a figure crested the top of the hill right in front of me. The girl was alone, perhaps nineteen years old, and ran as though being chased by Thulu himself. Her finely tailored clothes were dirt-stained and torn, probably from her head-long flight.

She collided with me, nearly bowling me over. A small burlap package fell from her hands, dashing its contents to the earth: a hairbrush, a few coins, a locket, some scraps of food.

She stopped and apologized, frantically picking up her spilled possessions as she spoke. She ran her dirty fingers through her tangled auburn hair, and muttered to herself—or maybe she was talking to me, though I didn't catch what she said. She glanced up at my face and momentarily froze. A question flashed across her brown eyes. For a few seconds, I thought she recognized me. Then she turned and fled down the road in the opposite direction to the way I had been walking.

"He's coming!" she cried. "Flee!"

That was it. Before I could even ask a question, she darted over the top of the next hill and was gone—a red-clad doe in the gathering twilight. I frowned. Then I turned about and followed in the same direction she had gone.

Oh, don't get me wrong. I've done more than a few heroic turns in my lifetime, but I've done my share of stupid things as well—more than my share. Doing heroic, stupid things is how I got into my unique predicament in the first place.

However, I've lived long enough to know that when a stranger tells you to flee, they probably have a pretty good reason for doing so. I may be brave, but I'm not foolish. So, despite my growling stomach, I decided to turn away from the town and whatever danger waited there.

Maybe tomorrow, I thought, *with a good night's sleep and a full stomach I'll decide to check it out. Maybe.*

It was a good plan, but it didn't work; the danger found me anyway.

I whirled at the sound of beating wings and dropped to the ground just in time to avoid the beast's flashing tail. A manticore. Another damn manticore. Lion body, human face, bat wings, scorpion tail, the whole bit.

Sometimes, the synchronicity of my life is almost too much to bear. If I didn't know how disorganized the gods were, I'd think they planned it this way.

I rolled to my feet, my sword already in hand. The monster's sting came at me again, but this time I was ready for it. In my last life, I'd been more worried about the manticore's sharp lion claws and its triple rows of teeth than about its tail. It had been a fatal mistake, and I wasn't about to make it again.

My sword found the crusty flesh of the tail and bit hard. The sting fell to the earth, still twitching as it landed. The manticore roared in pain. The man riding on the monster's back swung at me, and his mace nearly took my head off. I'd been so worried about the manticore's tail that I hadn't noticed the rider until it was almost too late.

I ducked aside at the last instant and the mace crashed into my left shoulder. I was lucky to escape with just a nasty bruise.

I spun away, retreating toward the edge of the nearby woods; the manticore and rider would be at a disadvantage there, no room to maneuver. To my surprise, they didn't follow immediately. Instead, the rider pulled back on the beast's mane. He gazed into my eyes and gasped: "You!"

Shit. He recognized me. Sometimes that happens when I run across people who knew my body before I moved in. I'm not sure how they do it, but they do. I always look more like *me* than I do like who I was—at least, I *think* I do. Nevertheless, it happens. And, when it does, I hate it. Old ties cropping up tend to make things a lot more complicated.

"I thought you were your sister at first," said the man astride the manticore's back. He was medium-tall and big-boned but not fat. He wore black leather armor on his chest and a tawny brown cloak on his shoulders. The cloak's hood covered much of his head. In his right hand he carried a nasty, spike-studded iron mace. His shirt and pants were drab green, his boots brown. Clearly, he had no fashion sense. "I thought you were dead," he said to me. I couldn't tell if he was pleased to see me alive, or not.

I shrugged. What else was there to do? Clearly he had mistaken me for someone else.

"You really should have joined us when I offered," he said. "I never would have extended the privilege if I'd known you'd turn me down. Your sister's the last, you know. If you'd *become one,* then the rest of your family wouldn't have had to die." As the man spoke, the manticore snarled and licked its lips, obviously happy at the talk of bloodshed. It seemed to have gotten over its wounded tail, at least for the moment.

"That must be a terrible burden to bear," the man continued. "After your mother's death, I thought you'd probably kill yourself and save me the trouble." His handsome face drew into a cruel smile. "I'm glad you didn't."

Now, despite the fact that I didn't know what the hell he was going on about, all this talk of family killing didn't sit well with me. If this manticore-riding bastard intended to make me angry, he got exactly what he wanted.

I sprinted forward, away from the safety of the woods. He wheeled his monster in my direction. Any winged manticore is a stupid manticore, though. The beast had already forgotten that I'd lopped off its stinger. It struck with its tail, but only succeeded in splashing its blood on my shirt.

I ignored the crippled tail and went for the rider. He brought up his mace to parry my sword, but I'd anticipated that move. I came at him with a two-handed attack. When our weapons met, I let my left hand carry the parry and let go with my right. I balled my free hand into a fist and smashed it into the rider's nose. The nose made a satisfying crunch and the rider's blood sprayed into the air.

The man toppled off the manticore, crashing to the ground on the far side of the beast. The monster wheeled on me as its master fell. It slashed with its claws, but I stepped back. The edge of my sword raked across its shoulder. The manticore howled and leaped at me.

I ducked.

It had forgotten how close we were to the trees. The beast's leonine body crashed into the bracken and stuck there. It beat its bat-wings furiously, but they only brought more branches down around its furry head. Like I said, stupid.

The rider got up off the ground. I met him before he fully recovered his feet. He swung at me, but missed. I swung high and slashed downward, taking off his right ear. The rider, whoever he was, screamed. I smiled and then thrust at his heart.

The bastard was lucky, though. The point of my blade caught in an amulet that hung on his chest; I hadn't noticed the talisman before. I slashed my sword up, but it remained stuck on the amulet. The necklace scraped the man from chin to forehead before its chain broke.

When the chain let go, I staggered—only momentarily, but enough for the rider to clout me in the side with his mace. The chainmail beneath my shirt saved me from serious injury, but the blow knocked the wind out of me. I fell hard onto my ass.

Surprisingly, the rider didn't come to finish me; he seemed far more concerned with his own wounds. He wheeled and ran to where his manticore had finally untangled itself from the undergrowth.

"I won't forget this!" he cried, jumping onto the beast's back. He spurred the monster's side and the manticore leapt into the air.

"See that you don't!" I called after him. They disappeared over the treetops, leaving only a spattering of crimson falling like red rain in their wake.

I smiled. Crimson. My parents had named me well. The smile dissolved when I looked at the amulet, still stuck to the point of my sword. I pulled it off and turned it over in my hands, making sure I wasn't seeing things:

The sign of the cult of Orlak, the demon-god of destruction.

I'd run into the cult before; they're a nasty piece of work. They infest the multiverse like cockroaches, being wiped out on one world only to spring up on another. Some evil gods just don't know when to quit.

I really hated the Orlakai.

They'd even killed me once. More than once. Only one time worth remembering, though—the first time. The first time I died....

*

I knew it would be a tough job when I signed on to do it. I was one of twelve mercenaries hired to protect the princess Aralyn on a dangerous mission. The princess had been disowned by her elfin clan; they considered her mad.

I wasn't too thrilled with her either.

The priest at my temple told me that she was destined to save the world. Personally, I doubted it. Sure, she was pious, but she didn't have sense enough to come in out of the rain. I often wondered how she got dressed without a retinue to help her tell her ass from her elbow.

My priest said she was favored of Chronalos, the Time God. The only way I could see that would be true was if Chronalos liked big hair and a bosom to match. Aralyn was a looker, I'll give her that. She was brave, too, foolishly brave—the kind of bravery bestowed only on idiots who think god is on their side, the kind of bravery that allows an elf to ignore the world around her, even when that world is falling apart.

At the end of our mission, we stood together trapped in a hellish world that seemed to be the princess' destiny.

Of the original thirteen, only the princess and I remained alive. My company had gotten Aralyn all the way to Orlak's inner sanctum, deep within the bowels of Mount Orl, but all the rest had perished in the task. A few of the dead had been friends of mine. Good friends. I wasn't too happy that the princess had gotten them killed.

Worse, she didn't even notice when they died; she was too busy with her mission. But, mission or no, I didn't intend to join my friends.

Aralyn and I barred the door to the great chamber behind us, locking Orlak's hordes on the other side. She fumbled with her scrolls while I looked around, assessing the situation. The room was large and circular, as tall as ten men and at least that in circumference. Hideous stone statues stood in niches around the perimeter—mute supplicants of the demon lord. The floor in the center of the room dropped away into an abyss of burning lava. Even standing by the door, the heat was smothering.

The thing that drew my eye, though, was the shimmering magical gateway in the center of the room. It floated above the lava like a mirage in the summer heat. Beyond it, I saw not the room, but the blackness of hell. Something else, too—something large moving in the blackness, taking shape.

I knew it was Orlak, the demon lord. I knew the princess and I were in deep trouble.

Aralyn continued to search through her scrolls, looking for the right one to complete her destiny. "I had it here just a minute ago," she said.

I watched the avatar of the demon lord form up out of the gateway, and I realized that every prophecy of doom that the priest had told me was true: Orlak was returning to the world, and the only people who could stop him were me and the bubble-headed princess.

I had no idea what Aralyn intended to do, and I don't think she did either. She remained sequestered in her own mind, muttering to herself, searching for the proper scroll. Obviously I couldn't count on her to save the world.

So I took the fight to the demon lord. Sure, Orlak was big, he was mean, he had claws like scimitars and iron scales—but I'm no slouch, either, not when it comes to fighting. I've had a sword in my hand almost since I could walk. It was no accident that I was the last of Aralyn's mercenaries to remain alive.

I jumped across the lava pit, landed on the small platform at the base of the magical gate, and laid into Orlak with my sword. He was one shocked demi-god, let me tell you. That momentary surprise gave me enough time to put my enchanted blade straight through his black heart.

To tell you the truth, I had no intention of dying to save the world. I thought I could slay Orlak's demonic avatar and get out of the way before the magical gate snapped shut. My plan almost worked.

But, at the last instant, the dying demi-god reached out and seized me in one huge hand. I didn't have time to struggle. The gate collapsed around us.

The last thing I heard was Aralyn crying, "No! *I* was supposed to be the one, not *her*!"

*

So, like I said, I hated the Orlakai, and not without reason. I had a pretty good idea what trouble that ragged girl on the road had been running from: not just the man on manticore-back, but the cult itself. Now all the talk of family killing made sense; the Orlakai were sadistic bastards.

I stood on the hillside, knowing I'd have to take care of the situation sooner or later. Tonight, though, was too soon. I remained ravenously hungry, and now I was tired and bruised as well. I took a deep breath and headed north, away from the "infected" town.

By the time I reached the next crossroads, the first stars were just peeking through the purple firmament. The main road kept meandering north, but I noticed a house atop a bald hill a short distance down the western road. The smell of frying pork hung in the air. I went west.

Luck favored me that evening. The house turned out to be an inn, the Lion's Head—a great stone building thrusting up out of the rocky hillside. The night had grown dark and chill, but warm light leaked out of the tavern's windows. I went inside.

The tap room was fairly large, with a number of chairs and tables scattered about. A large fireplace dominated the east wall; heavy timbers supported the building's upper story. A long oak bar stood near the north wall, and a wooden stairway ascended from near one end of the counter to the second floor.

The people in the main room regarded me suspiciously as I entered. I knew my mode of dress wasn't too odd for these parts, so I figured they must not be used to strangers wandering in after dark. Most of the people in the room were human, though a burley dwarf stood on a box behind the bar.

I walked up to the rail and ordered bread, cheese, meat, and beer. The dwarf looked at me skeptically. I fished into my pocket and pulled out a handful of local coins; the coins came with the weapons and clothing. At that moment, I felt profoundly grateful for small favors.

The bartender nodded and a smile cracked his weathered face. He clucked to a serving wench who went for the food while he poured my beer. "Need a room?" he asked.

I nodded. "Yes. Thanks." I took the beer from him. He swept the coins off the counter and nodded toward the nearby stairs. "Room twelve," he said. "Take the beer with you, if you like. We'll bring the food up. You look all in."

I downed the mug and motioned for another. The dwarf refilled it. I took the beer and mounted the stairs.

"Got a name, lass?" the dwarf called after me.

"Crimson," I called back. "Just Crimson."

*

The food came quickly, along with more beer. I had the maid draw a bath while I ate. The food tasted wonderful—but then it always does when I first come back.

The room was modest, but well kept. The walls were made of logs, carefully joined and pointed. The room had a window on the west with oiled sheepskin panes and shutters to keep out chill winds. Flames gently crackled in the hearth of the fireplace along the north wall; I felt glad for the warmth. A large fluffy bed rested opposite the fireplace, and a dresser, with a yellowed mirror, sat next to the window.

I ate, then washed, then cleaned my clothes and set them by the fire to dry.

I stood in front of the dresser and gazed at the face in the mirror. I saw a body both familiar and strange.

Brown skin, well-muscled arms, dexterous fingers, pale blue eyes, a scar on my right cheek. Same red hair, though short this time. I frowned. I like my hair long. Still, it would grow back, given time. The usual large breasts . . . Somehow I always have big boobs; I guess the gods must like them. Me, I'm not particular either way.

A thought crossed my mind, and I watched in the mirror as my white teeth bit my lower lip.

Could the girl I met on the road have been my sister? That was what the man on the manticore had implied. I supposed it was possible. I could see echoes of her face in my high cheekbones, the shape of my eyes, my thin lips.

It didn't matter. I was my own woman now. The girl's troubles were not mine. Not directly, anyway. The cult, though— I'd have to do something about them. Tomorrow.

Or so I thought.

At first, I didn't realize anything was wrong. I assumed that my lethargy was due to the fight, and the strain that always accompanies coming back to life.

My clothes had dried and I put them back on. They felt warm and good, even though I would have preferred a silk nightgown. I sat down on the comfy bed, letting the sensation wash over me. It was good to be alive.

I lay back, my thoughts drifting lazily. Too lazily. The last thing I remember before the blackness took me was seeing the fireplace slide away to reveal a secret passage. The dwarf bartender stepped through the hole and into my room, an evil grin playing across his leathery face.

If I hadn't been so sleepy, I'd have cursed myself. The sign out front should have been a karmic tip-off—the Lion's Head.

*

I didn't expect to wake up after Orlak's dimensional gate collapsed on me, but I did. *Where* I woke up was a surprise as well.

For a God of Time and Space, Chronalos wasn't very well organized. Stars lay scattered everywhere, a clutter of planets spun silently in the void, galaxies burst into luminescence on all sides. The whole of space seemed crowded with the fires of creation and destruction. And everything was happening all at once.

I suppose you needed to be a god just to figure it all out.

Chronalos sat in the middle of his eternal realm, planets and suns whizzing all round him, comets streaking through his vast ethereal body. For all his power, he looked like a wizened old man in a star-spangled robe—except, of course, that he had no face. None at all. Just twinkling galaxies where his eyes should have been.

He tinkered with one small world—the world of my birth—for what seemed like an eternity. Then he noticed me.

"You've really cocked things up, you know," he said.

"Excuse me?" I said, more than a little shocked.

"This business with Aralyn," he said.

"Well, pardon me for trying to save the world," I replied.

"I won't pardon you," he said sternly. "It wasn't *your* job to save the world; it was Aralyn's. That's what we made her for, you know, the other gods and I."

"I didn't think she was up to the task," I said.

"Well, despite what *you* think, it was her destiny, *not* yours. Now she's all upset. The other gods are upset, too."

I frowned. Somehow, this was not what I expected a conversation with god to be like.

"Not all of them, of course," he continued, "but some. Maybe not even a majority. It's always the brightest comet that gets the attention, you know. Anyway, what's done is done and there's nothing we can do about it now without mucking things up further."

"So, that's it?" I asked. "I saved the world and I'm dead. No eternal reward? No Valhalla? No Elysian Fields? No nothing?"

"Some among us were for rewarding you; some said you acted very bravely. They said you had no way of knowing what a mess you'd made of reality. They said you were only doing what you thought was right. Others said that you should be punished, punished severely—you tampered with things best left to the gods, and all that. We gods are quite jealous of our territories, you know."

I felt a knot of fear in my stomach, or whatever passed for my stomach in this timeless, bodiless place.

"Which side won?" I asked.

Chronalos looked at me with his face that was not a face. "Both sides, of course," he said. "Can't have the gods warring with each other over every small thing, can we? Been there; done that, ad infinitum."

"So...?"

"We're sending you back," he said. "Not the way you were, of course, but near enough for human purposes. You'll hardly notice the difference. Your real body was destroyed in the magical conflagration after you slew Orlak's avatar, naturally."

"I'm getting a new body?" I said.

"Well . . . not exactly a *new* body."

"What do you mean, not exactly a new body?"

"New used, if you must know," he said, setting a nearby planet to spinning faster. "Turns out there are a lot of people in the multiverse who have wasted their allotted time. You, on the other hand, still had a lot of time left when your little act of ... bravery ... sent things awry."

"How much time?" I asked.

"Well, a fair piece of your own," Chronalos replied, "plus the time belonging to Aralyn, too, now that you've ruined her destiny. We had to assume her into the firmament bodily, I'll have you know, just to quiet her down. Can't let Aralyn's extra lifetime go to waste, can we? It could tip the balance over into entropy, and we wouldn't want that to happen. Not again."

"So, I have my own life to live out, and hers as well?"

"In a manner of speaking, yes."

"What manner of speaking?"

"Well, you know the people I was telling you about before, the ones who've wasted their lives—folk whom the gods want out of the game, so to speak?"

"You're giving me their bodies? All of them?"

"Not exactly. And not all at once, in any case. But enough of them that you can live out your allotted span—and Aralyn's."

"But Aralyn was an elf," I said.

"Yes, she was," Chronalos answered.

"So I have a long time left to live."

"Yes, but only in pieces."

"I'm not supposed to do anything for you in return, am I?"

"Oh, no. You've done quite enough already, thank you very much. We'd appreciate it, in fact, if you could do your best to stay out of our way from now on."

I raised what passed for an eyebrow in this place. "How can I stay out of the way of the gods?"

"You'll have to figure that out on your own, I'm afraid. A bit messy for you, but that's the way it has to be. Preordained, and all that. I did say this was to be both punishment and reward, didn't I?"

"You did. So I'm supposed to live out my life in someone else's body—probably a multitude of bodies?"

"That's the idea, yes."

"Look, I don't mean to seem ungrateful, but. . . ."

That's when the bargaining began in earnest.

Eventually, I convinced Chronalos and the pantheons that I didn't want to finish someone else's life. I deserved to live my *own* life. I'd get the bodies of those who didn't need them any longer, people who didn't deserve or want that final chance, but I'd have those bodies remade into a semblance of who I was originally: the red hair, pale blue eyes, top physical condition, modest good looks.

I had to argue like a Rhetic minister to get to be a woman every time I came back. As if this wouldn't be confusing enough! Gods! Sometimes they just don't understand people.

The clothes and equipment were a sticking point, too. Originally, they wanted me to appear penniless, naked, and unarmed every time I was reborn. I pointed out that would be a bastard thing to do to someone who saved the world.

Besides, if they wanted to see me nude, all they had to do was peek in on me after my bath. That crack embarrassed enough of them that I got what I wanted: clothes, weapons, and coin of the realm—enough to get me started, anyway.

So, my reward was that I got to come back to life as Crimson, more or less, for a good long while. My punishment was that I'd wander the multiverse endlessly and I never know how much time I had in any given lifetime.

Overall, I think I came out ahead. Though, sometimes, one gets attached to one particular life.

*

I awoke with my wrists strapped in chains which were wound around a huge stalagmite. The rock pillar stood in the middle of a cavern somewhere in the bowels of the hill below the Lion's Head inn. The chamber smelled of mold and decay and manticore dung: familiar trappings for the cult of Orlak, all except for the manticore shit. That must have been a new twist for this lifetime. I could have done without it.

I looked around. This place wasn't nearly as elaborate as the Orl's grand mountain complex—but it wasn't the worst digs I'd seen the cult in, either. The room was a natural cave, modified by the Orlakai for their own dark purposes. Torches, set in sconces on the stone walls, lit the cavern. A high ceiling arched overhead; in the dim light, I couldn't see the top.

My pillar occupied the center of the room. Old dry straw covered the floor. Four dozen large kegs, smelling vaguely of hard liquor, lined one wall, stacked almost to the ceiling. Stalls for housing dim-witted manticores stood along the wall opposite.

Only three manticores were in residence at the moment, and one of them had his stinger missing courtesy of my sword. Perhaps the cult had only recently started their monster-breeding program on this world. The wounded beast snarled at me, twisting its human-like face in anger. It looked pretty silly, all things considered, but I didn't feel like laughing.

The two people in the room with me were not as amused as I, but they had so much more on the line than I did. One was the manticore rider. He stood by the entryway to the room, his face covered in bloody bandages. Boy, did he look angry.

The other person was the dwarf bartender. He wore that evil grin I'd seen when he came out of the secret panel to steal me away to this awful place. The two of them seemed unconcerned that I had woken.

"I don't see the resemblance at all, Parhun," the dwarf said to the rider. "She doesn't look like your fiancée to me. She said her name was Crimson. Besides, I thought your girlfriend killed herself after we tried to induct her into the cult."

"That's what we all thought," said Parhun, the rider. "But no one found her body, and there's something about this woman. . . ."

"The sister got away, then?" the dwarf asked.

"For now," Parhun replied, a snarl creasing what remained of his face. "I'll track her down soon enough, though."

"Don't bother," said the dwarf. "What can she do, anyway? The town is already in the thrall of our master's liquor, intoxicated with the power of the Orlakai. Who will believe one girl's fantastic story? Not the king, certainly, not until we have spread out from this hub and engulfed all the surrounding towns with the master's glory. By the time the king figures out what's happening, this wench, whoever she may be, will be gone to her greater glory, and it will be far too late to stop our plan." He looked at me and smiled more broadly.

"You drugged my food," I said.

"Of course. Our master requires a live victim, because. . . ."

I cut him off. ". . . Blood sacrifice will gain the master a foothold in this world. Yeah, yeah. I know. I've heard it all before."

That took them by surprise. I wasn't supposed to know what was going on. Nothing pisses fanatics off more than someone with a better line on god than they have. I watched a mixture of confusion and anger wash over their faces.

"Heretic!" the dwarf snarled, stepping toward me. "No one ..."

I finished his words again. "... can defeat Orlak the all-seeing, Orlak of the bloody hand, Orlak of the really bad teeth. Honestly! Your god needs to hire better help. All you cultists spout the same self-serving gibberish. Did you ever think that your god might be an egomaniacal sack of shit?"

The dwarf and the rider turned red with fury and took another step forward. I could see that Parhun held my sword clenched tightly in his fist. Apparently, the manticore rider liked my weapon better than his own. I could hardly blame him.

I continued. "Orlak's going to get you all killed, you know—if not by me, then by the next heroic type who happens along. Believe me, I've seen it all before. The only thing your deity is good at is getting his minions slain. He's all promise and no payoff. You should find yourselves a better god to work for."

The dwarf stepped close enough that I felt the spit flying off his lips. Parhun the rider stood, snarling, right beside him.

"Blasphemer!" said the dwarf. "Great Orlak will. . . ."

"Use my guts for garters. I know," I replied. "Same old loveable Orlak." All the time I was talking, I had been taking the measure of my chains. They were loose like a dog's leash, not tight against the rock. I had enough slack to execute my plan if the cultists would cooperate just a bit more.

Parhun looked at the dwarf. "Master, kill her," the manticore rider said. "We can find another sacrifice." The dwarf looked as though he might agree. I'd pushed him past his breaking point; silencing me had become more important than sacrificing me. Before he could reply, though, Parhun took another step forward and said, "Let *me* kill her now!"

"Not in this lifetime, asshole!" I replied. I yanked the slack out of my chain and looped it around Parhun's throat. Before he realized what was happening, I squeezed the chain tight, snapping his neck. A shocked look spread over Parhun's face as he died; my sword slipped from his hand.

I caught the weapon before it hit the floor. The dwarf staggered back toward his manticore friends, fear marking his leathery countenance. I swung my sword at the chain. Sparks flew where silvered steel met iron, and the chain broke.

"Kill her!" the dwarf sputtered to the monsters. He ran to throw the lever that would release their chains. The lever was on the wall by the doorway. My obsidian dagger sailed through the air and found his back before he got there; he and Parhun should have searched my boots more carefully.

The dwarf didn't die immediately, though. That would have made my life too simple. No, first he pulled the lever. The great bolts holding the manticore's chains slid into the wall and the beasts were free.

I swore.

Now, I've said before that winged manticore are stupid—and compared to their land-based brethren, they are. However, they still have the good sense the gods gave any pack predator. Immediately upon being released, they fanned out in three directions. One of them, the largest, prowled by the exit, a low corridor to my right. Another, the one I had wounded previously, crouched by the demonic liquor barrels to my left. The third leapt straight at me from the middle.

Fortunately, I wasn't there when it landed. I had already chosen ol' stump-tail as my opponent. Even before the dwarf fell dead, I was racing toward Stumpy and those barrels. The barrels, I figured, would make good cover—even if they were a long way from the door. Besides, which would you rather face, a manticore with a sting, or one without?

Stumpy hadn't learned his lesson from our earlier meeting. As I sprinted toward him, he came barreling right at me, gnashing his triple set of teeth and roaring. He jumped; I threw myself into a skid and slid under him.

When I cleared his front claws, I stabbed up with my sword. The point found his exposed belly and cut him from breastbone to loin. I rolled out from under him as he fell dead, spilling his stinking guts on the straw-covered stone floor.

The other two manticores howled and charged me. I reached the stacked liquor barrels and darted between the foremost ones.

The first manticore hit the barrels just as I slipped between them. She toppled two of them, and one smashed on the stone floor, splashing its contents everywhere. The noxious smell of demon alcohol swept over me, making my eyes tear up, nearly blinding me. This was the brew that the dwarf and Parhun had used to hold the nearby town in thrall. The woman whose body was now mine had been born and raised in that town. Her family had died there.

I knew that, logically, I had no connection to them, but I still felt responsible in some way for their fates. I needed to end this, for them if not for myself.

The she-manticore's tail darted toward me, but I ducked behind another barrel. The sting hit the cask and stuck there. As she tried to pull the poisonous barb out, I grabbed the barrel and pushed.

The recoil action of her tail and my shove smashed the barrel into her face. She staggered back, blood dripping from her nose.

With a roar and the fierce beating of bat-wings, the remaining manticore crashed into the barrels above me. His sting darted down, but I slapped it out of the way with my sword. The barrels he landed on began to topple; the manticore came with them.

I had no intention of being trapped in the barrelslide.

Before she could recover her wits, I ran toward the female. I jumped over her flailing paws, landed with both feet on her back, and swung my sword. The blade cut through the fragile membrane of her left wing. She shrieked in pain and lashed out blindly with her sting.

I ducked to the left and the sting caught her full in the shoulder. I had no idea if a manticore could die from its own sting, and I didn't intend to stick around long enough to find out.

The female lashed out in confusion and pain. She crushed a nearby barrel with her claws, splashing demon alcohol on her paws and face. It only increased her fury. The male shook his huge leonine body, trying to free himself from under a half-dozen fallen casks. The floor of the room was covered in alcohol, straw, and the bodies of my slain foes.

I ran for the exit.

When I got there, I pulled my obsidian knife from the back of the fallen dwarf. I re-sheathed the blade in my left boot and pulled its flint twin from my right boot cuff.

I looked back across the room only long enough to see both manticores extricate themselves from the mess I'd left them in. They looked mad as hornets and twice as ugly.

I smiled and struck the flint knife across the blunt edge of my sword. Sparks flew where the two weapons met. The embers fell to the floor and found the straw and liquor waiting there. The mixture ignited.

Fire ran across the room like rain down a steep-sloped roof. Before either manticore could react, the flames engulfed them.

They howled in agony, but I didn't stick around to savor the sound.

Instead, I raced for my life up the tunnel. I didn't know how volatile those barrels of alcohol might be, but I wasn't taking any chances. I may be virtually immortal, but that doesn't mean I like getting killed. Dying hurts. A lot.

The tunnel debouched from the side of the hill, not far from the Lion's Head inn. I broke into the light of early dawn and kept running. I spared only a brief glance for the inn. They'd need a new bartender, of course. The thought made me smile. Then the rest of the barrels ignited and an explosion shook the hillside.

A fountain of fire shot up out of the inn's roof. Stones and timbers flew into the sky, and the inn's walls tumbled down. I revised my earlier thought: the inn wouldn't need a new barman after all. I hoped no innocent people had been trapped inside the conflagration. I stopped and watched the smoke from the fire and explosion darken the morning sky.

That was the end of the first day of my new life. As always, the question remained—what next?

I thought about going after "my" sister—the girl I'd met on the road, the one whose family Parhun had killed. I wondered if she was all right. I wondered if she would ever recover from what he and his evil god had done to her.

But, no. I couldn't bring her anything but pain. I wasn't her sister, not any more. Only scraps of her sister's flesh remained in me, and even those pieces were unrecognizable. Whatever that haggard girl faced on the road ahead, she would have to do it without me. She had her own life to live. It was best if she got on with it.

As I had to get on with mine.

I found the crossroads near the inn and headed east, away from my past and toward the future. Ever onward, forever Crimson.

THE GIFT OF THE DRAGONS

Captain Ali al Shahar eyed the golden trinket in the girl's hand. "So, princess," he said, "why is this bauble so important to you?"

Princess Makachiko Sunrii averted her brown eyes from the captain and adjusted her carefully fitted silk garments. "It's been in my family a long time," she said. "I didn't want to see it lost."

The captain shook his head. "That may be your story, but I'm not buying it," he said. "Even with the pirate ship burning, and cutthroats all around you, you were more concerned with rescuing that necklace than with saving yourself. Why?"

Kor dar-Bek, the *Starcutter's* first mate, nodded. The half-ogre's huge frame completely filled the cabin door blocking the afternoon sunlight; his brutish countenance made the nod seem vaguely sinister.

Makachiko frowned. "It's really none of your business, Captain," she said. "You may have rescued me from my captors, but neither I nor my family owes you any explanations."

"True enough," Ali said. "All I was promised for your return was a fat reward. However," he continued, his hazel eyes growing cold, "I am captain of the *Starcutter*, and anything that may imperil my ship or crew concerns me. Rescuing you from the Purple Tern Brigands was dangerous. Taking you home, even with the pirates defeated, will be more dangerous still. Everything aboard this ship concerns me, including that necklace."

"What the captain is saying," Kor explained, "is that you either come clean about that trinket, or you practice up on your swimming." The half-ogre's eyes gleamed poison-green, and a wide grin cracked his gnarled face. He bowed slightly and added, "Yer highness."

The princess looked alarmed, too alarmed, really, for one of her breeding. She glanced hopefully from the captain to the half-ogre and then back, pleading with her deep brown eyes.

Princess Makachiko's looks were enough to sway the mind of nearly any man. She was round in the right places and slender in the rest. Her dark hair cascaded over her bare shoulders. Her silken clothes, rescued from the pirates, clung lovingly to her figure, and revealed much of her tanned skin. "Captain," she said, "please. . . ."

Ali folded his arms across his chest and gazed sternly at her.

"Give it up, girl," the half-ogre said, laughing. "You'll never win a battle of will against the captain!"

Makachiko sighed. "Very well," she said. "It seems I have no choice but to tell you."

She held the necklace out so that the captain and the half-ogre could see it better. The medallion glittered enticingly in the sunlight leaking through the cabin's starboard porthole. The necklace looked like a tiny silver dragon. Its bejeweled form dangled from the end of the stout chain twined through the princess' slender fingers. The dragon's body curved into a sinuous "S," and its blue gemstone eyes gleamed. It almost looked alive.

"This bauble, as you've called it," Makachiko said, "was given to my father by the dragon queen Argentia Lumus—for services rendered during the recent Wizard War."

Ali arched one dark eyebrow and studied the necklace carefully. "So you're saying its value is more sentimental than monetary," he said. "Somehow, I don't buy that."

Kor moved forward, ducking to keep his head from brushing the cabin's top timbers. He laughed. "The captain's heard enough fish stories to last his lifetime!"

Makachiko's face reddened. "This necklace is a gift from the dragons. Its price is beyond measure!"

Ali's eyes narrowed. "Why?"

"The dragon lady gave it the power to summon her people to my family's aid!" the princess replied.

Kor dar-Bek frowned. "That's a lot of fish-oil, too, Captain," he said. "If the trinket has that kind of power, why didn't she have the dragons save her ship from the Purple Tern Brigands? Or rescue her from their brig? For that matter, why doesn't she call them now to ferry her back to Sunrii Isle and save us the trouble?"

"It will only work once," the princess said icily.

The half-ogre scratched his stubbly chin. "Well, when your shipmates were being slaughtered might have been a good time to use it."

"The pirates caught us by surprise," the princess hissed. "And, besides, the necklace was immediately taken from me. Do you think I wouldn't have saved my crew if I could have?"

The half-ogre shrugged. "From what I've seen of you so far, it's hard to tell."

"Enough," Ali said. "Why the princess didn't use the medallion's magic—if it exists—is none of our concern." His handsome face melted into a smile. "Besides, if she used it to fly home, how would we collect the reward for her rescue?" He balled up his fist and affectionately slugged the half-ogre in the left biceps.

Kor dar-Bek rubbed his bony head. "Well . . . if we get into another fix," he said, "I hope her worship will be a bit more generous with her dragon-magic."

Ali looked from the half-ogre to the princess. "Don't worry," he said reassuringly to her. "I'm sure we'll have smooth sailing from now on."

"I agree," said a musical voice from the cabin door. "With their home base ablaze, the Purple Terns will be hard pressed to follow us. I saw no other Tern ships as I scouted the surrounding seas." In the doorway stood Sarifa T'Liil, the *Starcutter's* master-at-arms. The siren warrior folded her wings to duck through the cabin's human-sized portal. "I have assessed the damage from the skirmish, Captain," she concluded.

Ali nodded at the lightly-armored bird-woman. As usual, Sarifa appeared completely unfazed by the difficulties of the recent battle. Not one delicate red feather atop her head appeared out of place. "Go on," he said.

"Many minor scrapes and bruises," Sarifa reported. "Seven wounded, three severely—one may join his ancestors in the stars."

"Who?" Ali asked.

"Old Tifek," the siren replied.

Ali nodded grimly. "Is that Doran's assessment?"

Sarifa nodded. "The physician's Il-Siha training only extends so far. If you've any magic to spare, Captain, now would be the time to use it." She looked at him hopefully.

Ali shook his head grimly. "I used all the ship's blessing stones during the fight. I'm fresh out of miracles—even minor ones."

"Maybe her worship can help," Kor said. He turned toward the princess, bumping his brow on the rafters as he did so.

"I can't use the necklace for just one sailor," Makachiko said. "I have to save it for important things."

"Every life is important," Ali reminded her.

"Things that are important to my family . . . to my kingdom," Makachiko shot back. "The power of the medallion is not mine to throw away as I please. It belongs to the whole kingdom of Sunrii."

Kor glared at the princess. "What'd I tell you, Captain?" the half-ogre said. "The highborn are always trouble."

"It's not that I don't care," the princess explained. "It's just that I have to consider my responsibilities. If I wasted the dragons' gift on one lone sailor. . . . Well, what would the people of Sunrii say when the next typhoon struck?"

Ali looked from the princess to Sarifa. "Tell Doran to do what he can," the captain told his master-at-arms.

The siren woman nodded curtly. She folded her red wings tightly against her back and turned to go. As she paused at the doorway, the sunlight silhouetted her lithe frame. To those inside the cabin, she looked for a moment like a fiery-winged angel—a messenger of light and darkness, bringing portents for mankind.

Suddenly, the ship lurched hard to its starboard side.

"Rogue wave!" Kor blurted.

The *Starcutter* swayed precariously before pitching upright again. Princess Makachiko tumbled unceremoniously to the floor, and Kor crashed to the deck as well. Ali grabbed onto a support post and barely avoided losing his feet.

Sarifa fell to her knees. A look of pain flashed across her pale face. She clasped her hands over her delicate ears and squeezed her eyes shut.

Kor regained his feet quickly and lumbered to the siren's side. "Sarifa," he said, his big eyes turning purple with concern, "are you hurt? What's wrong?" The boat's sudden listing had ended as quickly as it had begun.

The winged warrior cocked her head to one side. "Can you not hear it?" she asked through gritted teeth.

Ali pushed past the siren and the half-ogre and exited the cabin door. His eyes darted from stern to stem, but he saw no immediate peril. Around them, the Azure Sea lay quiet and calm. The captain saw no sign of a rogue wave—or anything that might have caused the ship's sudden lurch.

He turned back to his siren master-at-arms. "What was it you heard?" he asked.

Sarifa caught her breath and rose. She fanned her wings out slightly to steady herself. "A high-pitched wailing hiss combined with a very low rumbling," she said, "as if the ocean itself were screaming. Very intense—but it has passed."

On deck, the rest of the *Starcutter's* crew wobbled to their feet. The sailors looked around warily, and a murmur of concern sprang up among them.

"Anyone hurt?" Ali called. "Sing out!"

The crew grumbled that they were all right.

Ali swung his eyes to the lookout atop the main mast. "What about you, Toshi?" he called.

The teenager clinging to the rigging called back, "Shipshape, Captain!"

"What happened?" Ali asked. "Did you see anything?"

"A queer shadow of some kind, Captain," the teenager replied. "It raced under the boat and away before I could even sing out."

"If not a wave, a rogue swell, then?" Ali asked.

"Maybe, Captain. I'm not sure. It was like nothing I've seen before." Toshi swung around the mast, shielded her eyes from the noonday sun, and peered into the distance.

"Can you see it still?" Sarifa asked.

"Aye," Toshi replied. "The shadow's still there, but it's a long way off and moving fast away from us."

Sarifa turned to Ali. "Perhaps I could see more from higher up, Captain," she suggested. Ali nodded. The siren unfurled her shimmering flame-colored wings and shot into the sky.

Princess Makachiko gasped as the siren took flight.

Kor's low chuckle echoed over the deck. "Still takes my breath away, too," he said.

"What do you think she'll find?" Makachiko asked.

"Allah willing, she'll find a rogue wave," Ali replied, "and nothing more."

Sarifa soared high into the air, quickly becoming just a speck against the cerulean sky. She circled amid the clouds for several minutes, and then dropped back down to the ship.

As her black-sandaled feet touched the recently-swabbed deck, she frowned.

"What's wrong?" Ali asked.

"I'm not sure," the siren replied. "The sea seems to have . . . risen up. A shadowy ring of water expands outward for miles in every direction."

"Not a rogue wave?" Ali asked.

She shook her head. "Not like any wave I've seen before. Your idea of a swell seemed more likely. It's fantastically large, though."

Kor spat over the rail. "Magic!" he growled.

"Maybe," Ali said. "Or maybe not. Sarifa, is this ring of water moving toward the *Starcutter*?"

"No, Captain," Sarifa replied. "It has already passed well beyond our position."

Ali stroked his beard and nodded. "The ship lurched as the swell passed under us."

"It would seem," Sarifa agreed.

"But what magic could do that?" the princess asked. "Are we in danger?"

Ali shook his head. "No way to tell," he replied. "Not yet."

"But you must have some idea what caused it," Makachiko pressed.

"I've got an idea, Captain," Kor blurted. "It's the girl's medallion! That magical wave hit us just after she touched it. The trinket's cursed! We should cast it overboard."

"No!" the princess cried, clutching the necklace protectively to her breast. "It's mine. It belongs to my people."

Ali cast a stern glance at Kor. "Don't worry, princess," Ali said. "I don't share Kor's superstitious nature. No one will take the medallion from you."

The princess looked very relieved.

Kor frowned and grumbled. "I suppose the reward said that she had to be returned in one piece?"

"Aye," Ali replied with a chuckle. "It did."

Kor dar-Bek crossed his huge arms over his barrel-like chest. "Well, we'd best get our pretty bit of baggage home, then."

"Set course for Sunrii," Ali commanded.

"Aye, Captain," Kor said. He climbed the short flight of stairs to the bridge. The pilot of the watch stepped quickly out of his way, and the half-ogre seized the ship's wheel in his huge hands.

"Thank you, Captain," Makachiko said.

Ali nodded at her.

"Er, Captain," Kor rumbled, "what if—during the course of our sailing—we should catch up to that magic . . . whatever it may be?"

"Toshi will keep lookout," Ali said.

"What about me, Captain?" Sarifa asked.

"Help Doran with the injured," Ali told the siren. "Your skills at battlefield medicine will come in handy, I'd imagine. Let Doran concentrate his Il-Siha training on Tifek and the gravely wounded."

Sarifa nodded.

"Get the Coralshell sisters to help out as well," Ali continued. "They can field dress a wound as well as anyone aboard."

Kor chuckled and shook his head appreciatively. "Those Coralshell sisters have more luck than a bag full of cats," he declared. "Even dressed like they are, I don't think either one of them got even a scratch during the whole battle!"

"Their Sisterhood pirate training serves them well," Sarifa noted.

"Put them to work," Ali commanded. "I want the whole crew back on its feet as quickly as possible."

"Do you anticipate further trouble?" the siren asked.

"No sense taking chances," Ali replied.

The siren warrior dipped her wingtips to him. "Aye, Captain."

"Captain," Princess Makachiko said, "what should I do?"

Ali al Shahar glanced from the girl's face to the dragon pendant hanging around her neck. "Return to your quarters," he said. "And if you know any prayers, you might say one for Tifek."

*

The *Starcutter* steered a straight course toward the isles of Sunrii. The Azure Sea rose in gentle swells around them, slapping the ship's red and blue sides with a steady, reassuring rhythm. Watching from the top mast, Toshi saw no further sign of the strange wave. After tending the crew's superficial injuries, Sarifa took flight again and patrolled the nearby waters.

Only minor tribes and petty kingdoms occupied the islands between the *Starcutter* and her intended destination. Most of the isles along the route were tiny and insignificant. With the Purple Tern Brigands in disarray behind them, Ali hoped for clear sailing all the way to the princess' home.

As the hours slipped past, the *Starcutter's* crew saw no sign of brigands, nor of any other people sailing upon the placid deep.

Toward evening, a puzzled frown drew across the captain's tanned face. He shielded his eyes and scanned the horizon. "Where are the fishers?" he asked, more to himself than anyone else. "Where are the tradesmen?"

Kor, still at his side, manning the wheel, looked at the captain and shrugged.

"Sarifa," Ali called. "Fly a patrol to the northeast. There's an islet a couple of leagues distant from our position. In the past, pirates have used that isle for a base."

"You think some sons-of-buccaneers might be plotting to ambush us?" Kor asked. The half-ogre's poison green eyes flashed yellow at the prospect of another fight. Like Sarifa, he never tired of battle.

The *Starcutter's* captain shook his head. "I don't know," he replied. "Something doesn't feel right. It's odd that we haven't seen any other ships—or a few fishing boats at least."

"Pirates might account for that," Sarifa agreed. "I will report back shortly." A few quick beats of her shimmering red wings lifted her into the air.

The captain prowled the quarterdeck, awaiting her return. As Ali paced, Makachiko peeked out of the ship's central hatch. When the captain spotted her, the princess climbed boldly onto the main deck.

"What have you been up to?" Ali asked. "I thought you were resting in your berth."

"I've been helping tend Tifek," she replied imperiously.

The captain looked puzzled, so she continued. "I'm not heartless, Captain. I don't want anyone to die on my account, but

I must put the good of my people ahead of the needs of others. Surely you understand."

"So, how is Tifek?" he asked.

The princess' voice softened. "His condition remains grave. One of those Coralshell girls—I'm not sure which one, they both look alike to me—is tending him while Doran gets some rest."

Ali smiled. "If anything can lift an ailing man's heart," he said, "it's the Coralshell sisters."

Makachiko frowned. "Their manner of dress is . . . different than that of my people," she said. "Their jewelry barely covers their modesty."

"They sailed with the *Sisterhood* before I 'rescued' them," Ali told her. "Wearing jewelry as clothing is their tradition, just as wearing silks is yours."

The princess' face turned pink. "Well, despite their immodesty," she said, "they seem quite effective as warriors, sailors, and medics."

"They're the best I have," Ali said. "You could probably learn a thing or two from them—if you're interested." He smiled at her. "Thanks for helping out, Princess. I'm sure your presence lifted Tifek's heart as well. Allah willing, it will be enough to see him through." He bowed courteously.

She dipped her lovely head just slightly. "It is the least I could do, Captain. He was injured effecting my rescue, after all. Your crew did save my life."

Ali mounted the steps to the bridge. "That's true," he called back to her, "and we expect to be well paid for it."

The princess followed him the stairs to the wheel. "Aye," she agreed. "Still, you did not take advantage of situations that you could have. And for that, I am grateful." She absent-mindedly fondled the dragon-shaped necklace at her throat.

The shimmering jewels caught Ali's attention, but he merely said, "Aye," and took the wheel from Kor.

An hour and a half later, Sarifa returned to the ship. She touched down lightly on the aftercastle, near Ali, who still manned the wheel.

"Well?" he asked.

"I saw nothing, Captain," she replied. She looked slightly concerned and cocked her head in a very bird-like manner.

"No pirates?" the princess asked hopefully. She sat cross-legged on the deck nearby, between Ali and the rail.

"No, your highness," Sarifa said. "Nothing at all. No pirates, no fishers, hardly even a sea bird."

"What?" Ali said, mirroring the siren's concern.

Kor was leaning on the stern rail, dragging a stout fishing line in the ship's wake. "It's that magic, Captain," the half-ogre suggested. "I ain't had a bite in all this time, either. And that ain't right in these waters."

Ali nodded. "Sarifa, I'm sending you back," he said. "Stop at one of the isle's small settlements and see if you can find out what's going on."

"But captain," the siren woman said calmly, "there are no settlements."

For a moment, only the creaking of the *Starcutter's* rigging and the soft hiss of the surf filled the warm sea air.

"But that's impossible," Ali finally said. "I've sailed these waters many times. There's hardly an outcrop of reef in this part of the ocean that doesn't have a handful of people trying to scratch a living out of it."

"Nevertheless," Sarifa said, "I saw no such settlements."

"What about the other isles?"

"Nothing. On any of them."

Ali's voice assumed the tones of command. "What's the course and distance of the nearest islet?" he said.

"A league away, fifteen points off the port bow," the siren warrior replied.

The captain nodded and spun the wheel.

"But, Captain," Makachiko protested, "that's not the way to Sunrii."

"It's not far out of the way, either," Ali replied. "We'll get you home as soon as we can, Princess. Since there was no telling how long your rescue might take, we're not bound to any schedule. Your royal parents will never notice the difference, I promise you. Something strange is going on, and I want to see what it is with my own eyes."

"What about the magic, Captain?" Kor put in.

Ali gazed seriously at Sarifa. "Did you sense any magic?" he asked.

She shook her feathery head. "No, Captain. None."

"Advise the crew of our course change," he told her. "Tell them it's probably nothing to worry about, but. . ."

"You don't believe that, Captain," the princess said. "If you weren't worried, you wouldn't be changing course." Her voice remained firm, but her fingers fumbled nervously in the folds of her silken dress.

Ali politely ignored her. "And send the Coralshell sisters up here. Just in case."

Sarifa nodded and went below deck.

"What about me, Captain?" Makachiko asked.

"Go to your cabin and stay there," he replied. "Watch from your porthole if you like, but don't come on deck unless I tell you it's okay."

The princess nodded and quickly retired to her cabin under the forecastle.

Moments later the Coralshell sisters appeared through the hatch amidships. The jewelry of their sparse clothing glittered against their tanned skin. Their hair glistened like spun gold in the fading sunlight; their sea-green eyes flashed with mischief. Each girl carried a saw-toothed sword in one hand and a finely-honed boat pike in the other.

With them came Doran, the ship's healer. He looked grubby and tired, but a smile creased his handsome young face.

"Tifek. . . ?" Ali asked.

"He'll pull through," Doran said, beaming.

Ali nodded. "Well done."

"I'd be considered a miracle worker in some circles, if I do say so myself," Doran added with a grin.

"Though not among *actual* miracle workers," Rina Coralshell put in. She laughed and her younger sister, Lia, laughed as well.

"Is there trouble, Captain?" Lia asked. She gave her sword a quick twirl to limber up her muscles. The thought of combat brought a smile to her pretty face and her sister's as well.

"I hope not," Ali said. "We'll know soon enough. Stay on your toes as we draw closer to the isle." He turned and called to Toshi atop the mast. "What do you see?"

"The island looks deserted, Captain," the girl called back. "We're heading straight for her."

Ali and the others peered into the twilit haze. A small, rocky islet loomed out of the encroaching darkness.

Doran squinted to try and make out details. "I can't see a bloody thing," he said.

"Me neither," agreed Rina.

"Pipe down," Kor rumbled. "You want every wizard in the whole World Sea to know exactly where we are?"

"With all that superstition filling your head, Kor," Lia said, "I'm amazed you have any room left over for courage."

"I'm just cautious," the half-ogre countered. "Something you and your rattle-brained sister should learn!" His eyes flashed yellow with annoyance.

"Lectures on caution from a half-ogre!" Rina gasped. "Next thing you know, basilisks will be teaching table-manners!"

"Quiet!" Ali commanded.

All of them fell silent.

After a few moments, Doran asked. "Do you hear something, Captain?"

Ali shook his head. "That's the problem. I don't hear anything. I've been to this isle before. There used to be a fishing village on that shore ahead. It was a small village, but full of life."

"And now it's just . . . gone?" Doran said, skeptical. "How is that possible? We're leagues from the Wild Seas. Islands don't just disappear in this part of the Azure Sea."

"Not without powerful magic, anyway," Kor noted.

"But it's not the *island* that's gone," Rina said.

"Just the people," Lia added.

"No," Ali said, peering into the growing darkness. "It's not just the people, it's the whole town." He turned to Kor. "Take the wheel. I'm going forward."

The half-ogre did as Ali commanded, and the *Starcutter's* captain sprinted from the bridge to the bow of the ship. He grabbed the bowsprit and leaned forward as far as he could, peering further into the gathering darkness.

"Toshi, see anything?" he asked, calling up to the lookout post.

"Nothing, Captain," Toshi replied. "No sign of life."

As the sun finally sank into the sea, the *Starcutter* drew within shouting distance of the rocky isle. By then, most of the crew stood armed and ready at the ship's rail, watching. Kor manned the helm as Ali kept lookout with the rest.

"You're sure there were people here?" Doran asked.

"Aye," Ali replied quietly.

"Well, there aren't any here, now."

"Aye."

"It doesn't make sense," said Lia. "If pirates took them, there'd be wreckage. The Purple Terns always make a mess of things, and even the Black Cliff pirates aren't that effective."

"Aye," her sister agreed. "It's almost as though something terrible scoured the island clean."

"It's that accursed magic," Kor said. "We should leave."

"I agree, Captain," Sarifa said. "No sense tempting the fates."

"Men make their own fates," Ali replied. "But, in this instance . . . we sail on." He took the wheel from Kor and steered the *Starcutter* eastward, around the island.

Princess Makachiko appeared at the bottom of the stairs leading to the bridge. "I felt the ship turning," she said. "What's happened? What have you found?"

"Not very good at obeying orders, is she?" Kor grumbled.

Ali gazed down at the girl. "We've found nothing," he said. "The island is deserted. We're merely returning to our previous course."

"Thank the gods," she said, very much relieved. She didn't notice as Ali fixed his eyes on Doran and gave a slight nod.

The healer immediately went over to Makachiko. "Princess," he said, "allow me to show you back to your cabin." He bowed deferentially and gave her a very winning smile. "After all the excitement earlier, you should try to rest. Physician's orders."

She nodded slowly. "Yes," she said. "I am feeling rather fatigued."

"Perhaps a draught to calm your nerves, then."

"Yes," she replied. "Perhaps." The two of them returned to her cabin in the forecastle.

Rina and Lia snickered.

"Enough of that," the captain said. Then, addressing the rest of the crew, he added, "All of you stay on your toes. Something strange is going on here, and I don't want anyone relaxing until we reach the Isles of Sunrii."

"But, Captain," an older seaman protested, "that's two weeks sail away!"

"The captain knows that!" Kor barked.

Ali put a steady hand on the half-ogre's elbow. "Aye, it's a long sail," the captain said, "and we've just finished a difficult mission and battle as well. However, our fatigue is the very reason we need to keep sharp watch."

"I will devise suitable shift rotations," Sarifa told the crew.

Ali nodded to her. "If we all keep our heads and stay wary," he said, "we'll get through this situation—whatever it turns out to be. Now, back to your tasks, all of you."

"And remember," Kor boomed, "keep your eyes peeled!" He used his huge fingers to pry his poison green eyes wide open.

The crew nodded and left the rail to go back to their regular duties.

Riana and Lilani Coralshell paused long enough to grin at the *Starcutter's* first mate. "Could you repeat that, Kor?" Lia asked playfully. "Yes," Rina added, "I'm not sure the princess and Doran could hear you in her cabin."

They laughed and turned away. The half-ogre reddened and his eyes turned a dangerous shade of yellow as he watched them go. The Coralshell sisters took no notice.

"One day," Kor muttered, "I'm gonna murder those girls."

"Not on my ship," Ali said.

Kor look startled. "Did I say that aloud?" he asked.

Ali laughed and even Sarifa cracked a smile.

Just then, the ship sailed around the point and into view of the far side of the island. Standing next to Ali on the bridge, Sarifa froze.

"What is it?" Ali asked quietly. He followed her keen gaze through the gathering gloom toward the isle's rocky shore.

"Wreckage," the siren announced, "scattered amid the rocks. I hadn't noticed it when I flew past before."

Kor strained his eyes. "I can hardly see it now."

"She's right," Ali said. "And look there . . . sharks!" He pointed toward a half-dozen red-tipped fins darting among the bobbing bits of wreckage.

"And there as well," Sarifa said, pointing further out to the darkening sea.

"Captain!" Toshi called down from the mast top. "Bodies! Bodies floating among the waves!"

She pointed in the same direction that Sarifa and Ali were looking.

The commotion brought most of the crew back to the rail. They murmured nervously as the ship sailed through the corpses.

Kor watched as a well-dressed carcass drifted past the stern. "Well, I'll be harpooned," he said. "That one looks more like a groom than a sailor!"

"He *is* a groom," Sarifa said. "See? The wedding kerchief is still knotted around his dead wrist."

"That don't make sense," Kor said.

"Unless he died before the ceremony was finished," Sarifa suggested. Her voice was soft and cold.

Kor shook his head. "It's powerful bad magic that can drag a man from his new bride before the wedding night! Captain, we should . . ."

He looked at Ali, but the *Starcutter's* master had gone suddenly pale.

"Powerful magic," Ali said, "or a powerful wave."

"What do you mean, Captain?" Kor asked.

Ali cast his eyes over the darkening, wreckage-strewn sea, watching the sharks as they sliced purposefully among the breakers. "It was that same wave that shook the *Starcutter*," the captain said. "A very long time ago, someone told me such a tale, on an island I visited during my youth. The people there spoke of a legendary wave that rose from the deep and washed over their entire island. Only the fishers who were at sea in their boats survived."

"That sounds more myth than reality," Sarifa said.

"I thought so, too," Ali agreed. "Yet, the whole island insisted on the truth of the tale. They swore it on the watery graves of their ancestors. And they had proof as well . . . the wreckage of an ancient galley, lodged halfway up a mountainside."

"Gods of Wrath and Mercy!" Kor gasped.

"That's what the islanders thought, too," Ali said. "They said their land shook with the fury of the gods before the wave came."

Sarifa watched stoically as a redfin shark circled a body floating nearby. "What could simple fishers like these have done to arouse the wrath of a god?" she asked.

"The gods are gods!" Kor said. "They don't need any reason to be roused!"

"Not everything in the wide World Sea is caused by gods," Ali said. "Some evils are done by people, and others just happen. That's the way of things. Sometimes a wave is just a wave."

Sarifa set her deep blue eyes on the captain. "And yet," she said, "something about this wave continues to worry you—even though it's passed us by and left us unharmed."

"Yes," Ali said, taking a deep breath. "I'm wondering how far a wave like that might travel."

"I pray to the gods that we never find out!" Kor blurted.

As night fell, they sailed cautiously through the wreckage, but they saw no sign of life among the flotsam and jetsam. The crew remained taciturn and largely silent. Even the former pirates among them had no wish to loot from the bodies of the floating dead. As the first rings of the moon peeked above the starry horizon, the scoured island and its grizzly sights disappeared from view—though not from memory.

"I'm glad the princess was spared that sight," Kor confided to Ali.

"I thought you didn't like her," the captain replied jovially.

"Well, I don't," Kor shot back. "But no one should have to look on such a thing—not even me."

Polishing the *Starcutter's* rail nearby, the Coralshell sisters chuckled. Kor glared at the girls, which only made them laugh more.

As night deepened, the crew kept careful watch and worked on chores, to dull the worry of the watching.

After the moon climbed from her watery bed, Princess Makachiko ventured from her berth to see the stars. Whispers of the floating corpses still circulated among the crew, but the princess either didn't hear the gossip or chose to ignore it. Doran appeared at the same time, and stood beside the princess at the rail for a while.

The physician spoke quietly to Ali about the progress of the ship's wounded. Then he flirted briefly with the Coralshell sisters before returning to his duties below deck.

Sarifa flew patrols by moonlight, but found no sign of life on the previously inhabited rocky islets nearby. "The war god himself could hardly have depopulated those isles more effectively," she told the captain.

Ali nodded grimly and ordered her below deck to rest. Exhausted from the day's trials, the siren warrior didn't object.

The captain set watches according to the order Sarifa had determined. The *Starcutter's* most reliable crewmembers were assigned to head the shifts, which meant separating the Coralshell sisters. Neither Rina nor Lia seemed to mind.

Kor would be piloting the ship during the night's last watch, so he was among the first assigned to sleep. Ali tended the wheel as the moon arced overhead. The Princess Makachiko stayed close to him while she remained on deck. She made polite conversation, but Ali sensed uneasiness beneath her careful words. Clearly as hard as this day had been on the crew, it had--in some ways--been even harder on the princess. After a few hours, she bade the captain good night and retired to her cabin.

Just before midnight, Ali turned the wheel over to Riana Coralshell.

The *Starcutter's* captain returned to his cabin below the bridge and settled into an uneasy sleep. He dreamed of pirates, and monster waves, and the dark eyes of an Acacian princess he'd once met.

Raucous shouts and the clang of weapons woke Ali from his slumber.

Cursing, he grabbed his sword and dashed onto the deck.

"Captain, watch out!" Lilani called as he came through the cabin door.

Ali ducked aside and a thrown dagger sailed over his head and imbedded itself in the door, near his left ear.

Fighting swirled on the deck of the ship, as Ali's crew clashed with a band of ragged-looking pirates. Lia stood in her night skirt, bare-breasted, defending the ship's central hatch from the intruders. Clearly the attack had roused her from a sound sleep, just as it had woken Ali.

Her lack of attire didn't slow Lilani down, though. She parried and slashed with all the force of her Sisterhood training. Rina battled on the aft deck above her sister, trying to protect the wheel from a pirate intent on seizing it. These brigands, like the ones they'd fought when rescuing the princess, wore the devices of the Purple Tern. Only a handful of the *Starcutter's* crew was on deck, helping to fight the violet-clad buccaneers.

Ali picked the nearest intruder and lunged. The pirate, who had been trying to sneak up on another crew member, sensed the attack at the last moment. He turned, and the captain's sword passed harmlessly under his arm.

Ali had expected that and, with his left hand, he clouted the brigand on the jaw. The pirate fell like a sack of dead fish. Ali stepped over him to engage the next brigand.

That one spun and faced the captain with a double-bladed boat hook. The weapon was rusty and ill-kept, clearly not from the *Starcutter*. The pirate stabbed the hook's point at Ali's midsection. Ali whirled inside the thrust and ran his sword through the man's belly. The pirate collapsed and Ali moved on.

Just then, the midship hatch opened and Kor and Sarifa emerged. It took the half-ogre and the siren only a moment to assess the situation.

"About time you two woke up!" Lia quipped.

The siren and the half-ogre smiled and waded into the battle.

Inside of two minutes all but four of the remaining pirates lay dead; the survivors threw down their weapons and surrendered.

"Please!" one of them, a ratty one-eyed sailor shouted. "We beg quarter!"

Lilani kicked the man to his knees. Kor did the same for the pirate's three comrades. "Pray our captain feels more generous than I do," Lia said. She wiped the blood from a long, shallow cut on her left arm. The kneeling brigands gazed around the ship nervously, pleading with their eyes.

Ali took a moment to evaluate the situation. Lia wasn't the only crew member bleeding, but no one seemed seriously injured; twelve pirate bodies littered his freshly-swabbed deck. Ali frowned and wondered why the brigands had tried to take his ship with such a small band of men.

"Go aloft," he ordered Sarifa. "Make sure there are no more of these cutthroats roaming nearby."

The siren nodded and took to the air.

Ali turned angrily to Rina. "It was your watch," he said. "How did this happen?"

The elder Coralshell sister stood straight and tall, ignoring the gore covering her lithe form; clearly, none of the blood belonged to her. "I'm sorry, Captain," she replied. "Chaka went to the head. When he didn't report back after a few minutes, I ordered Sallah to look for him. As I did, the pirates swarmed aboard."

Ali looked around but saw no sign of Chaka. He seized the one-eyed man by the shirt and shook him. "What did you do to my man?" he bellowed.

"M-mercy, Captain!" the pirate cried. "We didn't have no choice! Our ship was hit broadside by a monstrous wave! It floundered and we didn't have nowhere to go! We had to try and take your ship!"

"We had to kill him!" blurted another. He was quickly punched in the gut by his comrades before he could say more.

Ali's eyes blazed in the darkness. He clenched his bloody sword tightly in his fist. Murder blazed in his hazel eyes.

At that moment, Sarifa touched down beside him. "There's a ship about a half league away," she said. "It's a Purple Tern pirate vessel, indigo painted and rigged. Her masts are broken and she's heeled over to one side. Only her bridge and aftercastle remain above water. I'm not surprised our lookouts didn't spot her."

"There's a longboat roped to our port bow," Lia reported, returning from that quarter of the ship. "They must have rowed up silently and pulled Chaka overboard. He didn't stand a chance, Captain." She looked as though she'd be happy to slay the captured pirates herself.

"The night-camouflaged pirate ship doesn't excuse my error, Captain," Rina put in. "This ambush happened on my watch. I will accept your judgment."

Ali looked angrily from the blood-caked sailor to the desperate handful of pirates kneeling on his deck. When he turned back to Rina once more, his demeanor softened. "Chaka should have seen them," the captain said, "even if he was using the head. That was his quarter of the ship. Too bad his carelessness cost his life."

As the captain turned to the pirates once more, Doran appeared on deck to tend the *Starcutter's* wounded. Makachiko's face poked cautiously out of the door to her cabin. Ali noticed the princess, but said nothing.

"Please, Captain," the one-eyed pirate repeated. "We had no choice!"

"You could have asked for mercy *before* attacking," Ali said coldly. "Though you are pirates, I might even have granted it."

Rina and Lia nodded sternly and the rest of the *Starcutter* crew rumbled agreement.

"Put them off the ship," Ali commanded. "And sink their boat—so they can't ambush any other passing ship."

"With pleasure," Kor said.

"You can't, Captain!" cried the youngest pirate, a ratty looking girl barely in her majority. "It's inhuman! Our ship is all but sunk! We'll die!"

"You should have thought of that before you killed my man," Ali replied.

He turned his back on the captives and walked over to the princess. As he went, Kor seized the prisoners one by one and cast them far over the side. The pirates pleaded for mercy as they splashed in the night-dark waters. None aboard the *Starcutter* heeded them. Lia and Rina quickly sank the pirates' longboat.

"Seen enough, Princess?" Ali asked grimly.

Though she seemed frightened, Makachiko's eyes remained cold. "More than enough," she replied and then returned to her cabin.

Ali took the wheel once more and steered them away from the wreck of the Purple Tern ship. The cries of the pirates grew ever more faint and distant. The *Starcutter* crew ignored the pleas, but no one slept again that night.

*

Morning dawned hot and brazen over the placid sea. The wind blew barely enough to keep Ali's sleek caravel moving. No sign remained of either the pirates or the ship they'd left behind. The captain conducted a brief funeral service for their lost shipmate. Crew members who had known Chaka spoke kindly of him and cursed the shipwrecked pirates who had cut short his life.

The princess said nothing. Chaka had been the first sailor to lose his life during the mission to rescue her; she kept her head bowed respectfully throughout the eulogy.

More islands appeared as the *Starcutter* sailed toward the core of the Blue Kingdoms. Every one of the small isles had been scoured clean by the great wave, just like the unfortunate island they'd passed the previous evening. No island they spotted that morning showed any signs of remaining human habitation.

The continuing devastation began to wear on the crew. They went about their duties carefully, but their eyes often wandered to the blasted keys nearby.

"Could we be the only people left in this part of the isles?" Toshi wondered aloud.

"What are you worried about?" Kor asked her. "You H'Leng-Ru can't drown."

The captain shot his first mate a stern look. "Toshi's people could still be battered to death or crushed by such a wave," Ali said, "and their shoreline villages would suffer in any case."

"I meant no disrespect," Kor replied, half to the captain and half to the young lookout. "It's just that the H'Leng-Ru people make their homes a long way from these parts. That plague of a wave couldn't have run that far. There's other lands, other folks, as aren't so lucky." He cast his baleful gaze across the rest of the crew, working nervously on deck.

"The wave has to diminish as it goes," Toshi said. "Doesn't it, Captain?"

Ali nodded grimly. "I pray to Allah it does, my little flying fish."

As they continued sailing, the effects of the wave did seem to lessen. The islands ahead of the *Starcutter* became merely battered and crushed, not scoured clean. Still, the power of the monstrous surge remained so great that no human life survived on the islets the ship passed.

On mid-morning of the third day, they came in sight of larger islands—spits of land that were more than just a few snapped trees clinging to the remnants of rock or reef.

"Captain!" Toshi called down from the mast top. "The island off the starboard bow! I see people!"

Ali set the heading and gave the wheel to Kor. The captain fetched his spyglass from its case nearby, and went to the rail.

Those of the crew who were otherwise unoccupied followed, as did Princess Makachiko, who had been pacing the deck at the time. As one, the crew of the *Starcutter* peered across the ocean.

A mountainous island, steep-sided and rocky, loomed up before them. Once, green jungles had covered the landscape from the mountaintop to the pink sand beach at the island's base. Now, the bottom half off the mountain had been wiped nearly clean. Giant trees lay snapped and toppled like matchsticks across the mountainside. Shattered logs tumbled in the breakers at the isle's shoreline. Further down the shore, a ruined breakwater protected what must have once been a fine, small harbor with a fishing town at the mountain's base. Now only the ruined stumps of homes and the broken teeth of a stout wharf lined the bay shore.

A handful of ragged, sun-burnt people staggered amid the ruins. They waved their arms frantically and shouted as they spotted the approaching ship.

"Looks like all their boats've been swamped," Kor rumbled.

"I only see a dozen seaworthy vessels left," Rina noted, shaking her head. "Poor wretches."

"With their fishing boats gone, these people don't stand much chance this far from the big islands of the Core," Lia added.

Ali nodded. "Aye. Not without some help, they don't."

The princess quickly mounted the stairs to the bridge. "You're not thinking of stopping, are you?"

"Of course," Ali replied. "What would you have us do, sail on by?"

"Yes! I need to get home, I . . . !"

"How many of these people would you sentence to death so that you might return home a little quicker, Princess?" Ali asked. He gazed sternly at her, then handed the girl his spyglass.

"Take a look," he said. "Then tell me that we should keep sailing. Our mission to rescue you took less time than we'd expected, so we have more provisions than the return voyage to Sunrii requires––far more, thank Allah. We've food and water to spare, plus more than enough nails, rope, fishing line, and other essentials. The least we can do is give some to these unfortunates."

"As I would hope others would do were the people of Sunrii in such need, your Highness," Sarifa added calmly.

The princess's hand strayed protectively to the jewelry hanging around her neck. She said nothing and turned away.

"Prepare landing parties," Ali told Sarifa. "Send enough supplies to help the people sustain themselves and rebuild. Take Doran along as well. We'll anchor for the rest of today and move on at first light."

"Aye, Captain," the siren replied.

They loaded up the two small boats stowed amidships and ferried supplies from the *Starcutter* to the wreckage-strewn island. For the rest of the day, Ali's crew helped the handful of survivors clear debris and rebuild the isle's tiny fishing fleet. The islanders had suffered terribly from the great wave, but thanks to Doran, no more people died during the night. At daybreak, when the *Starcutter* lifted anchor, neither Ali nor his crew doubted that the survivors could make it on their own––at least until the islanders' local king sent help.

"Assumin' their king ain't dead," Kor muttered after the *Starcutter* had sailed out of earshot.

"What a terrible thing to say!" the princess blurted. Despite her initial reluctance to stop, she had actually ventured ashore with Doran and assisted the healer in tending to the island's wounded.

"It is possible," Sarifa reminded her, "that much more destruction lies ahead of us. The islands grow larger and more populous as we head deeper into the archipelago. If the wave did not spend its energy before reaching those larger islands, its effects could be far worse than they were here."

"Let's hope not," Lia said. She and her sister were using buckets of salt water to rub the island's grime from their tanned skin.

"Hope has little to do with it," Sarifa replied. "We are, all of us, under the wings of fate."

"Let us hope, then," Ali said, "that fate smiles upon the merciful."

*

The next day they sailed within sight of an even larger island. Again, the *Starcutter* lookouts reported the costal towns devastated. Because this island was larger and more populous, though, more people had survived the disaster.

"Their plight seems desperate, Captain," Sarifa reported after a brief scouting flight.

"Sail on, Captain," Kor urged. His poison-green eyes, tinged slightly darker with concern, scanned the mass of people swarming toward the shore. "Helping a mob this size will strip us of valuable supplies—supplies we need to reach home."

"Not if we resupply at Sunrii," Ali said. "And since we've rescued their princess, resupplying us is the least Makachiko's royal parents--and her people—can do." He looked hopefully at the girl.

"I . . . I think they would agree to it," Makachiko said. But, gazing at the wretched throng teeming the shores, she appeared worried.

"Whether Sunrii assists us or not, we've still enough extra supplies to help," Ali added. "Allah would curse us if we were not generous with what we have to spare."

The crew working the *Starcutter's* decks rumbled their agreement, though every man and woman of them looked wary. Kor and Sarifa nodded their assent, too, though the half-ogre did so with little enthusiasm.

The islanders began swimming out toward the skiffs even before the *Starcutter's* boats touched shore. The survivors swarmed the crew as the Coralshell sisters and the rest pulled the boats ashore and began unloading the supplies.

"Keep back! Wait your turn!" Rina cried as she and the other sailors unshipped casks of fresh water and sacks of flour. "There's plenty for all if you don't fight over it!"

"Who needs healing?" Doran called above the din of the crowd. "I've trained at the *Il-Siha* schools!"

Dozens of bruised and scabrous people surged forward, too many to help all at once. They pawed at the physician, each begging for his attention. "Not all at once!" he cried. "I'm no miracle worker! Form a line! I'll treat those hurt most badly first."

"Do as yer told, or I'll break heads until you shape up!" Kor dar-Bek bellowed. The half-ogre's watchful glare cowed the mob, and soon Doran and the other relief workers were able to continue their jobs in relatively good order.

A terrible odor arose within the destroyed village as the morning sun burned into afternoon. The stench of decaying bodies, both human and animal, mixed with the sweat of the populace and the filth of their living conditions.

Ali and the ship's carpenters helped build some primitive shelters and basic sanitary conveniences. They also repaired what fishing boats they could. By nightfall, the entire *Starcutter* crew felt exhausted, and there seemed little more that they could do.

The island's people were grateful, though they had nothing with which to replay their saviors.

"Your thanks is enough," Ali told them. "We must sail on." Turning to his crew, he said, "Everyone, back to the ship."

The survivors watched with forlorn eyes as the *Starcutter* sailed away.

More islands dotted the horizon as indigo night descended over the placid sea. On the distant beaches of the largest isles, wan fires burned and black smoke smudged out the stars.

From the bow of the ship, Ali gazed intently into the darkness ahead.

Rina and Lia appeared at his elbow. The sisters were dirty and tired, but each smiled brightly. The princess came with them, though she did not look nearly so enthusiastic.

"Another nameless island down," Rina said, "the gods only know how many to go."

"Yes," Ali said thoughtfully, "only Allah knows."

"Will we be stopping at any of those islands, Captain?" Lia asked, pointing to the dots that smoldered like embers in a dying fire.

"Aye," Ali replied. "If we're needed."

"And what of the islands after those, and the ones after the next. . . ?" Makachiko asked. "Will you stop to lend aid to every destroyed isle we encounter along the way to Sunrii?"

"For as long as we are able," Ali replied. "If Allah is merciful, perhaps the resources we have left will be enough. At the very least, we can save a few more innocent lives."

"And what of our lives, Captain?" the princess asked. "Are we to spend our days squandering our time and possessions on people we don't even know?"

"The princess is right, Captain," Kor grumbled from amidships. "I'm all for saving lives—so long as doing it doesn't cost us our own."

"I don't want any more deaths," Ali said quietly, "not among my crew, nor among the poor wretches in the path of that God-cursed wave."

Their previous stops had diminished the *Starcutter's* supplies by more than half, but they still had enough to finish their journey to Sunrii—plus a bit little extra.

Many of the crew grumbled quietly when Ali sailed toward the ravaged port on the next large island, but—under the captain's stern gaze—they all soon fell into the routine they'd established.

Ali, Doran, and the boat crew rowed ashore with supplies again. Makachiko went with them to help, despite the captain's misgivings. Again, refugees swam out to meet the skiffs as the boats neared the battered shore. The *Starcutter* crew did what they could to unload the extra supplies, but this time the mob of survivors became unruly, and not even the bellowing of Kor dar-Bek could quiet them down. They tore at the princess' silken garments, and she quickly retreated to the safety of the skiffs.

When it became clear they couldn't help any further, Ali, Kor, and the Coralshell sisters pushed their way back to the boats as well. The skiff crews quickly joined them and shoved off. Doran, though, remained behind, hemmed in by swarms of ragged survivors.

"Doran," Ali cried as the skiffs bobbed in the surf, "back to the ship!"

"Just another minute," the healer called back as Ali's crew unshipped the boats' oars. The physician worked frantically on an injured child, bandaging the girl's head and trying to straighten her twisted limbs. The child coughed, and blood seeped out of the corners of her mouth.

"That *Il-Siha* devil's killing her!" someone in the crowd shouted. The mob grew more hostile, but the healer remained intent on his work and didn't notice.

"Doran!" Ali shouted. The mob surged between the captain and the physician and the skiffs drifted into the bay, toward the *Starcutter*.

As the healer worked feverishly, a stone struck him on the side of the head.

"Ow!" he yelped. He looked for who had thrown the rock; only angry, worried eyes greeted his gaze.

"Are you people mad?" he asked. "Don't you want me to save this child's life?"

The mob surged in closer around him, their feral faces burning with hatred and fear.

Suddenly, strong hands seized Doran and lifted him into the air.

"It's time to go, healer," Sarifa said. Her flame-colored wings beat the air furiously as she plucked Doran from the beach.

"No! Wait!" the physician cried, trying to resist. "A moment longer! Just give me a moment longer!"

"I'm sorry, my friend," Sarifa replied. "If we wait any longer, neither one of us will reach the ship."

Doran watched forlornly as the beach and his young patient receded into the distance. "But I could have saved her!" he protested.

"And who would have saved you?" the siren asked.

The mob onshore surged into the waves, realizing too late that the mariners intended to set sail.

"Come back!" the mob wailed angrily. "Don't leave us!"

Ali's jaw clenched tight, and he didn't look back as his shipmates rowed. The *Starcutter* crew raised the smaller boats aboard ship, lashed them to the deck, and quickly sailed on. Even as the *Starcutter* left the harbor, a few ragged survivors swam futilely after them.

"Th-they were like wild animals!" the princess said as the ship left the bay. She rubbed her hands over her arms, as if she might smear the touch of the survivors from her body. "We never should have stopped to help them."

Ali shook his head. "Not animals," he told her, "desperate people. And in their situation, who wouldn't be?" He gazed sternly at the princess and she looked away. Her once-fine garments were soiled and tattered. She looked far less regal than she had, though her carriage remained proud and defiant.

"I'll be in my cabin, washing up," she said, and then turned and went to her room beneath the forecastle.

*

For two days after that, they saw only small, uninhabited spits of land. The crew cleaned the ship and themselves, and fished in the Azure Sea. Their spirits rose again, and they began to talk of reaching Sunrii and completing their mission. Then, on the third day, they spotted a smudge of smoke on the horizon.

Ali fixed his dark brown eyes on it.

The crew gathered on the main deck, expectant, worried. Sarifa and Kor stood beside Ali on the bridge.

"Sail on, Captain," Kor urged.

"This time, the half-ogre is right, Captain," Sarifa agreed. "Our supplies are very low. There is little we can do, even if the need is very great."

"Then we'll do what little we can," Ali snapped. He spun the wheel and turned the ship toward the new island. "We won't surrender our humanity—or our compassion—just because circumstances are difficult. All aboard, prepare to lend aid. We'll assist until our supplies run out or until Allah sends an angel to lift this scourge from the isles."

"Aye, Captain," the crew grumbled, and then began their preparations.

"That cursed wave!" Toshi said as she worked. "Is there nowhere that remains untouched?"

"Nowhere in this part of the World Sea it seems," Lia replied.

"Nowhere without a powerful wizard or a dragon to protect it, at any rate," Rina added.

The new island's inhabitants proved just as needy as the previous one's. The isle was a sharp, volcanic crag, thrusting precipitously out of the clear waters. Its rocky arms formed a narrow strait—barely two ship lengths wide—leading to a sheltered bay. But even the strait and the tall cliffs had failed to stop the onrushing wave's terrible power.

Once, a proud and prosperous port town had lain on the beach at the base of the mountain. Now only a few snapped beams stabbed out of the sea of wreckage piled against the coast. Bloated corpses bobbed in the placid waters of the wide bay.

Amid the ruins on shore, hundreds of squalid people scrambled like scavenger ants.

"Gods help us," Doran whispered. He rolled up his soiled white sleeves, tied on his white headband, and prepared to go to work.

The *Starcutter's* captain shook his head at the healer. "You're staying aboard this time, physician," he said.

"But . . ." Doran began.

"I won't risk sending you ashore until we know the situation is calm," Ali said, "not after the last incident."

Even as he spoke, the isle's wretched inhabitants splashed into the water, swimming for the *Starcutter*. Doran frowned but said nothing. The *Starcutter's* crew unshipped the two skiffs and filled them with supplies.

"Ready to cast off, Captain," Kor reported.

"So quickly?" Ali asked, concerned.

"We've loaded the boats with all we dare, Captain," Sarifa told him. "Any more and we risk starving or dying of thirst before we make Sunrii."

Ali nodded in resignation. "Would to Allah that we could do more," he said. "Kor, make ready to cast off from the ship. Sarifa, you have command until I return. I'll signal you if there's trouble." He turned and followed Kor over the side and down the ship's ladder.

As Ali reached the tiny, bobbing boat, someone jumped in after him.

"Princess!" he said, surprised. "Climb back up and stay with Doran."

"I'm going, Captain," Makachiko said firmly.

Ali frowned at her. "It would be better if you stayed aboard."

"You cannot order me," she replied, her eyes cold and stern. "I am a princess."

"On my ship, you are under my command," Ali said. "So, unless you'd care to swim to shore. . . ."

116

"Captain, I've seen too much suffering over the last days," she said. "I didn't do much but cower the last time. This time, I want to help. Please."

"Don't waste time arguing with her, Captain," Rina said.

"Aye," Lia added. "If she wants to risk her pretty neck, that's her own business."

"Not if she loses us our reward," Kor pointed out.

The princess' dark eyes met the poison-green eyes of the ogre. "Very well," she said. She reached around her neck, removed the dragon pendant, and handed up it to Doran, standing at the rail. "Keep this," she told the physician. "Deliver it to my family if I'm killed. Then they will know that you have fulfilled your obligation."

Slowly, Ali nodded. "Make room," he told the crew. "If she's coming with us, she might as well have a place to sit."

The crew aboard his boat reluctantly shifted to give the girl a seat. She settled in among them, taking only a moment to straighten her stained and tattered clothing.

A ragged throng of survivors met the crew well before they reached shore. The swimming islanders circled the boats like hungry sharks, crying for help and trying to scramble aboard. The skiffs' crews tried not to hit the swimmers with their oars.

"Get back!" Kor bellowed.

The desperate swimmers ignored him. They crowded in among the oars, grabbing and grasping.

"Please!" Makachiko cried. "Can't you see we're trying to help?"

The splashing and scrabbling of the refugees drowned out her words. Dozens of dirty hands seized hold of the skiffs' sides. The frantic people tipped at the boats, threatening to overturn them. The crew in both skiffs fought to keep their seats.

Above the clamor, Rina called, "Do we fight, Captain?"

"No!" Ali replied. "Hurting these people won't help anything! Cast the supplies overboard, and then row for the ship!"

"We're not just leaving them here!" Makachiko protested. "They'll drown each other."

"And us, too, if we stay!" Ali replied.

Immediately, the crew heaved the supplies overboard, into the water, amid the squabbling refugees. The desperate people grabbed for the casks and sacks, turning from the boats and fighting with each other.

"No! No!" the princess cried. "Don't fight! Help each other! If you don't fight, there's enough for all!"

The survivors didn't listen to her. Instead, they became even more frantic in their attempts to win the supplies.

"Pull for all you're worth!" Ali ordered his crew. The two skiffs jostled through the milling crowd and rowed out toward the *Starcutter*. A few wretches swam after them initially, but soon turned back to fight over scraps with the rest. Some of the survivors left the water and dashed along the shore, in a futile attempt to catch up with the boats. They screamed and howled as they ran.

"Why didn't they listen?" Makachiko asked. "Have they lost their minds?"

"No," Ali replied, "but they've very nearly lost their humanity."

"The disaster has turned them into animals," Rina whispered.

"What are your orders, Captain?" Sarifa asked as Ali and the crew returned to the *Starcutter*. "Shall we sail on to the next isle—see if we can be of any help there?"

"After those savages nearly sank us?" Kor replied, incredulous. He focused his poison-green eyes on the *Starcutter's* captain. "It's gotten worse at every isle, Captain. If we keep tempting fate this way, we'll end up dead just as sure as that unfortunate lot back there." He glanced from Ali to the shoreline, where masses of wild-eyed people ran along the beaches, fighting each other for supplies Ali's crew had cast overboard.

"There must be something we can do," Doran said. "'While life clings, there is yet hope.'"

Ali shook his head. "No, Doran. Kor's right, this time. Fate is against us. If we persist against such ill winds, we'll only be killed for trying." The captain's voice brimmed with bitter resignation. "Bring the *Starcutter* about. No more stops. We sail for Sunrii."

Doran sighed and gave the princess back her necklace.

"Perhaps the isles ahead won't need our help," Toshi suggested. "Perhaps the people there will be cooperating. Maybe they'll be helping each other, not fighting for scraps like frenzied sharks."

"Maybe the girl is right," Makachiko added hopefully. "Maybe they'll be able to save themselves, even without our help. Or perhaps the great wave went no further, and this is the last of the wave-cursed isles."

Her words rang hollow over the gently rolling deck of the ship.

The princess looked around, clearly hoping someone might confirm her wish. The faces of the crew remained grim. Makachiko's jaw began to tremble. "I-it has to stop sometime, doesn't it?"

No one answered. A floating corpse struck the side of the ship with a sickening thud.

The young princess fought to remain calm, but the trembling took hold in her whole body. Tears budded in her dark eyes.

"Please," she said, "tell me it will stop!"

Ali angled the *Starcutter* to pass between the rocky arms of the mountain and out of the devastated bay. "We'll have you home soon, Princess," he promised.

Makachiko and Toshi stared back toward the ruined town, unable to tear their eyes from the unfolding horror. The rest of the crew gazed forward, anticipating the freedom of the open sea beyond the strait.

"There are people running along the beach toward us," Toshi said.

"Let them," Ali replied. His hazel eyes remained fixed on the waters ahead. "Maybe when they've run enough, they'll be too exhausted to fight each other."

"But captain," Toshi said, "they have ropes and grappling hooks."

"What are they going to do," Kor asked, "swim out and try to board us?" His massive chest shook with a deep, ogrish laugh.

Simultaneously, Ali and Sarifa glanced up at the cliffs, looming close to either side of the ship, as the *Starcutter* passed through the narrow strait at the bay's head. Before captain or siren could speak, grappling ropes and nets rained down on the ship from the cliff tops.

"Damn!" Ali cursed. "They've gotten ahead of us!"

"Some must have climbed the heights even as we sailed into the bay!" Sarifa cried. "To arms!"

As she said it, a barbed and weighed net fell over her. She reached for the sword at her hip, but the net constricted around her and the hooks dug into her wings. The siren winced with pain.

Crude spears and rocks hurtled down from the cliff tops as the savage raiders pulled their grapples tight. The *Starcutter* groaned as the tethered ropes slowed it nearly to a halt.

"Princess, get below!" Ali called. He ducked, and a rough hewn spear sailed over his right shoulder.

The savages mobbed the ship. Some slid down their ropes, while others swung over and dropped onto the main deck.

Some of the crew, like Sarifa, had fallen under the hail of spears, rocks, nets, and ropes. Most of the *Starcutter* sailors remained on their feet, though. As the invaders attacked, the shipmates avoided the entanglements and drew their swords.

The Coralshell sisters fought side by side, protecting each other. Some attackers they cut down with their swords; others they pushed over the rail into the brine. "So much for trying to help," Rina hissed.

"I'm beginning to think humanitarianism is not worth the effort," Lia replied. She kicked one invader in the knee and cut a second down with her sword.

As the sisters traded barbs amid the battle, the rest of the crew struggled to stay alive. Toshi pushed past a half-dozen ruffians and scrambled up the masthead. Two raiders tried to scamper after her, but Toshi turned and drew two whalebone-handled daggers from her leg sheathes. She slashed at her pursuers, all the while clinging to the rigging with her toes.

Doran and Princess Makachiko stood next to each other, trapped on the forecastle. Barbaric attackers scrambled up the ship's stairs toward them.

"Is this the price of compassion?" the healer asked rhetorically. "To be dragged down and drowned by the very people we sought to help?" He clouted his fist against the chin of a man reaching for his throat. The man tumbled backward down the steps onto the quarterdeck, taking two of his companions with him. There, Kor grabbed the raiders and hurled them over the side.

"Stop philosophizin' and get below!" the half-ogre bellowed at the physician.

Doran pushed Princess Makachiko toward the forward hatch. As he did, a rough-cut spear struck his back, just below the ribs. The healer gasped and collapsed onto the deck. Makachiko screamed.

"Thrice-damned sons of dogs!" Ali cursed. "This is the thanks we get for trying to help you?" He put his sword through the eye of a man trying to skewer him, and then cut down two more attackers. The raiders kept coming, like a sea of pestilent crabs swarming over the ship.

Sarifa struggled in the barbed net. The attackers threw more ropes over her, pinning her to the deck. The net's hooks cut into the siren's flesh. Rivulets of blood trickled down her pale skin into the red feathers of her wings. Three savages stepped forward, surrounding the siren and raising their rough-hewn spears for the kill.

Ali charged into them, knocking two over and gutting the third with his cutlass. More invaders sprang forward to take their place. "Kill the siren demon!" screamed one. "Her evil magic's the cause of all this!" howled another.

Before the savages could reach Sarifa, though, Ali cut the siren free with a few deft slashes of his sword. The *Starcutter's* captain smiled as Sarifa rose from the deck. She looked grim and terrible, like an avenging angel.

"Snakes!" she hissed in her birdlike voice. "Flee while you still can!"

Instead, the pestilent mob surged forward. Ali laid into them, hacking and slashing with his cutlass. Sarifa threw off the last of her bonds and drew her sword.

At first, it seemed as though the siren's weapon had no blade. The air beyond the hand grip shimmered, like a mirage on a hot summer day. As Sarifa stood, a fiery blade grew from the pommel. The siren warrior spread her wings, buffeting two invaders over the sides of the boat. She looked around, her hawk-keen eyes assessing the battle.

Nearby, the ragged woman who had stabbed Doran pulled out her spear and reared back for a killing blow. Makachiko threw herself over the healer's body in a futile attempt to save him.

The woman stabbed at the two of them. Her spear descended, but then suddenly stopped. The scabrous woman jerked into the air as Kor seized her by the back of the neck. Before the savage could react, the half-ogre flung her over the side and into the cliff face. She hit with a wet crunching sound and slid into the dark water below.

Kor bounded up onto the forecastle, hurling raiders over the side as he went, quickly clearing a path to Doran and the princess.

The healer lay bleeding in Makachiko's arms. The girl wept quietly over the physician's pale body.

Kor's eyes went blood red. "Sawbones is hurt!" he bellowed. "We could use some help here!"

"Couldn't we all!" Lia called. She and Rina were bleeding from dozens of small cuts, though none were serious enough to slow them down. The sisters moved through the savages like twin whirlwinds, their swords dealing death to anyone unlucky enough to stand their way.

Sarifa T'Liil flapped her wings and rose into the air. The siren's face twisted with rage and her eyes blazed with fury. "By the Gods of Wrath," she cried, "you will all pay!" Her sword blazed bright in her hand as she dove on the raiders. Her keening war-cry echoed off the nearby cliffs.

The ambushers froze and their shabby faces went pale as the siren dived toward them. Ali cut down four savages trying to capture the *Starcutter's* wheel. Kor threw raiders overboard two and three at a time, protecting the princess and the wounded physician. The Coralshell sisters used their swords and fists to clear the port side deck of savages. Toshi sent a man tumbling from the mast into the dark waters at the base of the cliffs.

Though the savages still vastly outnumbered the *Starcutter* crew, fear ran like wildfire through the mob. As Sarifa dived on them, most of the invaders leapt over the side. Others caught fire as the blade of her sword passed near them. The burning wretches also dived into the water to escape. Those that didn't get out of her way, the siren cut in half.

Kor laughed, seized a boat hook, twisted it sideways, and shoved a half-dozen ambushers into the drink all at once. Having cleaned out the port side, Rina and Lia began fighting their way to starboard. Toshi dived into a mass of savages surrounding one of the deckhands. The H'Leng-Ru's blades pierced the backs of two ruffians before the invaders even knew what was happening. Ali cleared the aftercastle of raiders and then fought his way toward the quarterdeck.

The three dozen attackers remaining screamed in fear and leapt overboard. Ali sprinted back to the wheel and took control of the ship once more. Sarifa dove on the savages as they floundered in the blood-stained bay. Kor and the other members of the crew cut the ropes holding the ship, and the *Starcutter* surged through the strait and into the open sea.

"Sarifa!" Ali called.

The siren turned. A mask of blood covered her wrathful face.

"Sarifa!" he called again. "Doran needs you!"

For a moment, the siren hovered in the air, torn between bloodlust and duty. Then she wrenched herself free of her fury and flew back to the ship. Sarifa's sandaled feet touched down lightly on the forecastle, next to the unconscious healer.

Rina and Lia were already at Doran's side, putting pressure on his wound and unwinding a roll of bandages. When the siren arrived, the sisters made way for her and went to tend the other injured crew members.

"W-will he live?" Princess Makachiko asked the siren.

"If he does not," Sarifa replied, "those barbarians will wish they had never been born." She cast her hawk-like gaze back to the wretches floundering in the surf behind the ship.

Makachiko stood, confusion playing across her pretty face. "No," she said. "No. You can't. Desperation has driven them mad. They're starving. They don't know what they're doing."

"They know," Sarifa said. "And they will pay."

"Killing them in self defense was one thing," Makachiko said, "but killing them now. . ." Her eyes wandered from the surf to the ruined port, where the survivors still fought like dogs for the scraps of food the *Starcutter* had brought. Tears streamed down the princess' tanned cheeks.

The siren didn't reply. As the Coralshell sisters tended the rest of the ship's wounded, the remainder of the *Starcutter* crew began casting the bodies of their enemies overboard.

"Kor, take the wheel," Ali said. He sprinted to the foredeck where Sarifa knelt over the injured physician. "Well. . . ?" he asked the siren.

"It is too early to tell," Sarifa replied.

Makachiko looked from the bleeding man, over the carnage-strewn decks of the *Starcutter*, and out to the ravaged island and its desperate people. "It . . . it's all too much!" she whispered and buried her face in her hands.

Ali rested his fingers on the princess' bloodstained shoulder. "That's the way of the world," he said gently. "We all do what we can, but sometimes it isn't enough."

"Not nearly enough!" she sobbed. Her delicate fingers twined themselves around the amulet at her neck.

"Princess. . . ?" Ali asked.

"I . . ." she began, her voice quiet and uncertain, "I call . . ." She straightened up, seeming to draw strength from the medallion as she spoke. "I call on the power . . . of the dragons!" Her voice came loud and clear now, full of determination. "Argentia Lumus, hear my plea! Remember your promise to my people!"

A peal like distant thunder shook the heavens and the sea around the *Starcutter* quaked.

"Another wave!" Kor shouted.

"No!" Ali cried. "Look!"

He pointed to the sky. Amid the clouds and the clear blue heavens, brilliant stars suddenly flashed to life. For a moment, they blazed as brightly as the sun, before dimming to a silvery luminescence.

Toshi gasped. "Dragons!"

Argentia Lumus and her court swooped down toward the tiny ship. The dragons were huge, many twice as long as the *Starcutter*. They had teeth like swords, claws like lances, and armor that glittered like the purest metal ever forged. They glistened with the colors of the rainbow. The dragon queen herself was covered in scales of brilliant silver. Her sea green eyes sparkled with intelligence and a wisdom older than mankind.

She dipped toward the ship, and, as she came, she transformed into a beautiful maiden garbed in a diaphanous silver gown. Her bare feet touched down lightly on the deck next to the princess.

Ali and the rest of the *Starcutter* crew fell to their knees, all save Sarifa, who continued to work on Doran. Makachiko knelt as well.

"Daughter of Sunrii," said the dragon queen, "you have called and I have come. How may my people serve you and, thereby, repay our debt?"

"Queen of d-dragons," Makachiko said, her voice quavering, "help these people—the ones whose homes and lives have been destroyed by the great wave."

Argentia Lumus gazed from the princess to the blasted island, already receding into the distance behind the *Starcutter*. "But these are not your people, daughter of Sunrii," she said. "Your island lies safe and sound, beyond the wave's terrible reach."

"M-my heart thrills to hear it," the princess responded, "but my request stands. I want you to help the people who have been harmed by the wave, all of them, no matter who they are. No matter where they live."

"Some may be wicked people," the queen said, "pirates or slavers."

"Then help them so that they may see the error of their ways."

A smile crept over the dragon queen's face, and she slowly nodded.

"And what of you, princess Makachiko," she said. "Is there a boon I may grant you as well?"

"For myself I ask nothing," the princess replied. "But, if it is within your powers, heal the good people of this ship. They have risked much to help others—myself included."

Again, the dragon queen smiled.

"You have chosen well, daughter of Sunrii," she said. "For your sacrifice, your people will be thrice blessed. All those we help will know of your generosity."

"I . . . I'm not doing it to be rewarded," Makachiko said. "I'm doing it because it's the right thing to do."

"And so it is, child. Sometimes the only moral thing to do is to give up that which you hold most dear. Again, you have chosen well."

The silver-garbed woman spread her arms and her diaphanous gown flowed outward, like a great glittering cape. Silvery light blazed around the dragon queen as the garment transformed into her wings and she lifted into the air.

Renewed vigor flowed through Ali's body. The pain of fatigue and combat slipped away in an instant. He marveled as Argentia Lumus arced into the sky once more. She wheeled once around the ship, and then collected her retinue and sped off toward the ravished island.

The dragons quickly vanished into the distance, like stars winking out with the break of dawn.

For a long moment no one on the *Starcutter* even dared breathe.

Doran sat up and coughed. His eyes flickered open. "Did I miss anything?" he asked.

The crew burst out laughing, but Makachiko merely threw her arms around the healer's neck and cried.

"We'll be taking you home now, Princess," Ali said.

Makachiko fingered the dragon-twined medallion hanging around her throat. Its gems didn't glitter as brightly as before, but the princess didn't seem to notice. "Yes," she said, drying the tears from her face. "I'm ready to go home now."

"You did the right thing," Ali said, "to give up the gift of the dragons."

"I know," she replied. "I only wish I'd known it sooner."

"It's never too late to learn," the sea captain replied. "Never too late . . . for any of us."

"And that," Doran said, "is the hope of the world."

"Aye," Ali agreed. "There may be hope for all of us yet."

He smiled and steered the *Starcutter* toward home.

RENAISSANCE FEAR

"Lizard on a stick! Get your lizard on a stick!"

The street vendor loped through the dirt pathways between the colorful tents and muddy paddocks, holding aloft his sample of wares—a collection of brownish, lumpy ribbons of fried meat, each skewered on a thin strip of wood. The young scraggly-haired salesman eyed the crowd on either side of the path, looking for likely customers.

"Lizard on a stick!" he called again.

Caroline Shaw clapped her hands and squealed, as though she were a girl of half her actual age. She clung excitedly to her fiancée's arm, pulling him close, and spoke urgently into his ear.

"Let's get some!" she breathed in a voice too loud to be truly conspiratorial. "What do you think it *really* is?"

"Chicken, probably," Karl Lomax replied. "Spicy fried chicken."

"Untrue, milord," the vendor put in, his bright white smile belaying the "period" grunge of his dingy, rag-like costume. "'Tis lizard—as the Good Lord is my witness."

Karl shot him a very skeptical look.

"*Alligator*," the vendor added, whispering. Then, falling back into character, he threw his arms wide and made a comically frightening face. "This 'gator be a monstrous, dragon-like lizard, hunted in the wild swamps of the southland. Many knights fell riven beneath its claws to bring this delicacy to our fair land."

"I thought hunting alligators was illegal," Karl said.

The vendor frowned at him and spoke out of the corner of his mouth, as though trying not to let the others attending the fair hear. "Okay," he hissed, "it was raised on a gator *farm* down in the bayou."

"Not quite *period* fare, is it?" Karl said. "They didn't have alligator in Renaissance Europe."

The vendor shrugged, and the faux-rags on his skinny frame rustled. "Perhaps 'tis crocodile, from the Nile delta, then," he said. "My sources remain unclear on this point. But 'twer a terrible, great *lizard*, milord. And lizard be a well-known delicacy throughout this fair land." He held out the lumpy fried thing on the thin stick and added, "If you should but try it, your senses would thank you."

Karl remained unconvinced.

"Karl," Caroline said playfully, "they didn't have Renaissance Europe in eastern *Kentucky*, either! Get into the mood, would you?" She elbowed him playfully in the ribs. "We're on *vacation*. Seize the day."

"Thy fair maiden's advice be sound, milord," the vendor agreed. Then, laying his hand next to his mouth and speaking in a stage whisper, he added. "'Tis said that the flesh of the dragon has powerful *aphrodisiac* qualities, milord."

Caroline laughed and clapped again. "Let's get some."

"Yeah, okay," Karl said, a begrudging smile tugging at the corners of his lips. "How much?"

"That be four single paper notes per skewer," the vendor said.

"Is this where I should haggle?" Karl asked hopefully.

"Alas, haggling be outlawed by the master of the Vendors' Guild, milord." The lizard seller frowned. "My deepest and most sincere apologies."

Karl nodded at the vendor, then smiled at Caroline as he handed the money over. Keeping his eyes fixed on his fiancée was the only way Karl could avoid wincing at the price—real alligator or no.

The ragged-costumed vendor handed over the food and then bowed, flashing his twenty-first century smile once more.

"Thank you, milord, milady," he said. "Fare you well." He turned and hobbled theatrically down the muddy street.

Caroline Shaw put her arm around Karl Lomax's waist, and the two walked down the crowded marketway as they chewed on their fried 'gator. Colorful tents of many shapes and sizes lined the sides of the unpaved thoroughfare. Each pavilion shared the common goal of separating the fairgoer from his money. Most were dedicated to selling wares, though a few provided services— massage, body painting, soothsaying.

Karl didn't need a fortune-teller to know his wallet would be a good deal lighter by the time he and Caroline continued on their vacation that evening. The sign outside the town had read, "*Knightshead Kentucky*—Sister City to *Knightstor, England.*" Karl thought that if they stayed at the Renaissance Faire long enough, it might have been cheaper just to go to England.

Fog surrounded the tent city, making it seem strange and unreal. The mist added to the period effect that the fair sponsors were trying so desperately to achieve. In the fog, attendees could almost overlook the electrical lines snaking into the backs of most of the tents, or the Velcro fasteners that held so much of the fabric together. The mist made the participants' costumes look better than they were, too. From a distance, Karl could almost believe that he was looking at historical English peasants going about their daily business—historical peasants with great dental work.

This fair midway seemed larger than most of the others he'd been to, though perhaps that was a trick of the light as well. When the fog parted a bit, Karl almost thought he saw a medieval, or early Renaissance, town beyond the woods on the far side of the tents. And was that a *castle* perched atop that distant hill? Probably no more than a painted facade. The AAA guidebook hadn't mentioned castles—or reconstructed historical towns—in Knightshead, Kentucky. Maybe it was something new, though— something tied into the "Sister City" campaign mentioned on the road sign.

Whether a fake or not, the looming castle did add to the atmosphere. Karl almost felt impressed. If he hadn't been to so many Renaissance Faires over the years, he probably would have *been* impressed.

Caroline sighed and snuggled up against him. The neckline of her low-cut top bunched up a bit, giving him a nice view down her blouse. "I just *love* this place," she said. "Don't you?"

Karl smiled and nodded at her. When Caroline wore a scanty top and cut-offs, it was hard *not* to love anyplace they went together.

If the truth were known, though, Karl Lomax *didn't* love the place. Despite the number he'd been to, he didn't much like Renaissance Faires at all. Karl knew the fair circuit well, and there were plenty of things *not* to like about it: too many weirdoes, too many aging hippies, too many "arts & crafts" booths (exhibiting neither art nor craft), too damn much strange (and overpriced) food, too many out-of-work actors hoping to be spotted on the off chance of getting their big break, too many dopers hiding out after the dissolution of the Grateful Dead, and *way* too many poseurs speaking with fake accents.

Most of the "history" came from old Hollywood films; Renaissance and medieval cultures were haphazardly blended into a commercially viable whole. The music wafting through the air was often painfully slow and crude (and frequently off key). The colorful tents were fabricated mostly from materials created in a laboratory after World War II. The costumes of the participants were usually about as convincing and historically accurate as the tents.

Not that Karl didn't find some of the costumes the *women* wore attractive—even *alluring*. (Despite his engagement to Caroline, the sight of a chainmail bikini still made his pulse quicken.) Women, in fact, were the whole reason he started coming to Ren Faires in the first place.

Long ago Karl had discovered that women were suckers for *chivalry*.

They loved the colorful tents, the sensual costumes, the whole "dress-up" nature of the events. Ren Faires were great places to pick up girls—and they were great places to go on a date.

You could catch a few knights bashing each other and getting all sweaty, listen to some mushy music, dine on exotic foods, knock back a couple of home-brewed drinks, and then finish it all off with a torchlight stroll through a tent city or a fake medieval village. The net effect of all that romance and chivalry practically *guaranteed* a quick score.

Which was why Karl put up with all the other Ren Faire shit he didn't much care for. The fairs had been good to his libido—very good indeed.

Of course, Caroline didn't know that. *She* thought Karl was interested in the whole historical re-creation bit; she thought he was just another *rube*, like her.

The two of them had met at a Renaissance Faire very much like this one. Karl had been on his usual babe patrol, and Caroline had come for all the romantic stuff that women like. The two of them hit it off immediately.

Much to Karl's surprise, the initial attraction blossomed into something deeper. An intense period of courtship had followed, and now they were engaged. Happily engaged. There was only one problem.

Karl had never told Caroline the *real* reason they'd met at that Ren Faire eighteen months ago. He didn't have the nerve to tell her that she was just the latest pick-up in a long line of conquests. Nor did he dare tell that he was sick to *death* of fake Renaissance events.

He knew she wouldn't understand. She would think it was some reflection on his love for her. (It wasn't.) Or, worse, she would think that their entire relationship was based on a lie. (Maybe in the beginning, but they'd moved far beyond that point now.) In either case, he couldn't tell her. Not now.

The only thing to do was to carry on with the charade; to be as phony as every peasant, knight, and noble in the fairs themselves.

Karl didn't much like the corner he'd painted himself into, but Caroline was worth it. One day, after they'd been married for fifteen years and had a couple of kids, he'd tell her. Until then, he'd keep his chin up and try to find things to admire in a series of increasingly repetitive and boring semi-historical attractions.

He *had* tried to steer Caroline away from them. He'd planned out-of-town vacations when he knew the local fairs were returning to town. He discarded flyers and sections of the local newspapers before she could see Ren Faire ads. Karl had been pretty successful—until today's stroke of bad luck.

He'd never expected to be "ambushed" by a Renaissance Faire while driving through Knightshead, Kentucky on vacation. The sign for the fair had just appeared out of the fog. Naturally, Caroline *had* to go. Naturally, Karl couldn't refuse—not without revealing his "dark secret."

So, here he was, munching alligator fritter and getting his new Nikes muddy while the chill haze pressed in around them. The fog, Karl decided, was a blessing. Not only did it make the fair look less shabby, but it had the added benefit of making Caroline snuggle close.

"We should have brought our coats," she cooed.

"Yeah," he replied, glad they hadn't. His T-shirt and shorts weren't as brief as hers, but he didn't get cold as quickly as she did. Which always served to bring them closer together, much to his delight. "Do you want to go back to the car?" he asked hopefully.

"Not yet," she said. "We haven't been here that long." She hugged him as they walked. "I sometimes feel like I was born *too late*. That *here* is where I really belong."

"In Kentucky?"

"No, goofball. In the Renaissance. Things were so much simpler then. Life didn't run at you headlong; things were more laid back. Everyone knew their place in society; everybody had a job to do—a niche to fill."

"That's simpler, all right."

"Don't you wish we lived back then?"

"I had a namesake who lived back then," Karl said. "He was burned at the stake."

Her eyes grew wide. "Really? What for?"

"Consorting with witches," Karl said. Consorting was probably a Renaissance euphemism for chasing skirts, he thought.

"Well," Caroline said, putting her arms around him, "*I'm* the only witch you consort with now." She smiled and gave him a quick kiss.

Karl wondered if a man could inherit a tendency for "consorting."

"So, witch burnings aside, don't you think it would have been fun to live during the Renaissance?"

"Forgetting witch burning, and plague, and famine, and all that stuff?"

Caroline frowned playfully. "Yes. All that aside. Wouldn't it be nice to live in a world that . . . *Unspoiled*?"

"Sure," Karl lied. "Isn't that why we're here? No sense re-living history if you can't cut out the nasty bits. Of course, living in the Renaissance would be easier if we got the coats out of our car."

"Silly man," Caroline replied. "I'm not *that* cold. Let's look around a bit more. What about that?" She pointed past the tents and small forest to the village looming out of the fog. "We haven't seen that, yet. It looks like a re-creation of a town."

Karl squinted and peered into the mist. Night was fast approaching, and the twilight had taken on a gray, dreamlike quality, so he couldn't be sure what he was seeing. She was pointing to where he thought he'd seen a town before, though.

"Is that a castle?" Caroline asked excitedly.

"Maybe. I caught a glimpse of it earlier, through the mist. It's probably just a facade, though."

"It looks real. Let's go see."

"It'll be dark soon," Karl said.

"We've come this far," she replied. "It would be a shame to miss the rest. It's not like we'll be back this way any time soon."

"I guess that's true," Karl answered, thoughts of escape fading from hope. Still, he preferred being "trapped" at a Renaissance Faire with Caroline to being alone most anyplace else. He smiled at her. "Let's check it out before the light goes."

They finished their lizard and dumped the sticks in a trash barrel, then walked through the fog toward the dim, angular shapes in the mist. At the edge of the tent city, the couple passed through a small, wild, woody area with an open clearing—probably used for outdoor shows during better weather. The tiny, tree-lined paddock looked like a gloomy wasteland—its surface muddy and rutted with the passage of people and animals. Hoof prints and other animal tracks were clearly visible in the wet earth.

"I wonder where they're keeping the horses?" Caroline asked, glancing around. "I didn't see any in the pavilions." She peered back the way they'd come, but already the fair tents were disappearing into the mist.

"We'll look for them on our way back to the car," Karl said. "The 'village' up ahead doesn't look too promising."

The houses looming out of the fog ahead of them appeared shabby and ill-kept. There were a *lot* of them, though—far more than usual for a fair this size. In fact, they looked more like part of a historical attraction, or perhaps a theme park (a very run-down theme park).

"Do you think this is some kind of permanent display?" Caroline asked, mirroring his thoughts.

"It could be," Karl replied. "I didn't see anything in the AAA guidebook, though. Maybe we should go back to the car and check."

"After we've walked all this way?" she said. "Honestly, Karl, it's almost like you can't wait to leave."

Karl winced invisibly and reminded himself that now was *not* the time to reveal his Ren Faire history to Caroline. He shrugged sheepishly. "I guess I'm more in the mood for necking than exploring foggy shacks," he said.

She smiled. "Don't worry. We won't stay long. I just want to scope out what's here. It looks pretty deserted, though."

It did. Standing near the first building, they didn't see another soul. The motley village stretched off into the fog, toward the castle on the unseen hill. The exhibit was as big as a real town—but no other fair-goers seemed to be visiting it.

"Maybe this part of the fair is closed for renovation," Karl suggested. The buildings looked as though they needed repairs. Actually, it occurred to Karl that they looked *more* historically accurate than anything else in the fair.

The roofs of the buildings were thatch; the walls largely wattle and daub—a primitive form of plaster. Karl spotted several wood frame and stone buildings in the distance, though those didn't seem in much better shape than the rude shacks nearby.

Many of the houses had small vegetable gardens next to them, and one or two even had barns. The barnyard fences were roughhewn rail affairs, certainly good enough to pen livestock, but not much to look at. The barricades surrounding the small gardens were even less appealing. They were cobbled together from sticks, crooked tree limbs, and the weathered trunks of saplings. The vegetables in the tiny patches of protected earth looked stunted and sickly—though this might have been a trick of the failing light and the fog.

The houses seemed deserted and, while this could have been expected in a disused exhibit, it still had a disquieting effect on Karl and Caroline. It seemed as though the couple had walked into a village of ghosts. Caroline leaned closer to Karl and tried to rub the goosebumps from her arms. Karl put his arm around her and held her close.

"Creepy, isn't it?" she said.

Karl nodded. "No electric lights, no music, no amenities," he said, "just like the *real* Renaissance."

"Ugh." Caroline replied, shivering. "If this is the real Renaissance, I've changed my mind about wanting to live there."

Impending dusk filled the fog with ominous shadows. In the distance, Karl could make out a few flickering orange lights—though he couldn't tell if they came from the ramshackle houses or somewhere else.

Humanlike shapes began to move in the mist. For a moment, the couple felt relieved to see other fairgoers amid this strange and disquieting tableau. Something about the figures seemed odd, though.

They moved slowly, hesitantly, as though they were afraid, or perhaps crippled in some way. As the fog parted slightly, Karl and Caroline saw that the people were dressed in clothes much shabbier than the fried-lizard vendor's faux rags. All of the "villagers" were short and stooped. Greasy, unkempt hair dripped down over their foreheads and shoulders. Their skin looked sallow and spotted. Their feral eyes glinted in the rapidly failing light.

"Maybe this is a re-creation of a leper village," Karl whispered.

"Ew! Yuck!" Caroline replied, giggling nervously.

The half-dozen decrepit figures shambling nearby stopped at the sound. They eyed the couple warily and made the sign of the cross. Gathering together, the villagers spoke to each other in hushed whispers.

"Okay," Karl said, "I've reached my limit on 'period' charades. This is too much."

"Mmm," Caroline agreed. She kept her eyes focused on the congregating inhabitants of the weird village.

"Let's skip the castle and head back to the car," Karl said.

Caroline nodded. She slipped her trembling hand into his and gave a hard squeeze. The couple turned and walked quickly back the way they'd come. As they did, the voices behind them rose as if arguing, or perhaps angry.

"Maybe the attraction wasn't open for visitors yet," Caroline said. "Maybe they're mad at us."

"They should have posted a sign, then," Karl said, laughing nervously as they walked through the fog. "What are they going to do, arrest us?"

"I hope not."

"We'll be back at the car soon," he replied. "I'd like to see them catch us after that."

"Karl . . ." she said, ". . . Why can't we see the tents yet?"

Karl stopped suddenly, his anger fading quickly into concern. They looked around, peering into the fog, but saw no sign of the fair.

"I'm *sure* we came this way," Karl said, fighting down the worry in his guts. "How could we have gotten lost? The place isn't that *big*."

"Bigger than we thought, I guess."

Trees hung ominously over the path where they stood, and thick scrub lined the trail on either side. Ahead, the trees looked even denser.

"I'd *swear* this is the way we came."

"Me, too," agreed Caroline. "Maybe we should double back."

"And risk getting even *more* lost? No thanks." He pulled his cell phone out of his breast pocket, turned it on, and punched 9-1-1.

"Karl . . ." she said, her blue eyes peering questioningly at him, "we're just a *bit* lost. It's no big emergency."

"We're strangers here, so being lost *is* an emergency," he replied. "I'm not going to wander around all night, trying to find that damn fair. It's getting colder and damper by the minute. Do you want to be stuck out here for the night?"

"I'd rather be somewhere toasty," she agreed. "We could keep following the path, though."

"And what if it just leads deeper into the woods? No. Let's talk to the cops and let them sort this out." He frowned and punched the buttons of the cell phone again. "What the hell. . . ?"

Pulling the phone away from his ear, he tapped the case with his fingertips.

"What's wrong?"

"No signal. How the hell can that be? The signal was fine when we called the hotel from the parking lot."

"Maybe the battery's dead."

"No. It's low, but it's not dead. Not yet."

"I guess we're in one of those cell-phone sinkholes."

"This close to the highway?" he asked angrily.

Caroline shrugged. "Don't get pissed at *me* about it."

Karl sighed and gave her a quick kiss. "Sorry. I guess we'll have to backtrack after all."

"Someone at the village *must* have a cell phone," she said.

"Unless they're taking this Renaissance business *way* too seriously. C'mon."

They retraced their steps down the wooded path, and soon came to the outskirts of the shabby village once more. The fog parted a bit as they left the woods, and they could clearly see the outline of a castle atop the nearby hill. Overhead, stars began to peek out of the indigo sky. Warm yellow lights burned within the castle's windows.

Lights flickered in the village, too—but these were orange, moving lights.

"Torches?" Karl asked incredulously.

Caroline shrugged. "That would be in period."

"Let's find that phone."

They walked to the nearest house, and knocked on the roughhewn door. Though they heard some movement within the dilapidated walls, no one answered.

"Is anyone home?" Caroline called. "We need to use a phone."

"Or could you just give us directions back to the fair?" Karl added.

Still no one came to the door.

Karl cursed and headed toward the next house. "Talk about lousy customer service. . . !" he fumed. "Hey, you!" he called to a man hurrying across the street ahead of them. "How do we get back to the fair?"

The man turned frightened eyes toward the couple, then darted between two nearby houses without saying a word.

"Karl, this is giving me the creeps."

"Well *somebody* here has to know the way back to the fair." Spotting a man carrying a torch nearby, Karl ran up to him. "Hey! You there! Stop!"

The man, a ragged fellow like the ones they'd seen earlier, turned and thrust a burning torch in Karl's direction. "*Back*, spawn of the *Devil*!"

Karl stepped back, barely avoiding the torch's flame. "Hey!"

"The people of Knightstor are God-fearing folk!" the torch-wielder said. "We reject Satan and all his works! Begone!"

"Knightstor?" Caroline said, puzzled. "But this is *Knightshead*, Kentucky. Not Knightstor. Knightstor is in *England*."

"You're taking this period role-playing shit *way* too far!" Karl snapped. "You either take us back to the parking lot, or I'll have your manager stick your head on a pike!"

"Get thee back, minion of evil!" the peasant said, thrusting the torch at Karl once more.

"Shit!" Karl said, barely avoiding the flames again.

"You *asshole*!" Caroline spat. "That'll cost you your *job*!"

"Better my job than my immortal soul, vile temptress!" Turning, the ragged man called to his fellows. "They're *here*! I've found them! The witches are here!"

"Right!" Karl said. He lunged forward and smashed his fist squarely into the man's face. The peasant fell backward into the mud, and the torch skidded out of his hand.

Karl scooped up the firebrand. "Now are you going to *help* us, or do I have to call a cop?"

"Here! The hellspawn are here!" the man shouted, ignoring Karl's threat.

They heard other people coming now. Angry voices filtered through the fading mist; a dozen torches danced toward them through the darkness.

"Shit, Karl!" Caroline said. "Let's get out of here!"

"Yeah."

As the torch-wielding mob closed in on them, the couple turned and ran back the way they'd come. As they went, Karl tossed his torch into a nearby pig pen.

"Why'd you do *that*?" Caroline asked, a note of panic creeping into her voice.

"The light would lead those psychos right to us. I'd rather take my chances in the dark."

They fled down the wooded roadway they'd taken before. As the dark forest closed in around them, Karl spotted a small path branching off to the left. He grabbed Caroline and pulled her from the main track down the narrow game trail.

"Is this the way back to the fair?" she asked.

"The last way we took was wrong. Maybe this is the right one."

She nodded hopefully, but her eyes told him she doubted it.

As they continued running, the voices of their pursuers grew more distant. For a moment they hoped they might be on the right track at last. The woods opened up before them and they paused at the edge to catch their breath.

"Damn," Karl whispered.

"What?" Caroline asked. She had fallen slightly behind as they ran, and had to peer around him to see what lay beyond the end of the path.

"We're back at the damn village," he said quietly.

"Shit. Try the phone again."

The cell phone beeped as Karl pulled it out of his pocket. Caroline looked at him hopefully.

He shook his head. "It's just the low battery warning. Shit!" He punched the numbers into the keypad, with the same disappointing result. "Nothing. Shit!"

"What are we gonna do?"

"We can't stay out here all night," he said. "Let's try that barn." He pointed to a nearby ramshackle building. "Maybe we can hide out until morning."

Cautiously, they crept from the woods to the barn. No lights or sounds came from inside the structure—a good sign that they might use it for refuge. In the distance, torches moved through both the forest and village. The couple carefully opened the barn door and slipped inside before anyone could spot them.

The building was two stories high, with a hayloft above and animal stalls below. The middle of the room stood open, giving free access to both levels. A wooden ladder leading to the loft leaned against the wall in the back corner of the room. They saw no sign that any animals had been housed in the barn recently. Old, dank straw covered the bare earth floor. Stacks of moldy hay filled the upper level. Several bundles had fallen from the loft and smashed onto the floor below. The shattered bales looked like small haystacks amid the moldering groundcover.

"It could be worse," Caroline said, though her tone made it plain that she didn't think it could be *much* worse.

"It's a good hiding place," Karl replied. "C'mon. Let's get behind some of those hay bales in the loft."

They climbed up the rickety ladder to the second floor and secreted themselves amid the moldy stacks. Outside, the voices of the angry villagers drew nearer.

"This is crazy," Caroline whispered. "Why are they chasing us?"

"Union troubles on the job?" Karl replied, but the jest fell hollow. "Maybe we've stumbled onto a secret government project or something."

"Maybe they're a terrorist cell, hiding out in the castle."

Karl shook his head and shrugged. "It's possible, I guess."

"Maybe they're on drugs."

Karl nodded. Another reason to dislike the fairs—though it seemed a very petty reason at the moment. Perhaps all his reasons for disliking the fairs were petty. Right now, he wished he'd just told Caroline the *truth* and kept driving this afternoon.

They huddled in the hay for long hours, not daring to move. Their scant clothing ensured that neither of them spent a comfortable night in the chilly loft. Several times, Karl drifted briefly into uneasy sleep. Caroline's shivering woke him, though. Her breathing seemed labored, too. He pulled her closer to him, but it didn't fend off the cold very much.

Near dawn, exhaustion finally took him.

He woke suddenly, and in pain. Caroline was squeezing his arm hard enough to draw blood. "They're right outside!" she whispered frantically. "I think they're coming in!"

"Keep it down," he hissed back. "They won't find us if we're quiet."

They ducked down into the stale hay and, moments later, the rickety barn door rattled open.

". . . thought I heard something," came a gruff voice.

"Maybe it were a trick," replied a more nasal voice. "Witches be good with trickery."

"Aye," said the first. "Be careful while ye search. They may have transformed themselves to deceive us."

The light from the searchers' torches flickered in the dismal barn, casting eerie, dancing shadows on the walls. Karl glanced nervously at Caroline. He said nothing, but even hiding in the semi-darkness, he could see his own fear reflected in her eyes. This was madness! They had to find a way out of this insane village.

The sounds of the men searching the barn below drifted up to the frightened couple.

"Did ye see their manner of dress?" the gruff voice asked.

"Not I," the second replied. "But my good wife said it were most un-Godly. She said the woman—if woman she be—were a brazen *succubus*, sent to tempt us and lead us all to damnation."

"Aye, and the man be her warlock keeper."

"Devils from Hell."

The men searched without speaking after that, poking into the barn's corners. Suddenly, a sound broke the rustic quiet.

*Bee*p!

"What's that?" said the gruff man, a note of fear in his voice.

"A bird?"

"Like no bird *I* ever heard."

Beep!

Terror clutched Karl's heart as he realized what the sound was—his cell phone's low power warning!

Frantically, he dug in his pocket for the device. He hit the power button, but the phone *beeped* again before it died. His sudden movement caused one of the hay bales hiding the couple to tumble from the loft.

"Look out!" called the gruff man. He sprang out of the way of the falling straw.

"It's *them*! The devils!" answered the other. He pointed his pitchfork toward the frightened couple in the loft.

"Please! We're *not* devils! Just people like you!" Caroline called.

"Don't listen to her! She's trying to tempt ye!"

"Away, vile succubus!"

"No," Karl said, "you have to *listen*! We're just lost travelers …."

"Travelers from the pits of Hell!" the gruff man replied. "Back away, William! We'll lock them in the barn!"

145

Holding their pitchforks and torches in front of them, he and the high-voiced man quickly backed out of the ramshackle building. They slammed the door shut, and Karl and Caroline heard the brace being dropped across the front of the door.

A cry went up outside. "They're *here*!" "We've caught them!" "They're trapped in the barn!" The voices grew louder, as the whole village gathered around the structure.

"What are we going to *do*?" Caroline asked.

Karl shook his head. The building was shabby, but not shabby enough to break down the walls. Trying to leave by the door was futile with the mob outside. He scanned the barn for some other means of egress.

"The hayloft door!" he said, pointing to a square opening on the far side of the loft.

"But it's right over the main door."

"Maybe we can climb to the roof," he said, "and then slide down and head for the woods."

"Maybe we should just stay here. Maybe they'll calm down. Listen! Someone's opening the door again!"

The two of them looked hopefully toward the crude portal. "We won't hurt you," Karl called. "We don't mean any harm!"

"Deceivers!" someone shouted from outside.

Beyond the portal stood a huge mob. They brandished torches and rusty farm implements. The shabby people gathered outside looked both frightened and angry. The torchlight made their decrepit faces seem demonic.

"We'll send you back to Hell!" a woman called.

At that, three flaming torches sailed through open door. The firebrands bounced across the barn floor. One landed harmlessly on the bare earth near the ladder. The second sputtered on the damp straw covering the floor. The third, though, skidded into the fresh bale that had just fallen from the loft.

The straw went up like dry tinder.

"Shit!" Karl said. He swung down from the loft and ran to a wooden water trough near one of the stalls. It was only half-full, and the water inside smelled like sulfur. He pushed it across the dirt floor and dumped it onto the burgeoning fire.

The fire hissed and sputtered, but didn't go out. The flames spread rapidly to the other hay spilled nearby, then flicked up toward the loft.

"It's no use!" he called to Caroline. "Go to the hay door! Climb out!"

Caroline rushed frantically around the perimeter of the loft toward the hayloft door as he climbed up the ladder to join her.

She threw open the hatch, then shrieked and staggered back, nearly toppling off the walkway. Three flaming arrows arced through the opening where she'd stood a moment earlier. The arrows stuck in the underside of the roof and set it alight.

Karl ran to Caroline's side and seized her in his strong arms. Caroline alternated between screaming and weeping. "They're going to *kill* us!" she cried hysterically. "Why are they *doing* this?"

A flaming section of the thatch roof fell in. Clearly, the villagers had set the outside ablaze even before shooting arrows through the hayloft door. Beyond the flames, Karl saw the sky, deep blue, the stars fading with the approach of dawn.

The crackle of the fire and the cries of the mob outside built to a deafening roar.

"Burn, ye witches!"

"Burn!"

More of the roof fell in, revealing the sleepy countryside beyond the barn.

Holding tight to each other, Karl and Caroline staggered toward the hayloft door again—only to be driven back by another hail of arrows.

"We're going to die here, aren't we?" she said, her voice a hoarse whisper.

Karl didn't reply.

"I'm *so* sorry," she said, looking at him with tearful eyes.

"Me, too," he said. He wished he had the time to tell her all the things he was sorry for; all the lies—the lies that, somehow, had led them to this point.

They embraced and waited for the end. The smoke stung their eyes and burned their lungs.

As the flames licked higher around them, more of the barn fell into ashes—opening gaping holes in the ramshackle walls and roof. The morning sun crested the eastern hills, revealing the landscape beyond the village. A green swath of unspoiled forest and brown farmland greeted the new day. The castle on the hill's summit stood proudly, its walls untouched by the ravages of time.

Karl saw no sign of anything he remembered from the previous day. No fair. No highway. No road signs. No phone lines. No jet trails marring the smog-free sky. No sign of Kentucky—or modern America—at all.

Before him stretched barely-tamed wilderness, farm land, and a proud stone castle—newly completed—standing guard over a shabby Renaissance village.

Despite the fire and smoke, despite the burning in his lungs and the scorching of his flesh, Karl's last thoughts were that everything looked *beautiful*, unspoiled—very much as it must have looked in Knightstor England, five hundred years before he was born.

Caroline was right. This *would* have been a good place to live.

But it was a terrible place to die.

DR. NARCISSUS' HOUSE OF MIRRORS

Madeline Poole tottered in her high heels across the ever-widening puddles, following her husband from one brightly-lit trailer to the next. Every year the carnival came to town, and every year Nick turned out for it—despite the weather, despite the creeping decrepitude of the attractions. In his heart, he still held a child-like love for the raucous gaudiness of it. His eyes grew wide and his voice bold immediately after passing through the front gate.

This fall, he'd been particularly anxious to come. So she, in heels made precarious by her weight and a red dress that clung to bulges in all the wrong places, wobbled after him through the rain and fog.

Her thirty-seven years had not been kind. She was wide in the hips and sagging under the chin. Her love of cooking and eating had done most of it; lack of exercise accounted for the rest. But when did she have time to exercise? She worked long hours at her clerical job, then came home, cooked supper for Nick, washed dishes, relaxed in front of the TV for a few scant moments, maybe had some sex, then collapsed into bed only to wake and do it all again the next day.

Small lines eroded the corners of her mouth and eyes, roadmaps from years of smoking. They made her smile less attractive, but Nick didn't seem to mind. He didn't seem to mind anything she'd done lately, whether for good or ill. Not that he wasn't affectionate—at times. Though his job at the factory kept him busy and tired, there were hugs, pecks on the cheek, and sometimes subdued groping in the darkened bedroom.

Nick's body had fared a little better. His belly didn't bulge a lot, despite his love of greasy food and alcohol. His arms were still strong, though his back bothered him from time to time. His job wore on him, just as hers often did on her, but he still found time for household chores and repairs, and he occasionally played touch football on Sundays—though he'd lost a step or two. Come autumn, he always went deer hunting for a weekend, but infrequently brought home venison.

The two of them had lived together comfortably for thirteen years now, eleven of those as a married couple. Every Thanksgiving they spent the day watching football with friends. Every Christmas they went to Nick's aunt's house in Duluth, Minnesota. Every spring they visited the House on the Rock in Spring Green, Wisconsin. Every Fourth of July they went out on Lake Superior in Joe Ordog's cabin cruiser. Every summer they took a weeklong vacation to the Upper Peninsula of Michigan. And every fall they went to the carnival when it came to Frosthaven.

Usually, the weather was miserable. Madeline could never figure out why the carnival came so far north just as autumn began to show its teeth. Still, the crowds were usually large, despite the weather. And, of course, Nick *always* had to go.

He wandered in a happy daze amid the shabby trailers—now hastily converted into rides and midway booths—his eyes saucers, his hands twitching. He drank in the gypsy atmosphere of it all, savored its greasy food and overpriced drinks. He tossed baseballs at milk cartons, and he tried to shoot wooden clowns. He didn't win anything tonight, but once—years ago—he'd won a giant pink and white panda bear and given it to Madeline. She still had that animal somewhere, hibernating behind boxes of old magazines in a dark corner of their basement.

Madeline trudged behind Nick, occasionally tripping over the electrical cables that sprawled through the carnival like infinitely-long snakes, occasionally stopping to wipe off her pumps with a napkin pilfered from a vending stand, occasionally dipping into her purse to pay for a ride, or a bit of food or drink. She would have preferred wearing something more practical, but the heels and the red dress were favorites with Nick. She knew that wearing them tonight would enhance her chances for the intimacy she craved.

The evening wore on and the storm gathered the darkness around the Frosthaven fairgrounds. Madeline's dress and shoes got wetter. Nick moved more slowly, but still with a sense of purpose. Every nook and cranny of the carnival must be explored, every ride and attraction sampled, every sight seen. The Ferris wheel, the Tilt-A-Whirl, the Cyclone, the Python all spun together into one long blur. The big slide, the haunted castle, the fun-house took on a shabby sameness that spoke of long hours and long hauls and short pay. The exotic, tired faces of the attraction operators looked like wax masks—some benign, others malevolent, a few bizarre.

Madeline absorbed it, not with the same enthusiasm as her husband, but with the familiarity of visiting an old friend slipping into a long, slow decline. Fond memories bubbled to the surface of her mind, mingling with the sopping, noisy reality—filling this strange, impermanent world with a sense of both comfort and longing.

She bumped into Nick, and nearly lost a heel in the mud, when he stopped abruptly. Leaning against him, she gazed around his shoulder. They had come to the backwater of the midway, sheltered from the lights and loud music of the larger, more popular attractions.

A jagged shape, like a Victorian manse, loomed out of the fog and the rain. Mirrors—many grime-covered, a few fractured into crystal shards, some merely painted on—decorated the trailer's propped-up sides. The pointed gables of the faux-mansion groped toward the lightning-dappled sky. Within the attraction, dim lights flickered, as though the house's connection to the carnival's life-giving web of power cables was tenuous at best. A hand-painted sign above the shadowed doorway read: *Dr. Narcissus' House of Mirrors.*

An old black man with spidery limbs and short gray hair leaned against a ticket stand by one side of the yawning door. He was shirtless, but wore a long black coat with tails hanging down the back and a battered top hat. The coat sleeves crept only part way down his long arms, leaving his bony wrists exposed. The hem of his black pants covered his feet and dragged in the mud. Nick and Madeline couldn't tell if he wore any shoes. Around his neck dangled a thick golden chain.

"I don't remember seeing this before," Madeline said. "Is it new?"

"Does it look new?" Nick replied.

The question seemed absurd as soon as she'd voiced it, and his answer was unnecessarily snide. Years of dirt and grime covered the attraction's exterior. The paint from the mawkish advertising on its side was peeling in strips as big as Madeline's handbag.

"I meant, is it new to the carnival?" she said.

"I've seen it before," Nick said distractedly. "I saw it last year."

"Well, we've never gone inside," Madeline said. "At least, I haven't. What's it like?"

"I didn't say I'd gone in," Nick replied. "I only said I'd *seen* it. It was late, and I only caught a glimpse as the carnival was packing up."

She turned to the man, Dr. Narcissus she presumed, and said, "Excuse me, but what's inside?"

He smiled, showing one golden tooth in front, and several missing ones to the rear. "Mirrors," he said, "reflections, memories, dreams, desires. We got all kinds of mirrors. Something for everyone. Step inside and see for yourselves."

"Reflections of ourselves?" Madeline asked. "Is that all?"

"What else is there?" the doctor said. "In yourself is everything. Inside my maze you see everything: everything you ever seen, everything you ever *will* see. Everything you want. You see the good, the bad, the ugly, the beautiful, the young, the old, the needy, and the satisfied. People who see my mirrors, why, they don't never see themselves the same again." He grinned wider, the smile reaching his dark eyes.

"Let's give it a try," Nick said. "Pay the man, would you?"

Madeline fished a few bills out of her handbag and laid them on Dr. Narcissus' weathered palm. He tipped his hat to her. Then he winked at Nick. "You see anything you like," he said, "you just let me know."

Nick nodded slowly. "Thanks, I will."

The threshold of the House of Mirrors was dark, and Madeline had to watch her step so as not to catch her heel. Inside, glass walls closed in, and scattered mirrors cast their flickering images around the maze.

Madeline giggled. "Looks like the fun house," she said. "Except darker. Maybe we could have some *fun* here." She smiled at Nick, but he didn't smile back. Instead, he gazed through the maze of glass and toward a line of mirrors at the back of the labyrinth.

"There's something funny about those mirrors," he said.

Madeline peered through the glass into the darkness. "I can't tell from here," she said. "Maybe I can see when we get closer."

Slowly, they groped their way through the maze toward the long row of mirrors at the back.

"I bet Dr. Narcissus' Windex bill is murder," Madeline said, suppressing another giggle. She ran her fingers along a pane of glass, and was surprised when it didn't smudge. She crinkled her nose and muttered, "Must be the dim lighting."

Three times they walked into panes of glass that they didn't see and had to backtrack and find a new route. Scuff marks on the floor were no help, as all the paths seemed equally worn and dingy.

"At lest we're getting our money's worth," Nick said after ten minutes.

"I'm surprised this place isn't more popular. No one else is in here."

Indeed, since they'd entered, the couple hadn't seen another living soul—unless you counted their own reflections. The farther they went into the maze, the more muffled and distant the carnival sounds became. As they approached the back wall, everything grew eerily silent.

"It's cold back here," Madeline said. "I can see my breath. Maybe we better go. Get some hot cocoa someplace." Beyond the far wall of mirrors burned a red exit sign.

"We've come all this way," Nick said. "Let's take a good look. Who knows when we'll have the chance again? Who knows if the carnival will be back next year?"

They walked down the row of mirrors slowly. The first few were outrageous—making their heads vanish, or squashing their bodies, or making them as tall and gaunt as Dr. Narcissus.

Madeline stopped in front of the fourth. "This one isn't doing anything," she said.

Nick looked at it closely and then shrugged. "It's made your crows' feet go away," he said.

Madeline crinkled her forehead, but the reflection remained placid and happy. Madeline frowned. No change to her image.

"Hey, look," Nick said. "I can't see my tattoo in this one."

He'd rolled up his sleeve and was peering at his right shoulder. His reflection in the mirror showed no sign of the coiled cobra Nick had tattooed there three years ago.

"That's weird," Madeline said. "How can it make your tattoo go away?"

"You look thinner, too," Nick said. "And so do I."

Madeline shook her head, and droplets of rain fell from her dark locks. "This is creepy. We should get out of here."

"No," Nick said, a familiar boyish enthusiasm burning in his eyes. "I want to see what's next."

"I'm even thinner in this one," he said, "and my beard is gone. Your hair is curly, like it was years ago."

"It's just the rain," Madeline said. "It always curls when it gets wet."

Nick looked at her and then at the reflection. "It's different, I tell you."

"How can it be?" she said. "It's just a reflection."

"Let's check the next one." He dashed the few steps to the next mirror and broke into a broad grin. "Look at my muscles, now," he said. "And look at your tits."

Not waiting for her to catch up, he ran to the final mirror.

"Nick," Madeline said, "this is *very* creepy."

"It's not creepy," he said. "It's cool. Come here and check out this last one."

Madeline walked to the final mirror. Moths took wing in her stomach and, for a moment, she didn't dare look. Her eyes seemed to have closed of their own accord, and they didn't want to open.

"What's the matter?" Nick asked. "Are you afraid? Afraid of a mirror? Afraid of what you'll see?"

She pried her eyes open and looked.

The woman in the mirror was her, but not her. The legs were longer and leaner, the bust higher and firmer, the hips slender, the face smooth, the hair shiny, and the smile altogether more genuine.

Nick grinned. "Now that's the girl I fell in love with." His reflection, too, looked different: younger, more muscular and lean, and lacking the beaten-down countenance of the man Madeline had lived with for so many years.

"Oh, my God, Nick," she said. "This is impossible. No mirror can do this."

"Dr. Narcissus said everything that ever was or ever will be is in here," Nick muttered. "All our dreams and desires."

"But this isn't a dream," Madeline said. "This is the past—or maybe a dream of the past." Tears began to well at the corners of Madeline's eyes.

Her reflection's brown eyes twinkled with mischief.

"This can't be real," she said.

Slowly, tentatively, Madeline reached toward the woman in the mirror. She shuddered as fingertip met fingertip. Her eyes went wide, though the reflection remained smiling and placid.

"I-it doesn't feel like a mirror," Madeline said. "It feels like I'm touching flesh!"

The reflection's grin broadened. The hands in the mirror reached out and grabbed Madeline by the wrists.

Madeline shrieked. "Nicky! Help me."

Nicholas Poole put his hands on Madeline's back and pushed.

For a moment, Madeline felt as though she were falling into an endless pit. She screamed, but no sound came out. She flailed but felt nothing. Then she just stopped.

Standing, Madeline gazed out of the mirror at Nick and the other woman—the one who'd formerly been just an attractive reflection. "Yes," Nick said, holding the woman's arm, "this is the girl I fell in love with."

The other woman smiled at him, mischief still flashing in her dark eyes. The New Madeline looked better in the pumps and red dress than the real Madeline had.

Madeline ran forward and pounded her fists on the glass of the mirror. But it didn't help, it didn't make a sound, it didn't feel like anything. She was *trapped*.

She pounded on the glass of the mirror for two full minutes before finally giving up. She wiped unfelt tears from her cheeks. *After all*, she thought, *how could I feel anything? How could I feel anything at all? I'm only a reflection.*

She stood in the timeless, endless space of the mirror and wept as Nick and the New Madeline left the maze.

Only a reflection. Soon only a memory.

Madeline wept for a long time, an infinite time, as she stood in the unfeeling darkness of the mirror.

She wept until her tears ran out, until every moment of pain had been wrung from her body.

She wept until she felt no more substantial than a wavering image in the glass.

And in her wraithlike state, a realization slowly dawned.

A smile tugged at the care-worn corners of her mouth.

She remembered the way that the other woman—the New Madeline—had glanced back while leaving the maze with Nick. The perfect reflection hadn't been looking at the Real Madeline, and she hadn't been looking at Nick—not the Real Nick anyway.

The New Madeline had looked to another mirror and then back to Nick—real, flabby, beaten-down Nick—and then back to the other mirror: the mirror that reflected the strong, handsome, young, insubstantial *reflection* of Nick.

Madeline somehow knew that next year—because the carnival most certainly would return to Frosthaven—next year, the New Madeline would return to the maze. She'd bring the Real Nick with her. Bring him to the far bank of mirrors where the younger reflection of Nick would appear once more.

Then the Real Madeline would get her husband back.

She smiled. She could wait. A year wasn't so long, after all. They'd had thirteen years together, and soon they'd have an eternity. A year apart would give Nick time to discover how hollow reflections were, how unsatisfying memories could be.

Here, behind the glass, Madeline had all the time in the world. And there would be plenty of room for two in Dr. Narcissus' House of Mirrors.

INTO THE FIRE

Tiberius Faustino tugged the fire-retardant sleeve of his sequined costume over the exposed skin on his wrists. He adjusted his matching white gloves, pulling them down to meet the sleeves. Even an inch of bare skin could mean terrible burns and, worse, failure.

Ty adjusted his helmet, blazoned with the family logo—"The Flaming Faustinos: Human Cannonballs Extraordinaire"—and buckled the strap securely under his chin. He glanced at his family: uncle, aunt, cousin, mother, and sister. All bore the brands of their ancestral profession, all but he and sister Angela. The pasty white scars and disfigured skin made the Faustinos look as though the entire family had lived through a terrible, fiery car accident.

The circus patrons would never see those scars. Costumes and stage make-up covered them expertly. The Faustinos had long years of practice behind them; the show *must* go on.

Ty glanced at the Ringmaster, standing in front of the tent flaps near the Faustino dressing room. He noticed the man's lecherous eyes caressing Angela, admiring her long dark hair, her smooth skin, the generous curves of her young body. The Ringmaster's beady pupils shone in the Big Top's semi-darkness.

"You won't have her," Tiberius vowed silently. "You won't have any of us. Never again. Not after tonight."

"You're next," the Ringmaster said flatly to Ty. They locked eyes and, for a moment, Tiberius felt the man peer into his soul. Could the Ringmaster read his mind? Ty didn't doubt it. The thought made him despise the man all the more.

He hated the Ringmaster. He hated the circus. He hated the torturous nightly ritual his family had to endure. Tonight, he would end it—this he vowed.

Ty felt the weight of a hand upon the padded shoulder of his sequined jacket. "Good luck," his uncle Angelo whispered. The old man's voice was hoarse and strained, his tones as scarred as his body.

Tiberius nodded once. There was no need for anything further; no need for more good wishes or last minute tips. To do more would have been to tempt providence. The Faustino family had done that enough already—more than enough.

The other members of the family put on their helmets and made last-minute adjustments to their costumes.

Ty swallowed, but found his mouth dry as desert sand.

The Ringmaster smiled and stepped through the flaps into the spotlight.

"Lay-deez and gentle-men," he boomed, "it is with immense pleasure that I present our next act. Direct from their exclusive engagement performing for the crowned heads of Europe, the most exciting Human Cannonball act in the world—nay, the entire universe. I give you . . . the Flaming Faustinos!"

He stepped back and the curtain parted as Ty led the small parade of his family into the Big Top. The older generation of Faustinos pushed the huge cannon out onto the sawdust. It was three times as long as a man, and wide enough to accommodate a human body. Bright green scales decorated its painted sides, and its mouth was blazoned with flaming orange, red, and yellow. The decoration made the cannon resemble a hideous, fire-breathing dragon.

Tiberius gazed into the monster's bright yellow-and-green eyes as he stepped into the center ring and waved to the crowd. The dragon didn't blink; neither did Ty.

His mother, uncle, and aunt wheeled the monstrosity to one side of the three-ring circus, the ring on Ty's right. Angela and his cousin went to the ring on his left and began to raise the net Ty would be shot into—if all went well.

Tiberius suppressed a shudder.

"Tonight," the Ringmaster barked, "we have a special treat. A new generation of Faustinos takes the center ring for the first time." Grinning, he stepped up beside Ty and held out a wide, black hoop, about the size of a hula hoop.

"The profession of a human cannonball is perilous, as I'm sure you can guess," the Ringmaster said. He turned full-circle so that the whole audience could see his perfect grin. "One mistake can mean death, disfigurement or, perhaps, something even worse!"

The crowd murmured apprehensively.

The Ringmaster, still holding the hoop, pointed to the net being raised by Angela and Ty's cousin. "There are members of the Faustino family who have never walked away from that net," he continued. "Some eventually recovered from their injuries; others remain crippled for life. Few who make this perilous flight return unscathed. The list of casualties stretches back to the beginnings of the circus and beyond."

He smiled at Ty again. "'Why do they do it?' you may ask. Is it for glory? For fame? For riches? Or is it simply," and here he held Ty with his eyes once more, "that the show *must* go on?"

The Ringmaster turned in a circle again, twirling the hoop above his head. "For most people," he said, "soaring through the air would be dangerous enough. The Faustinos, though, are more daring than that. Behold!"

The Ringmaster attached the hoop to a slender wire hanging down in the center of the tent. A clown ran forward with a fiery torch and handed it to the master of ceremonies. The Ringmaster set the hoop ablaze. Tiberius' mother, now at the side of the ring, hauled on a black rope and raised the flaming hoop high into the air above the center ring.

"Tonight," the Ringmaster announced, "young Tiberius Faustino will attempt to fly through that hoop, and into the net on the far side."

The crowd roared its approval, but the Ringmaster hushed them with a wave of his arms. He looked across the sea of faces, as if confiding a secret privately to each one. "The price of failure," he said quietly, "would be very high indeed." He stopped, and his gaze came to rest on Ty. The Ringmaster's eyes blazed nearly as brightly as the burning hoop.

"See you soon," Tiberius hissed at the man.

"Doubtful," came the circus master's whispered reply.

Tiberius waved to the crowd. He shot a final, defiant glance at the Ringmaster and then strode to the dragon-faced cannon.

His aunt and uncle propped a metal ladder up against the cannon, and Ty climbed to the monster's mouth. Beneath her helmet, a single tear rolled down his aunt's cheek. Ty nodded at her, but said nothing.

With a final wave to the crowd, Tiberius Faustino lowered himself, feet first, into the dragon's maw.

The metal tube was long and immensely dark. It smelled of sulfur. A thin shaft of light from outside shone down the narrow tunnel. The small circle of the world beyond the cannon's blackness seemed remote and unreal—a picture painted on a disc as far away as the moon.

Ty felt his stomach lurch as his relatives made the final adjustments to the cannon's angle. The big top swirled by in a dizzying kaleidoscope. He couldn't see the net at the far end of his flight; he couldn't see the flaming hoop, either. It didn't matter. Trust was all that mattered. Trust in his family. Trust in fate.

Trust—and keeping his mind focused on the ring.

Sounds echoed down the barrel of the cannon. Ty recognized the boisterous tones of the Ringmaster, but couldn't understand the words. The words didn't matter. He'd heard them all before, though never from inside the cannon.

"Quiet, please, ladies and gentlemen. The Faustinos need quiet. Their utmost concentration is required to avoid disaster!"

To avoid disaster. That goal stood out in Ty's mind.

Trust. Avoid Disaster. Focus on the ring.

A thunderous roar shattered the momentary silence as the Ringmaster, ignoring his previous admonition, now exhorted the crowd to count down.

Ten ... Nine ... Eight ... Seven ... Six ...

Ty tensed, then remembered his training. Tense was bad. Tense broke bones. Relax.

Five ... Four ... Three ...

Relax and concentrate.

Two ...

Father...!

ONE!

The world exploded in a sudden rush of sound and fire.

Ty felt himself blasted forward, out of the serene darkness of the barrel and into the light of the Big Top. The roustabouts tried to focus the spotlights on him, but he was moving too fast.

The tent, the crowd, the Ringmaster, his family . . . all blurred around him.

Before him, a circle of fire—a blazing eye in the night.

To miss it was to fail.

Failure meant death.

Tiberius Faustino reached out for the burning ring.

*

He saw the flames spring up around him, felt himself pass into the hoop—felt the heat of the flames, even through his costume. Too much heat for a simple ring of fire.

He looked for the net at the far side of the Big Top, but saw only fire—endless fire—in front of him. A fathomless tunnel of flame.

Then, suddenly, empty air.

But no net.

He fell.

A blasted, ruinous landscape rushed up to meet him.

This was the heat he had felt in passing through the hoop— heat stronger than the best protection his family could devise, the heat of this flaming purgatory.

Tiberius crash-landed with bone-jarring impact and lay still.

The world screamed around him, a tortured banshee wail begging for release. It took him a moment to realize that he had not been killed.

He hurt too much to be dead. His bones ached, his skin burned, and his ears pounded with the sound of his own heartbeat. Slowly, painfully, he stood.

Around him stretched a hellish, alien panorama. Razor-sharp rocks sprang up in every direction. Great, yawning pits opened unexpectedly before him. Geysers shot gouts of steam high into the air. The sky overhead burned with blazing orange light and clouds of fire. It took long moments to drink it all in.

Ty blinked to clear both his eyes and his mind.

He peered intently at his strange surroundings, trying to find the way out—seeking the object of his desire.

In the far distance hung a tiny black circle, like a shadow moon in the fiery sky.

That was his goal.

How much time had he wasted taking in his surroundings? He didn't know. He was told time meant nothing in this place. At least, time meant nothing until it ran out.

When would that be?

Reflexively, he glanced down at his wrist. He hadn't worn his watch, of course—watches, any jewelry, could be dangerous or fatal upon launch. Instead of the watch, he saw a reddish, blistered patch of skin between his glove and his sleeve. Images of his relatives, scarred and burned, flashed through his mind. He pulled up the sleeve once more, ignoring the pain that shot through his wrist as he did so.

How much time?

He had no way of knowing. He might be out of time even now.

Ty focused on the distant black orb and ran.

He ran with all his might, ran as if pursued by the hounds of Hades.

The howling, torturous sound built around him as he went—obscene wind, rushing through the blasted landscape.

The brittle reddish stones beneath his feet betrayed him. They cracked, turning to powder and then becoming treacherous, pointed shards. They reached up, pawing at his ankles with sandy fingers, trying to pull him down.

Ty stumbled. His hand touched the sharp, rocky surface and the outer layer of his glove ripped away. His palm scalded, and he cried out in pain. He staggered to his feet and kept running.

The landscape twisted and turned unexpectedly. Great gaping chasms of blackness opened up suddenly in front of him. He tottered at the edge, the boisterous laughter of the Ringmaster echoing in his head.

A vision sprang up before him: Angela unburnt, unscarred, worry playing across her smooth brow.

He needed to end this curse. He *must* be the one that changed the hellish gauntlet his family faced every night back into a mere circus act. He owed it to the generations of Faustinos that had gone before, as well as Angela and the generations to come. It was his fate to do so.

Ty veered away from the precipice and kept running.

Family. Fate. These things mattered. Nothing else.

It was his fate to be a Faustino, his fate to do this.

No one else could. No one else dared.

Nothing else mattered.

Slowly, the black orb on the horizon grew larger.

The scarred and blasted landscape assailed him. It reached out with sudden, bony fingers and flayed at his protective suit. Long ribbons of fabric ripped away. Beneath the torn cloth, boiling welts rose on Ty's skin. He felt as though he were being scourged by fiery, demoniac claws.

A geyser billowed up, pushing him back. He fell and tumbled down a rocky hillside. Beneath his costume, his skin bruised and scraped with every gyration. The faceplate of his helmet cracked. Hot air leaked in. The sulfurous atmosphere scorched his lungs.

Above the wail of the wind, another sound grew—a sound that brought flashes of memory within Ty's frantic, confused mind.

The image of an old man formed in his brain. The man laughed and smiled and patted Ty on the head. *Caesar Faustino*—his father. More memories: fishing, family dinners, festivals, skiing. Finally work, the tools of the trade, the craft of their ancestors. The cannon, a terrible, flaming maw. The hellish curse.

Tiberius Faustino topped the obsidian, crag-like rise and saw the otherworldly black orb hanging in the sky before him. In the orb's darkness he perceived the faint outline of the Big Top, and the life-saving net hanging in the third circus ring.

The sound in his head grew, and he recognized it for what it was—a scream, a *real* scream hidden within the banshee howl of the wind. He turned, seeking the source of the mournful cry. As he did, the blackness of the waiting big top whispered to him.

Time!

No time!

"No!" he thought. "I *must* end the curse! I *will* have time!"

Flames crackled up from the ground, licking at his heels. He felt their sting through the tatters of his fireproof garment.

The landscape changed around him, moving as though a living thing. It tried to obscure his sight with scalding fog and rocky thorns.

"Father!" he cried to the angry wind. "Father! Where are you?"

The fiery tempest caught his words and swept them away into the burning darkness.

In his mind, Ty saw rot and decay and despair—a body flayed of its flesh; muscle and sinew burnt to the bone.

"Ti-ber-i-us!"

His call returned on the wind.

Trust in family. Trust in fate.

The scars mapping his relatives' bodies told him it was possible.

All he needed was time.

"Tiberius!"

He heard the call again.

No delusion. Real. Real in this place of madness and terror.

He could end this, once and for all.

"Father!" he cried.

The scalding mist and smoke and fire parted, and he glimpsed a figure through the burning maelstrom. The man writhed within a burning ring, his every moment agony, his very breath stolen by the scorching wind.

Tiberius Faustino ran through the hellish whirlwind, ignoring the demoniac phantasms that leapt up to bar his way, ignoring the pain of his scalded body.

He closed the distance to the fiery prison quickly. Clawing rocks shredded what remained of his clothing; the hot earth blistered his feet. It didn't matter. The man within the ring of fire had suffered far worse.

At first, Ty barely recognized his father. Caesar looked old—unbearably ancient. His body showed scars from ages of abuse. The hot wind whipped the frizzled gray hair around the old man's head. In his father's eyes, Ty saw pain and torment.

"Father. I've come to take you home," Ty said.

"Tiberius . . ." Caesar replied, as if in a dream. His eyes did not focus on his son.

"Take my hand," Ty said, thrusting his arm into the ring of fire.

The old man reached tentatively forward.

Harsh winds buffeted Ty, and his body shook violently. He felt as though a cyclone might tear him away at any moment. He stretched his hand forward, but it moved slowly, like pushing through layers of hot blubber. The farther he reached, the more unbearable the heat and agony became.

Tiberius twined his fingers around his father's skeletal hand. He pulled with all his might.

Both men screamed from the effort. Around them the wind, the noise, and the heat built to hellish proportions.

Just when it seemed both would perish, something gave, and the Faustinos fell free of the infernal prison.

"Father. . . ?" Tiberius asked.

"Run, fool! Run!" the old man replied. He staggered to his blistered feet and began running himself. Tiberius got up and sprinted after him.

The thunderous noise around them changed. The howling gradually faded away, and an even more unsettling sound took its place. It began as little more than a chattering whisper, the claws of a thousand crabs scuttling over a stony beach. It built to the scurrying of rats, meeping with frustration and rage. Then a pack of hounds, scrabbling and fighting over a dead man's bones. It grew ever louder, thousands of strange, inhuman voices clamoring in the fiery void.

Tiberius turned and looked back. His breath caught in his throat. He stumbled and nearly fell.

Behind them, a tear rent the alien sky. Within the breach loomed black, fathomless space and out of the fissure streamed an endless parade of demons. Tiberius formed no clear impression of them, save for wings and claws and flailing tendrils, sinuous bodies and slavering fangs. Their red eyes burned into his soul. In his mind, he heard them calling, commanding him to cease his futile efforts.

Return to us! they whispered. *Return to your home! Your true home! Stay!*

"Don't look back!" his father cried as they ran. "Never look back!"

Tiberius ripped his eyes away from the terrifying sight. The demons closed in on them. Every second the fiends drew nearer, as inexorable as fate.

Tiberius and Caesar Faustino ran desperately across the blasted plains. They kept their eyes focused on the black circle hanging in the sky: the portal back to the Big Top. The sounds of the demoniac pursuit grew louder by the second.

"Jump, son! Jump!" the old man called.

They jumped with the legions of hell biting at their heels. The shadows of the monsters swept over them. Flailing limbs clutched and scratched and tore their bodies.

The Faustinos reached out for the faint circle of reality.

So close.

Falling.

*

The crowd gasped as the sequined figure flashed through the flaming hoop and fell into the net on the far side of the circus. For an instant, the circus patrons imagined they glimpsed the figures of two men emerging from the hoop. For an instant, it appeared as though one of the figures had caught fire.

Then the human cannonball bounced into the net, and the second, fiery phantom vanished. The audience burst into frenzied applause as the acrobat quickly stood and waved to show that he was all right. His costume was burnt and scorched, the dark faceplate of his helmet cracked. It seemed amazing that so much damage could have occurred in the split-second it took to pass through the hoop. It seemed impossible that the ring of fire could be so blazingly hot.

The human cannonball climbed to the side of the net and lowered himself down a rope ladder to the floor of the arena. The other members of the Flaming Faustino family rushed up to greet him. They surrounded him with their costumed, helmeted bodies and embraced him.

The group waved and bowed as the roustabouts quietly removed the cannon and other gear.

The fact that the human cannonball seemed shaken, perhaps even hurt by his daring exploit, made the crowd love him all the more.

His family supported him as the tent-flaps parted and the Faustinos left the arena. The roar of the crowd followed them out.

*

The man in the fireproof suit staggered to a nearby stool and sat, the life nearly drained out of him.

He reached up and removed his blackened, scarred helmet.

Caesar Faustino shook his head and his white, grizzled hair fell over his bony shoulders.

"We almost made it," he said, exhausted. "Almost. . . !" He buried his face in his hands and wept.

His wife threw her arms around the old man and sobbed. The rest of the family removed their helmets and stood silently nearby, tears rolling down their cheeks. Caesar removed his wife's helmet and caressed her face with his scarred and burnt hands.

"Tiberius?" Angela asked. The canvas of the circus dressing room nearly smothered her quiet voice.

Caesar shook his head. "So close. You never should have sent him. You should have left me there. What does an old man like me matter?" He drew a ragged breath and asked, "How long was I gone? A month? A year? More?"

Caesar's brother shook his head. "A day," Uncle Faustino replied. "The performance where you rescued me and were lost yourself was yesterday."

"A day?" Caesar asked. "Just a day?"

Uncle Faustino nodded. "It's always a day—no matter how long it *seems*. You rescued me yesterday, and I rescued mama the day before that, and. . . ."

"A day. . . !" Caesar moaned and collapsed into a tearful heap.

The Ringmaster stepped from the shadows and smiled. "Quite a good show tonight," he said. "As always."

Angela turned on him, her youthful eyes blazing. "We will *never* give up!" the youngest Faustino said defiantly. "We will try tomorrow, and the day after that, and the day after that if necessary. We will keep trying until we succeed—until the curse is lifted, until *all* come home again. We will keep trying until this rotten circus tent becomes your shroud. Other family members will join us and try."

The Ringmaster nodded slowly. His burning eyes lingered over Angela's nubile body. "Tomorrow," he said coldly, "it's *your* turn."

Angela Faustino glanced down at her smooth skin, unmarked for the last time.

She shuddered and nodded just once.

Tomorrow.

TRICKS & TREATS
a Frost Harrow story

HARRASSMENT OR HALLOWEEN PRANKS?
Frosthaven Chronicle, October 31

Stanislaus Kaminski claims local business tycoon Abner Winslow is trying to force him from his home. Following a recent rash of vandalism on his property, Kaminski—a longtime Winslow Hills resident—said, "Winslow [has] been after me a long time. But Noah Frost give [sic] me this land. Ain't none of Winslow's hooligans going to drive me off."

According to court documents, Winslow obtained the land in question from Frost over a decade ago. Kaminski has been "squatting" on the property since at least 1950. So far, Winslow has been unable to evict Kaminski. "The court process can be slow," a Winslow spokesman said, "but Abner Winslow is a patient man. Kaminski has no deed, and, sooner or later, he'll be evicted."

As to Kaminski's charge of vandalism by Winslow's associates, Winslow's spokesman said, "Pranksters, that's all it is—pranksters getting an early start on Halloween by tormenting an addled old immigrant. Mr. Winslow has nothing to do with it."

*

The cold October wind cut through Dotti Zigler's coat as Jeff pulled her out of the front seat of the battered Chevy.

"I'm coming," she told him. "I'm coming. You don't have to be so rough."

"I just want to get this done," Jeff replied. He looked grim, almost supernatural, in the moonlight. His unruly blond hair cast dark shadows over his handsome, angular face. He peered into the woods and down the trail leading to the old man's shack, almost as if he could see the dark deeds ahead of them.

171

Marquis and Lynn tumbled out of the car's back seat, laughing, their bodies half-entwined. They were high, as usual. They never did anything important without getting high first. Tonight's mischief was no exception.

Lynn took a last hit on the crack pipe. "Are you sure you don't want some, Dotti?" she asked.

Dotti shook her head. She felt frightened, scared right down to the bone. She wanted to get high, but she'd never liked crack. And she knew being stoned wouldn't help, not tonight. The only thing to do was to push through this and get it done—not for herself, but for Jeff.

"Let's go," Jeff said, trudging down the trail without glancing back.

Marquis and Lynn giggled and followed after him.

"For God's sake, keep quiet!" Dotti whispered. She glanced around nervously, fearing someone would spot them at any minute.

"Don't get your panties twisted," Marquis replied. "We got a ways to go yet."

"How do you know that?" Dotti asked. "Have you ever been here before?"

"Winslow said it was a mile and a half from the road," Lynn replied. "Or was it half a mile?" She giggled again. Marquis planted a sloppy kiss on her lips.

Jeff glanced back and hissed, "Shut up, all of you."

Marquis frowned and Lynn pouted mockingly, but both of them clammed up. Dotti did, too.

They didn't dare use flashlights, but the full moon shone through the bare trees, illuminating the overgrown path through the woods. An early snow had fallen a week before, and patches of half-frozen slush still dappled the forest floor between the tree trunks. The air temperature hovered a bit above freezing, and wisps of fog rose from the ground and whirled into the sky.

To Dotti, the mist looked liked dancing ghosts. She hurried to catch up with Jeff but snagged her foot on a root. She sprawled to the ground, landing hard and crunching into the dry leaves and brittle grass. The impact jarred her elbows and knees, and her breath rushed out in an anguished gasp.

Jeff stopped and spun, angry at first, but his face turned sympathetic when he saw her lying on the ground. "Are you all right?" he asked, giving her a hand up.

"I'm okay," Dotti said, dusting herself off. Her knees stung and her elbows tingled, but she knew if she stopped walking, she might not start again. "Let's just get this over with."

"Sure thing, babe," Jeff replied. A slight smile tugged at the corners of his mouth, and for a moment, his brown eyes sparkled in the darkness. In that instant, Dotti remembered why she loved him. Then he turned serious again and resumed walking. Dotti and the others followed.

It didn't take them long to reach Stanislaus Kaminski's cabin. The building was a ramshackle affair—more a hovel than a home—crouching in the middle of a small clearing at the end of the path. Mismatched, ill-fitted boards formed its walls, and rough-hewn shingles covered its roof. Leaning timbers propped up an overhang on the front, but the whole porch looked as though it might collapse at any moment. Moss dangled from the building's roof, and grime covered its two tiny windows. No light came from inside.

Dotti and the rest moved off the path and crouched behind a low, rock-strewn mound at the edge of the clearing. The rise hid them from view of the house. As they crept to the top of the hill, Dotti's hand brushed against something cold. She gasped.

"What is it?" Jeff whispered.

"T-this rock," Dotti said quietly, "I think it's a *tombstone*!" She ran her hand over the stone's smooth, cold surface, her fingers playing across a row of incised letters. In the darkness, she could barely make out the inscription: S-O-F-I-A.

"Maybe the old man knows we're coming and dug his own grave in advance," Marquis joked. He reached into his coat, pulled out an automatic pistol, and checked the action.

Jeff grabbed his arm. "Put that away," he said. "We won't need it."

"What if the geezer's got a gun?" Lynn asked.

"We won't be here long enough for him to use it," Jeff replied. "Just take whatever's out on the porch and go. That's the plan. That's what Winslow told us to do. He hired us because the guys working for him last night were fuck-ups. That's why he *fired* them. Do you want to fuck this up?"

Dotti shook her head, and Marquis and Lynn did, too.

"Good," Jeff said. "'Cause fuck-ups don't get paid. Let's just stick to the plan. Got it?"

Marquis and Lynn nodded. "Stick to the plan," they repeated. Dotti nodded, too, though her stomach felt twisted and queasy. Reluctantly, Marquis put the gun away.

They peered over the top of the hill at the cabin. Nothing stirred; no lights flared from within; only the sound of the vandals' own breathing broke the autumn silence.

"You think he's sleeping?" Marquis whispered.

Jeff shrugged. "Let's go," he said. "And for God's sake, keep quiet."

The others nodded again. Quickly and silently the four of them crested the mound and stole over the clearing in front of the house.

Dotti nearly gagged as they reached the porch. The place smelled foul, like rancid grease and rotting meat. A dozen shallow tin pots lay near the edge of the porch. Strange mottled lumps sat in each pan. In the moonlight, it was impossible to discern what the lumps might be, but they seemed to be the source of the stench. Dotti looked around, but saw nothing else on the porch to steal. Jeff looked confused, too.

"Is this is?" Marquis whispered, incredulous.

"Must be," Jeff whispered back. "Leave the pans. We don't want them clanking and waking the old man up."

He opened a pull-tie garbage bag and began shoveling the lumps inside. Dotti and the others helped. The lumps felt cold, greasy, and squishy in Dotti's hands.

"It's like gross sausages or something!" Lynn whispered.

"It's disgusting!" Marquis agreed. "This stuff reeks!"

"Why would anyone leave stuff like this on their porch?" Dotti wondered quietly.

Jeff smiled sarcastically. "Maybe it's for trick-or-treaters," he suggested.

"Some sick Halloween treats!" Marquis scoffed.

Dotti looked around nervously. "Who'd come trick-or-treating out here?"

"Guy must be some kind of weirdo pervert," Lynn added.

"He's just an old backwoods coot," Jeff insisted.

"We shouldn't steal this stuff," Marquis said. "We should bury it!"

"And the old man, too," Lynn put in. "Isn't that what Winslow wants?"

"That's not what Winslow told us to do," Dotti protested. "Let's just take the stuff and go home." She glanced fearfully at the cabin door as she shoveled the last of the grizzly bits into the bag.

"Okay, we're done," Marquis said. He cinched up the handle on the garbage bag and hefted it onto his shoulder.

A creaking, shuffling sound from nearby made Dotti's blood run cold.

Jeff gasped, "Run!" and bolted for the woods. Dotti and the rest followed without looking back.

*

Stanislaus Kaminski woke with a start. Someone or something was prowling around outside his house. He heard them shuffling near the porch. The stench of their fear wafted to his nostrils.

No lights burned inside Stan's ramshackle cabin, but since he had no electricity, he'd long ago grown accustomed to the dark. The smudges of moonlight leaking through the grubby panes of his windows were more than enough for him to see by.

Silently, he rolled out of bed and picked up his shotgun from where he'd placed it on the floor. No intruders would catch him unaware this night! He grabbed his knife from the top of the slatted box that served as his nightstand and tucked the blade into the waistband of his pants—just in case.

He crept to the door and threw it open, leveling his gun to fire. But the intruders were already fleeing into the woods.

"Come back, you hoodlums!" Stan cried, giving chase. "Come back and fight like men!"

Rage flared up like a bonfire within the old man's emaciated body. How dare they? How dare these ruffians trespass on his land tonight of all nights? How dare they run through the family graveyard without even saying a prayer or crossing themselves? How dare they disturb the slumber of his late, beloved wife Sofia and their long dead children?

The old man fired his shotgun after the brutes. The report shook the night, but Stan couldn't tell if he'd hit anyone. Four shapes scampered between the trees, like rabbits fleeing a wolf.

Did the hoodlums have any idea what they were risking by coming here tonight, or were they merely pawns of Abner Winslow?

Winslow . . . Thought of his old enemy made Stan's guts twist and curdle.

He'd show Winslow that Stanislaus Kaminski was *not* to be trifled with! He would teach Winslow and his ruffians a lesson! He would teach them if it was the last thing he ever did!

Shoving another cartridge into his gun, Stan hurried into the forest after his prey.

*

Dotti's heart pounded in her chest. The woods flew by in a great gray and black blur. The snap of twigs and leaves under her feet echoed like breaking bones. The air smelled of mold and mist.

She looked at Jeff, but he didn't return her glance. He kept running, his fearful, wild eyes focused straight ahead. Marquis and Lynn lagged behind, panting.

"Slow up! Slow up!" Marquis gasped. "What are we running from?"

"I saw something move," Jeff said. "It came up behind us. It might have been the old man."

"It *might* have been the old man?" Marquis said. He staggered to a stop, and the rest of the group halted as well. "Shit! You nearly give me a heart attack because it *might* have been the old man?"

"I thought I heard a gunshot," Dotti said.

"Me, too," Lynn agreed.

"I didn't hear nothing," Marquis said. "I was too busy running for my life through the woods. And I didn't see nothing, either." He glared at Jeff. "Do you know where we are?"

Jeff didn't reply. He gazed around the woods looking worried, annoyed, and disoriented.

"Do you have any fucking idea where we are?" Marquis repeated.

"Why didn't we stay on the trail?" Lynn whined.

"We didn't have time to get to the trail," Jeff said. "Besides, the old man knows it better than we do. If we'd used the trail, he would have caught us."

"The old man probably knows these woods better than we do, too," Marquis said. "Did you ever think of that, smart guy?"

For a moment, Dotti thought Jeff might hit him. Then Jeff's eyes fell on the tell-tale bulge of the automatic in Marquis' jacket. "If we just keep going," Jeff said, "we're bound to hit South Road sooner or later."

Lynn shivered, clutching her arms around her shoulders. "You want us to wander around in the woods all night?" she asked.

"Fuck that," Marquis said. "I'm going back to the trail, and if the old man gets in the way, I'm going to cap his ass." He pulled out the gun and re-checked the action. "C'mon, Lynn."

He turned and stomped back the way they'd come.

"Wait!" Dotti cried. She didn't know what to say next. She didn't want Marquis and Lynn to leave, but she couldn't explain why. A feeling of cold dread clutched at her guts.

Marquis waited for her to speak a moment and then shook his head. "Hey, I almost forgot," he said. "Catch!"

He threw the offal-filled garbage bag at Dotti. She caught it reflexively and then dropped it, disgusted. It slumped onto the leaves with a nauseating slosh. The stench wafting from inside made her eyes water.

"Trick or fucking treat," Marquis said, flashing a nasty grin.

"Go screw yourself," Jeff shot back. He put his arm around Dotti protectively.

"Maybe when I get back to my nice, warm apartment," Marquis replied snarkily. "You can watch—*if* you ever find your way home." He and Lynn laughed and walked through the trees, back the way they'd come.

Dotti stared at the putrid garbage bag. Was this what they'd risked their lives for? "Should we take it with us?" she asked Jeff.

"Hell no. Let's just get going."

"Do you know which way the road is?"

He pointed. "It's gotta be this way. I think." Taking a deep breath, he trudged off in that direction. Dotti went with him, clinging to his hand as though it were a lifeline.

They hadn't gone very far, though, before a scream and the crack of gunfire shattered the stillness of the night.

Jeff stopped in his tracks. "Shit!" He looked at Dotti. "We have to go back. It's that old man. We have to help Marquis and Lynn."

Dotti gazed at her lover's face, trying to suppress the fear gnawing at her insides. "Maybe they killed him already."

Another shot rang out. Another scream, higher and longer this time. Then three more shots.

"We have to help them *now!*" Jeff said, running back the way they'd come.

Despite her fear, Dotti ran with him. Terror clawed at her spine. She felt as though she might throw up at any moment. The two of them dashed through the woods in the direction of the shots—the direction of the terrible old man's cabin. Cold wind bit into Dotti's cheeks and low-hanging branches clawed at her face. It was all she could do to keep from screaming.

To Dotti, it seemed as though they ran for an hour, though she knew it was only a few minutes. Suddenly, Jeff pulled up short, and she almost plowed into him. She stumbled to a halt and leaned against her boyfriend, panting. They'd come to the edge of a small clearing.

"What?" she asked, trying to shake the fear from her brain. "Why did we stop?"

Jeff didn't reply, but his body began to quake.

Dotti looked up, following his gaze.

On the far side of the clearing lay Marquis and Lynn. They were sprawled side-by-side, limbs splayed, mouths gaping, dead eyes staring at the night sky. Terrible gashes covered their bodies from throat to groin. Their guts lay strewn on the ground around them; their blood stained the forest floor dark red. The stench of death hung in the damp air.

Dotti fell to her knees and vomited.

"Run," Jeff whispered.

"What?" Dotti managed to gag.

"Run!" Jeff wailed.

Dotti staggered to her feet, turned, and ran. Tears streamed down her face. The chilly night air nipped her face and tugged at her hair. Her stomach twisted into a cold knot, and fear smothered her brain.

Someone pushed her from behind, and Dotti sprawled headfirst to the ground. She shoved her hands out in front of her and scraped her palms raw on pine needles and dead leaves. The impact of the fall jolted through her body, and stars burst behind her eyeballs. She rolled over, gasping, eyes tearing with pain. "Jeff, why did you. . .?"

Jeff knelt in the dry leaves a dozen feet away. His head was tilted back, his mouth frozen in a soundless "O." His belly had been torn open and his bowels lay heaped out upon his lap. Wisps of warm steam rose from his entrails and curled into the night sky. The air stank of raw meat, blood, and excrement.

Over him crouched a terrible emaciated creature. Ragged clothes hung in tatters from its sallow skin. Blood covered the thing's claw-like hands, and its eyes burned red in the darkness. As it smiled, gore dripped from its rotted teeth.

Dotti screamed. She kept screaming until the creature ripped her throat out.

*

Stanislaus Kaminski leaned against the porch rail and panted, trying to regain his breath. His hunting knife dangled from one hand and his shotgun from the other. He set them down carefully and rubbed his knotted fingers to chase away the chill.

He'd failed. He'd chased the hooligans into the woods, but failed to catch them. They'd eluded him somehow, even though he'd heard their screams and the crack of their gunfire.

Perhaps they'd run into a wild animal. Bears and mountain lions had been known to haunt the woods near Frosthaven.

Or perhaps they'd had a falling out. Stan understood such things often happened among criminals. Whatever the case, Stan hoped they were gone for good.

"I beat you Winslow," he gasped. "I failed, but I beat you anyway. I chased your ruffians off. You won't get this land from me! Not tonight!"

He slumped onto his backside and rested his elbows on his knees. His chest still felt as though someone were sitting on it. He shook his head and muttered, "I'm getting too old for things like this."

Only then did he notice something odd. The treat pans he'd carefully arranged on the porch had been moved. Not only that, but every pan lay *empty*.

But it was *too early* for them to be empty!

Stan scrambled to his feet, worry gnawing at his insides.

The hooligans had taken them! They had taken his offerings!

He turned and gazed into the woods. Did the hoodlums still have them? Could he find the gifts in time? He wasn't even sure where to look.

A noise from the far end of the porch caught his attention—a creaking, groaning sound. With it came the scent of fresh-turned earth and a rustling like dry leaves.

Stan wheeled as someone emerged from the shadows on the far side of the deck. The person was very thin, with scraggly, unkempt hair and long, bony fingers. Blood covered the front of her tattered shift. Her eyes burned red in the darkness.

Stan squinted at her, trying to be sure he wasn't dreaming. But no. Even after all these years, he knew that face almost as well as his own.

"Sofia?"

*

181

GRUESOME DEATHS ON HALLOWEEN NIGHT
Frosthaven Chronicle, November 2

Five bodies were discovered by police yesterday in Winslow Hills. Four of the dead were local teenagers. The fifth body was Stanislaus Kaminski, an elderly recluse who lived near where the bodies were found. The teens have not been identified, pending notification of next of kin.

"All four were known drug offenders," a police spokesperson said. "They were apparently caught in the act of vandalizing Kaminski's property. There was some damage, including overturned gravestones and digging at the family burial site. We believe Kaminski confronted the teens, which resulted in the deaths of all parties involved."

Police denied rumors that any of the victims had been killed by wild animals. "Animals will feed on human remains," the spokesperson explained. "Any unusual wounds on the victims can be attributed to post-mortem predation."

Kaminski had been involved in a long-standing dispute with Abner Winslow, local businessman, over ownership of the property where Kaminski resided. A police spokesperson indicated that there appeared to be no connection between that dispute and Kaminski's death.

Abner Winslow's spokesman also dismissed any such connection, stating, "We always believed Kaminski's troubles were being caused by Halloween pranksters, but we are deeply saddened to be proved correct in such a horrifying manner." The spokesman declined to comment on how Kaminski's death would impact Winslow's effort to reclaim the disputed real estate.

GHOSTS OF 9/11

The stories that follow were written in the days and weeks immediately following the terrorist attacks of September 11, 2001.

The stories have been lightly edited, but remain largely unchanged from when they were first written.

9/11/2001
THE LAST TERRORIST

The master terrorist sat in his posh room and sipped his bottled water. Wine was forbidden to him by religious faith, so he disdained it. Murder, too was prohibited by his religion, but the master terrorist ignored that commandment; it stood between him and his goals.

It had been a good day, a good month, a good year. Images of the burning, crumbling towers—still fresh in his mind—brought a smile to his lips. It had all been so perfect, like a movie script, a script endlessly rehearsed by his operatives and flawlessly performed, a script in which thousands of unwitting "extras" had died on cue. A script that he, himself, had written.

The master terrorist chuckled and took another sip of Perrier. The response, of course, had come quickly. But the terrorist was nothing if not a master of misdirection. Even now, US forces battered a city miles from where he sat drinking. They were destroying a set of buildings he had long since abandoned. Come dawn, they would discover their victory hollow—again. He had beaten them once more, though the victory had its price.

He frowned. The endless shell game of eluding the authorities tired him. The result, though, was worth it. Headlines and pictures flashed all round the globe, showing the Americans for the fools that they were. The choices of airlines had been symbolic, of course: United, American. The fools should count themselves lucky there was no "States" airline. Symbolic airplanes, symbolic towers, symbolic deaths—symbolic of the weakness of the Great Satan.

How he had showed them! Showed them that missiles weren't needed to strike at the heart of America. Showed them that billions spent on high-tech space weapons couldn't foil low-tech terrorism. Showed them that even the mighty could be brought low by a man prepared to do anything to achieve his cause.

The cause. In his mind, he gave lip service to the service he had done it. In his cruel heart, though, he knew what his cause had become—chaos, destruction, death. His own glory. That was enough in itself, now. It made no matter that other people died at his behest, people on both sides, caught in the crossfire between two superpowers—the US, and the terrorist.

He smiled again, feeling the warmth bubble up inside him as the water fizzled down his throat. The Americans were fools. They attacked the wrong target. They were weak and would never catch him. Soon, he would strike again.

The explosion caught the master terrorist by surprise. He dropped the bottled water. It splashed across the expensive Persian carpet at his feet. The lights in the overhead chandeliers flickered. In the distance, he heard shouting and the sound of alarms. Gunfire followed.

The terrorist's pleasure melted as fear stabbed his icy heart. The room shook again, and gray smoke began to leak from beneath the door on the far side of the room. The master terrorist glanced around, frantically.

Where were his bodyguards—the people who kept him safe? Someone should have responded by now. His men should have arrived at the first sign of trouble. He walked toward the door, but the gray snakes of smoke brought him up short. Beyond the door, more shouts and gunfire.

He couldn't go that way. Where were his weapons? He looked to the antique desk nearby. A few quick steps brought him the right drawer. He opened it and pulled out the automatic pistol secreted inside.

Another explosion; the building shuddered once more. The lights went out, and the terrorist groped in the darkness.

The other exit—where was it hidden in this safe house? He tried to remember, but the many hideaways he used clogged his mind. He had used the hidden exit here before, but then there had been aides to guide him. His mind ran through the hundreds of hiding places, hundreds of exits he had used over the years.

Behind the tapestry?

No.

Behind the bookcase.

The shouts and gunfire grew louder. The smoke grew thicker. Why didn't the emergency lights come on? His heart pounding, he groped his way to the bookcase and pulled the books from the shelves until he found the hidden button. He pressed the button and stepped back as the secret door slid open.

Smoke leaked through. Smoke . . . and light!

The master terrorist brought his gun up—too late.

A sharp crack thundered in his ears and hot pain seared his wrist. Involuntarily, he dropped the gun. He looked down and saw blood streaming down his hand. "H-how dare you?" he gasped.

The figures stepping through the smoke didn't answer. They wore fatigues and carried guns and powerful floodlights. The lights cut through the smoke, revealing the terrorist in the darkness.

A lone commando stepped out of the crowd. The terrorist turned to run, but tripped and fell to the floor. Sweat beaded on the master planner's forehead, fear glistened in his eyes. "Do you know who I am?" he roared.

"A coward," the commando replied.

"And you are a fool," the terrorist said, slowly getting to his feet and regaining his composure. His arm throbbed but he ignored it; the bullet had passed cleanly through. "A fool to think you've caught me."

"You are caught," the commando said. As he spoke, a camera team in fatigues stepped from the passage behind him. He nodded and the cameras whirred to life. "You are caught before the eyes of the world."

"It will make no difference," the master planner said. "Put me on trial—execute me if you like. In the end, hundreds will rise to take my place."

"That there are more rabid dogs in the world is no excuse for allowing a single rabid dog to live."

The terrorist scowled. "Look at you, entombed in your high-tech finery, a walking advertisement for western decadence. You are a tool of a capitalist society that cares nothing for you."

"As you care nothing for those you've killed," the commando said. "As you care nothing for laws of man or God."

The terrorist raged. "I am a man, yes! A man who will set the world free of your kind!"

"The only freedom you offer is death," the commando said. "I offer you that same freedom."

The master terrorist's face went pale. His stomach knotted and sweat beaded down his nose and fell on his trembling lips.

"You don't dare," he said. "Your weak nation will not condone it. You must bring me back, for trial."

The commando glanced at the camera. The red broadcast light atop it blinked.

"We're stronger than you think," the commando said. "And I'm not here as a representative of my government. I'm here as a man who lost brothers, sisters, cousins, and friends to your continuing acts of insanity. I am here as a free man." He raised his pistol and pointed it at the terrorist's head. "A free man who will end your reign of terror."

"You cannot!" the master planner said frantically.

"I must," said the commando. "Someone must. As you spent your money to cause terror, I've spent mine to end it. As you've trained your assassins, I've trained myself. As you've plotted revenge, so have I."

"We are alike then!" the terrorist said, a glimmer of hope sparking in his eyes.

The commando nodded. "In some ways, we are alike. But you strike from hiding then crawl back into your plush hole. You skulk and hide, denying your actions while perpetrating the most heinous crimes. I do this now, before the eyes of the world—declaring that I alone am responsible, and I alone will bear the consequences. Where you've struck at innocents on purpose, I've targeted only you, and those who aid you."

"Your government has killed thousands of civilians!"

"Never on purpose," the commando replied, shaking his head wearily. His eyes glistened wetly in the darkness. "Never like you. And when we did, we wept. Where are your tears, madman?"

The terrorist blinked the sweat from his eyes. He gazed wildly at the cameramen. Cold, accusing lenses stared back at him. "Help me!" he pleaded.

"They've come only to observe," the commando said quietly. "Besides, they can't hear you. The roar of falling buildings and the screams of innocents have made them deaf."

Slowly, deliberately, the commando pulled the trigger.

The brains that had conceived brilliant plans of fire and death filled the air with a gray and crimson haze. The body of the master terrorist crumpled backward, his blood staining the expensive carpet that cushioned his fall.

The commando turned to the cameras. "I have done what I must," he said. "But you cannot fight violence with violence. This madman—and so many before him—have proven that. I am now his victim as well—his last victim. I will not allow his cancer to spread from me to anyone else.

"It was necessary this man should die," the commando said. His face was sleek with sweat and mottled with green and black paint. "Now, I, too, pay the price. God save America."

He raised his gun to his head and pulled the trigger.

Eventually, the echoes of gunfire died away.

The sounds of weeping lingered much longer.

9/12/2001
110 STORIES

All the stories presented here are fiction.

At 8:44 AM, Tuesday, September 11, 2001 in the north tower of New York City's World Trade Center . . .

110) Abe pulled his cleaning equipment out of a closet and prepared to ascend to the observation level, to make it ready for the hundreds of tourists to come.

109) Glynnis pulled off her shoes, swung her feet under her computer desk, and wiggled her toes against the carpet.

108) Robert walked to the coffee machine and put on the first pot of the day.

109) Adam leaned back in his office chair and mentally replayed the events of the hot date he'd had last night.

107) Claudia worried about telling Jeff that he was being fired.

106) Jarod typed up his fifth report of the morning.

105) Jamal stuck his head under the copy machine, wondering how the damn thing could be jammed so early in the day.

104) Shawna changed her tampon.

103) Mitchell scratched the mosquito bite he'd gotten while jogging in Central Park the previous evening.

102) Toren wondered if that cute little temp would be working again today.

101) Her high-heel shoes caught in the nap of the office carpeting, causing Paula to tumble to the floor.

100) Inez emptied the cigarette and cigar butts from last night's meeting out of the ashtrays in the executive meeting room.

99) Lori closed the door of her office so that she and Jeff could be alone.

98) Chaim smiled as he finished his repairs on the office computer system.

97) Jeanne came up with a great idea for a novel and wrote it on a piece of paper so that she'd remember it later.

96) Asa combed his hair and straightened his tie. Damn! He was a good-looking man.

97) Shelly tossed her copy of USA Today into the waste basket.

96) Bert called his secretary into his office.

95) Lars tried to stay awake in a boring meeting.

94) Moera crossed her ex-husband's phone number out of the phone list in her Daytimer.

93) Paul zipped up and left the bathroom, heading for his office.

92) Yusef placed a person-to-person call to his cousin in South Africa.

91) Marc checked the baseball scores.

90) Hating the shade of purple she'd chosen just that morning, Lara began to repaint her nails.

89) Bette heard a funny noise outside the office, but couldn't see what it was over her cubicle wall.

88) Logan closed his eyes to rest them for "just a moment."

87) Jim moved an entire pile of papers from his "In" box to his "Out" box without glancing at one of them.

85) Bruce rubbed the corns on his aching feet.

84) Collin read the front page of the New York Times.

83) Gus finished fixing one of the building's emergency lights.

82) Allanis fought off the cramps and reached for the toilet paper.

81) Geoff turned up his radio, just to bother his officemates.

80) Winston looked out his window and saw an airplane that was flying far too low.

79) Theresa took her first phone call of the day and had to tell a customer that the boss would not be in for another 45 minutes.

78) Ahmed glanced at his watch in the elevator, worrying that he might not get to his office on time.

77) Frank fretted that his homophobic boss had discovered Frank's "little secret."

76) Grace argued vociferously with via long-distance with a Hong Kong customs agent.

75) Christie pounded her fist onto the monitor and, amazingly, the computer sprang to life once more.

74) Taking his green card out of his wallet, Barima smiled, happy to be in the U.S.A.

73) Maria whistled Bernstein's Mass.

72) Schlomo thought, "Not another damn bill!"

71) Lobo stepped on a pushpin that he had lost yesterday.

70) As her boss bawled her out, Carol dug the toe of her Gucci shoe into the carpet.

69) Sidling up to the urinal, Juan unzipped his pants.

68) Jullienne scrubbed a mysterious stain out of the office carpet.

66) Since the multiple copy function wasn't working, Walt hit the "print" button for the 50th time.

65) Katerina wondered if the dark roots of her hair were showing beneath her dye job.

64) Knowing he could put it off no longer, Adolphus began to sort through the huge pile of papers in his "In" box.

63) Wally looked in the washroom mirror and checked the new post in his aching, pierced tongue.

62) Annoyed by the song the radio was playing, Francis switched to another station.

61) Julia went to the bathroom and took her birth control pill, which she'd forgotten to take the night before.

60) Arlene signed the first in a stack of thirty papers, all of which needed her signature before 9AM.

59) With his office door open, Paul spoke quietly with his new girlfriend on the phone.

58) Orlando built a deck of cards on the table, waiting for his boss to arrive for the morning meeting.

57) Juanita cursed in Spanish as her mop got caught on something in the broom closet.

56) Shaneale checked the policy of a distressed car-accident victim and assured the woman that she was covered.

55) Because her three-year-old was upset at being left at daycare, Yolanda told the girl a comforting story over the phone.

54) Wiping the vomit from his lips, Harold hoped the doctor's prognosis was wrong, and told his co-worker in the next stall that he was "all right."

53) Gaylord walked from his office to the break room and felt annoyed that no one had put on any coffee.

52) Josh looked up at the clock and was dismayed to find he'd only been at work for fifteen minutes.

51) Against company policy, Bob pinned a picture by his kindergartner on his cubicle wall.

50) Jerri finished filling out her application for employment form.

49) Martin yawned and took a Vivarin.

48) Shaniqua realized that someone had stolen the wallet out of her purse.

47) Aldo gazed lovingly across the cubicles at a woman who didn't even know his name.

46) Sheila turned on her radio to listen to the morning news.

45) Xavier called the hospital to check on his sick son.

44) Camille opened a fresh bottle of White-Out.

43) Wilson checked his gun in its holster, and prepared for another day at security duty.

42) When Don's computer screen went dead, he calmly restarted and waited for scandisk to finish.

41) Anna looked at her calendar, checking the time of her appointment to give blood.

40) George washed the cleaning liquid off his palms and refilled the mop bucket.

36) Andre had a second cup of coffee.

35) Cleo called the local FBI office to report a suspicious neighbor.

34) Rufus wondered if he'd left his car's lights on.

33) Despite his doctor's orders, Julio ate a glazed donut.

32) Jake fantasized about what Miss May looked like before her plastic surgery.

31) Georgina accidentally set the waste basket on fire with a cigarette butt.

30) Todd finished his morning calisthenics routine and plopped down behind his desk.

29) Sure that he had no real problem, Arthur took his third drink of the morning.

28) Bonnie played an impromptu game of hopscotch on the carpet outside her mother's office.

27) Trevor hit the "panic" button on his computer's Tetris game as his boss walked past his cubicle.

26) After a seemingly endless shift, the elevator doors opened in front of Li.

25) Darlene inserted the wrong diskette into her computer— again.

24) Kobe wondered what his wife was doing at that very moment.

23) David finished his mineral water.

22) Stephan put a classical CD into his Walkman, cranked up the volume, and turned back to his computer screen.

21) When her daughter's toy fell out of her open purse, Seema put it on her desk to cheer herself up during the day.

20) Taking a deep breath, Wilfred looked out his window at the spectacular view toward the Empire State building.

19) Brett, God's Gift to Women, put the moves on an attractive officemate.

18) Bernard talked to his mother on the phone for the first time in three weeks.

17) Rachel adjusted her bra strap.

16) Jillian reached for the ringing phone.

15) Bobby reached under his neighbor's desk to retrieve the subway token that he'd dropped—his last one.

14) Bernie called security because he'd forgotten his key once again.

13) Aliya washed her hair in the bathroom sink, as she'd been too busy to go home last night.

12) Manuel tripped on the stairs.

11) Becky quietly talked to her lover on her cell phone, praying her boss wouldn't hear.

10) Counting his change, Fisher discovered that he'd given the cabby a twenty instead of a ten.

9) Karl wished he hadn't given his last cigarette to Ralph.

8) Ahmala hoped that her daughter would make the US Olympic team.

7) Itzak called his wife to see if he'd left his glasses on the bedroom dresser.

6) Ralph got off the elevator, puffing already, though he hadn't taken the stairs this morning.

5) Otto opened the breakfast that he'd picked up at McDonalds.

4) Millie kissed her new husband and walked him back to the elevator, happy in her job and confident that their marriage would last forever.

3) Grace found a basket of flowers on her desk and slowly opened the card to see who'd sent them.

2) Remembering something that he'd left in the cab, Mike hurriedly turned around on the stairs and headed back down to the lobby.

1) Sophie from South Carolina walked her young son Ben through the front door. They'd arrived early, but soon they'd be going up to the observation tower for a great view of the New York skyline.

One-hundred and ten floors, one-hundred and eleven possible lives.

Moments later, at 8:45 AM, American Airlines Flight 11 slammed into the north tower of the World Trade Center.

Of the hundred and eleven, these survived:

Ahmala, Anna, Asa, Bette, Camille, Francis, Geoff, Georgina, Harold, Itzak, Kobe, Jeff, Julia, Julio, Li, Martin, Manuel, Mike, Orlando, Otto, Paul, Paula, Rachel, Ralph, Shaniqua, Schlomo, Shelly, Sophie, Wilfred, Yolanda.

Now multiply these stories by four hundred.

9/14/01
STRUGGLE IN THE SKY

Jason Wu pressed the button on the side of his chair and leaned back, listening to the quiet thrum of the airplane engines. The leather first-class seat felt soft and warm against his neck and shoulders. After a hectic week on the east coast, he was looking forward to getting back home to California once more.

The woman sitting between Jason and the aisle worked nervously on her knitting. She'd been at it all during the takeoff, and only now seemed to be easing off. She let out a long relieved sigh and looked at him for the first time during the flight.

"I hate takeoffs and landings," she said, putting her knitting into a cloth bag at her feet. "They're the most dangerous parts of the flight, you know."

Wu nodded.

"Once we're in the air or back on the ground I'm okay," she continued, "but until then. . . !" She adjusted the pillbox hat on her bluish white hair. "I'm Mrs. Millie Schwartz," she said, extending her hand.

Wu took the hand and gently shook. "Jason Wu," he said.

The matron's blue eyes went wide. "The martial artist?" she asked.

He nodded again.

"Imagine finding *you* on a plane next to *me*," Mrs. Schwartz said. "I always wanted to ride next to a celebrity. But shouldn't you be off looking for lost treasures or protecting movie stars or something?"

Wu chuckled. "Don't believe everything you read in the supermarket checkout line," he said. "I'm really just a simple teacher. I spend most of my time visiting my dojos in Hong Kong and the US, checking on my students."

"Well, I'm certainly pleased to meet you, nonetheless," Mrs. Schwartz said.

"Nice to meet you as well," Wu said, smiling.

"Coffee? Tea? Wine? Soda? Something else to drink?" asked the stewardess as she pushed the serving cart up the aisle next to Mrs. Schwartz's seat.

"Could I have a bit of bubbly?" Mrs. Schwartz asked.

The stewardess nodded and smiled at her. "And for you, sir?"

"Just sparking water, please," Wu said.

Mrs. Schwartz smiled indulgently at him. "Don't want to break training, eh?" she said knowingly. "Or is it some kind of religious prohibition?"

Wu shook his head. "Drinking on a plane makes me giddy," he said. "I like to keep my head clear when I'm flying."

"Well," said Mrs. Schwartz, taking her drink from the stewardess, "sometimes we need a bit of giddiness, I think."

As the stewardess leaned over to give Wu his drink, though, she stumbled forward, spilling it—then lurched back suddenly, as someone pulled her from behind. A short razor-knife appeared at the stewardess's throat. The knife was clutched in the hand of a well-groomed, bearded man in a dark suit. With his free hand the man wrestled the stewardess' left arm behind her back.

Mrs. Schwartz screamed.

"We have a bomb," the bearded man said. "We are hijacking this plane. Everyone cooperate and no one will be hurt."

Wu saw now that the man was not alone. A second terrorist, this one wearing a gray suit, was making his way through first class toward the cockpit. In front of him, he held another stewardess. At her throat, he held another small but deadly knife. Cries from the coach section of the plane, behind first class, told Wu that there were other hijackers on the plane as well.

A man seated across the aisle from Wu and Mrs. Schwartz stood up. He wore a black suit and a parson's white collar. "Please, son," he said, "don't do this. There's no need for violence."

In response, the bearded man kicked the preacher in the gut.

Springing to his feet, Jason Wu reached across Mrs. Schwartz and seized the knife hand of the bearded man. With an expert twist, he shattered the wrist, and the knife tumbled to the floor of the airplane. The stewardess struggled out of the hijacker's grip as the bearded man stumbled back.

Wu dived over Mrs. Schwartz, who was still screaming, and tried to grab the knife. But the bearded man recovered enough to kick the knife out of the martial artist's reach. The blade skidded down the aisle and came to rest under a seat in the last row of first class.

The terrorist aimed his next kick at Wu's head. Wu grabbed the man's foot and heaved, sending the hijacker over backward. The bearded man cracked his head on a seat back and slumped to the floor, unconscious.

While Wu fought with the first man, the second hijacker had been banging on the cockpit door, threatening to kill the stewardess he'd taken hostage. But the commotion around Wu quickly caught the gray-suited man's attention. The skyjacker looked from the martial artist to his unconscious compatriot. "You move, I kill her!" he said to Wu.

Wu held up his hands in surrender.

"Get on the floor!" the gray-suited man said.

Wu did as he was told, lying on his stomach in the aisle. As he did, he caught a metallic reflection from the knitting bag under Mrs. Schwartz's seat.

Others in first class had now joined the chorus of Mrs. Schwartz's screams. Several people nearest to the gray-suited man rose as if to attack, but he warned them back, cutting the stewardess across the cheek to prove that he'd kill her. She screamed and fainted dead away. The hijacker had to hold her up to keep his knife at her throat. As the terrorist struggled with the weight of the stewardess, the door to the cockpit opened.

"Don't hurt anyone! Please!" the co-pilot said, poking his head out of the cockpit door.

"Get out, both of you, and give me control of the plane or I kill her!" the hijacker barked, shifting his attention from Wu to the co-pilot.

Wu grabbed one of the needles from Mrs. Schwartz's knitting bag and threw it as he rose to his feet. The knitting needle sailed straight and true, stabbing the hijacker in the neck, just below his right ear.

The gray-suited man gasped in shock, and, at that moment, the passengers nearest him pounced. They wrestled the knife from his hand and pummeled the skyjacker into unconsciousness.

The co-pilot stumbled back into the cockpit, yelling, "Radio SOS and take us down! We need to make an emergency landing!"

A smile cracked Jason Wu's lips as the plane's "Fasten Seatbelts" sign came on and the nose of the plane edged down. "Stay in there!" Jason called to the pilots. "Don't come out no matter what!"

"Look out!" cried the parson, who had finally regained his wind.

Wu spun and saw a hijacker with a red bandana burst through the curtains from the coach section. The man's eyes flitted over his fallen comrades. He didn't say anything, but roared incoherently as he charged, brandishing his razor knife.

"What is going on?" a gruff voice called from the coach section.

The man in the red bandana didn't have time to answer. As the hijacker came in, Wu kicked him in the knife hand. The knife flew straight up and stuck in a ceiling panel.

The hijacker grunted and tried to punch Wu in the chest. The martial artist grabbed the bandanna wearer's wrist and pulled. At the same time, Wu smashed his other elbow down hard on the terrorist's arm, just above the elbow.

A resounding "Crack!" filled the cabin as the hijacker's arm shattered. Wu's backswing broke the man's nose.

From the other cabin, the gruff voice yelled. "Shut up, you stupid Americans! Don't you understand we have a bomb?"

The bandana wearer tried to burble a warning, but the blood streaming out of his nose and mouth smothered his words. A quick chop on the back of the neck sent him into oblivion.

"What's the matter in there?" called the gruff voice. "Why are we going down so soon?"

At that moment, the captain's voice came over the intercom. "I'm sorry ladies and gentlemen, but we will be making an emergency landing. Please fasten your seatbelts and hang on."

The final terrorist burst through the curtain separating first class from coach. "I have a bomb!" he screamed. "You understand? I have a bomb?" His shirt had been ripped open to expose the plastic explosives strapped to his chest. Fear and anger filled his eyes when he saw the rest of his compatriots lying unconscious on the floor.

He reached for the detonator button at his belt.

Jason Wu leapt the distance between them. He grabbed the hijacker's hands and wrestled them away from the detonator. The terrorist lunged forward, smashing them both into the back of the nearest seat. Pain shot up Wu's spine, but he didn't relax his grip.

For long moments, Wu and the terrorist grappled in the aisle of the plane. Wu snapped his head forward, but the hijacker jerked back, avoiding the head butt. The terrorist tried to trip Wu, but Wu heaved them both backward, dragging the hijacker down with him.

Wu landed hard on the floor in the aisle between Mrs. Schwartz and the parson. The seat next to the preacher lay empty, and beside it was an emergency door. The parson had followed the captain's orders and refastened his seat belt. Wu said a silent prayer that the rest of the passengers had done so as well.

The preacher started to get up to help Wu, but Jason shook his head: no. As Wu struggled with the bomber, he gazed into the preacher's eyes, hoping that the clergyman would understand his plan. Wu glanced from the preacher, to the emergency door and back.

"I . . . I can't!" the parson whispered.

"Do it!" Wu cried.

With a muttered prayer, the parson leaned over and threw the latch on the emergency door. He pushed on the bottom and the door flew out into the open sky.

Instantly, the air began to rush out of the airplane. Oxygen masks fell from the ceiling and everything that wasn't strapped down got sucked toward the door.

Wu and the hijacker were the first things to go.

As they hurtled toward the opening, Wu let go of his enemy. The hijacker reached for the detonator as he hurtled out of the plane. Wu grabbed for the seatbelt on the empty seat next to the parson and caught hold.

The final hijacker sailed into the cold, thin air just as he hit the button. The terrorist burst into a ball of orange fire and black smoke, but he was too far away from the plane to do any harm.

The plane dropped precariously as the pressure equalized and the pilots struggled to maintain control. Wu clung desperately to the seatbelt, trying not to join the skyjacker in oblivion.

Just as his fingers lost their grip, the parson grabbed him by the wrists and held tight. A moment later, the airplane leveled off at five-thousand feet. With the pressure equalized, the horrible vortex stopped, and Wu struggled back into the plane.

"Thank you," he said to the parson.

"No," the parson replied, "thank *you*."

Jason Wu smiled. "I guess I better get back to my seat," he said.

He stepped past the parson and over the body of the bearded terrorist, which had been wedged under the nearby seats.

Wu gazed at Mrs. Schwartz and smiled. "Excuse me, Mrs. Schwartz," he said. "I'd like to sit down."

A smile flickered across the matron's eyes, but quickly turned to fear.

Before Wu could react, the bearded terrorist surged up and wrapped his arm around Jason's throat. The hijacker was bleeding from the mouth and nose from the sudden depressurization, but still seemed to have enough in him to finish Wu off.

The martial artist yanked on the man's arm, but Wu's limbs felt like lead. He'd used all his strength hanging onto the seatbelt to avoid being sucked out of the plane. Frantically Wu turned toward the dumbfounded preacher. The parson fumbled with his seatbelt, trying to get up and help. Wu's world began to go black.

"At least . . ." the hijacker burbled, "*you* will di—!" He stopped in mid-sentence.

The terrorist gasped once and went limp. As Wu stepped way from him, the hijacker slumped to the floor, a knitting needle embedded at the base of his skull.

"You owe me a new set of knitting needles, young man," Mrs. Schwartz said with a grim smile.

"And you would have made a fine acupuncturist, Mrs. Schwartz," Wu gasped, rubbing his throat.

After making sure that all the remaining hijackers were either dead or securely tied, Wu staggered to his seat and leaned back into the soft leather.

"You know, young man," Mrs. Schwartz said, "Maybe I was wrong about take-offs and landings being the most dangerous part of flying. In fact, I think I'm going to *enjoy* this landing."

Wu merely chuckled and closed his eyes.

With the emergency door open, the thrum of the engines was much louder. Still, as the wounded plane made its final approach to Pittsburgh, Jason Wu couldn't think of a more comforting sound in the world.

FIGHT THE DARKNESS

Darkness surrounded the small, mud brick building. Darkness, though the sun had not yet set. All the land was covered in darkness—or, at least, all the city. And in the darkness, shouting and gunfire.

Terrified, Aliya peeked out the crack between the aging wooden door and the worm-eaten door jam. Turmoil reigned outside: smoke, fire, blood, thunder, and death. Aliya knew that the Americans had come.

Slamming the door shut, she leaned against the flimsy wood, knowing that it would not keep the invaders out. If they wanted revenge, if they wanted to slaughter everyone in the house, they would do it. She would not be able to stop them. The house's sole window had been shuttered, and though that kept out the smoke, it would not stop the invaders.

The oil lamp lighting the room cast flickering shadows on the walls: ghosts and demons—monsters from a far-away land. A whimper from the children gathered on the far side of the room, near the two straw-tick beds, told Aliya that she was not the only one who saw the encroaching devils.

She recited a silent prayer to Allah to steel herself, then crossed the room and said, "Hush, little ones. Hush. The angel of death will not visit us tonight. Allah knows we have done no wrong. He will protect us." Aliya gathered the three children into her arms and hugged them.

"Where is papa?" wailed Sarifa, the youngest of the brood. Her face was blotched red from crying. In the dim light, the blotches looked black—like the plague.

"He's at work, little one," Aliya said. "He's safe."

"Ali says papa's building was blown up," Mohamud said, with the pride of a nine-year-old contradicting a parent. "Ali says no one is safe. He says anyone who's smart is fleeing the city."

Jamal, the middle child, began to bawl, rubbing his dirty hands into his clear brown eyes. "Papa's dead! 'Mericans killed him!"

The other children began to wail as well at the thought, even Mohamud who had spurred the idea on.

"Hush, now, and stop all this nonsense!" Aliya said, though in her heart she feared it might be true. "Papa is not dead. He's merely working. He can't get home right now, because it's dangerous to be outside. That's why we're inside, safe. Safe inside."

"Is this like the plagues we hear about during teachings at the mosque?" Mohamud asked, drying his eyes.

Aliya shook her head, biting her lip to keep from crying. "Not like the plagues," she said, "though it is a trial—a test of our faith. Allah will watch over us if we have faith. Allah does not allow innocents to perish."

"What about the people in New York?" Mohamud said. "Papa says they were innocent, but they died when the buildings fell."

Aliya stood and walked to the small, wood-burning stove in one corner of the room. She had set out vegetables and a few eggs to make into a soup for dinner. She turned her face from the children so that they would not see how upset she really was. She kept her voice calm. "And Allah watches over them even now. Innocents go to paradise, to live at God's side."

"What about the people who did the killing?" Jamal asked. "What about the killer 'Mericans outside?"

"They will suffer the torments of damnation," Aliya said with total conviction. She picked up the long, sharp cutting knife and began to dice the vegetables into small bits. Her hands shook as she cut, but she avoided losing any fingers. "Sarifa, fetch me some water to boil."

The smallest child rose from where she had been cowering with her brothers and fetched the water from a rusty tap. Aliya put it on the stove to boil.

"Shouldn't we hide?" Jamal asked.

"No," Aliya said. "We will do what we must, not varying from our usual tasks, so if the devil comes, he will find us doing the work Allah has assigned us."

A hollow knock echoed from the battered door.

"Should I answer, mama?" Mohamud asked sheepishly.

Aliya shook her head, and her long, black robes rustled. "No. I will answer it." She set her knife on the table next to the eggs and partially chopped vegetables and turned toward the door.

"What if it's the devil?" Sarifa asked, looking as though she might cry again.

"What if it's the *'Mericans*?" Jamal asked.

"I don't think either the devil or the Americans would knock," Aliya said. "They would just come in."

Another knock came, just as Aliya reached the door. The knock seemed more frantic this time, less patient. For a moment, she almost didn't answer it. Then, summoning all her bravery, she opened the door.

A man staggered in, the door fairly flying open with his weight. The man was dirty, covered with smoke and sweat and blood. He had a long beard and hair, and wore the clothes of a nomad. "I need a place to rest," he said in a calm, controlled voice. His eyes darted around the room, taking in all the details of the small house.

"It is not safe here," Aliya said, knowing she was contradicting what she had told the children minutes earlier. Gazing at the man, she felt she had seen him before. She knew that she didn't want strangers in the house during this crisis.

"I'll be no trouble," he said. "I need only stay a minute. I'll be gone before you know it." His eyes were deep and liquid. Calming, like those of an Imam, or a prophet. The simple robes and headdress of an ascetic adorned his thin frame. "My people will come for me, and I will be away from here," he said. "The Prophet encourages hospitality. If you will, I shall wait by the door."

Slowly, Aliya nodded.

"Have you been in the fighting outside?" Mohamud asked, somewhat awed by the stranger's presence.

The man leaned against the door jamb and nodded. "Yes," he said, "and many battles before."

"Are you a hero?" Jamal asked.

The man hesitated a moment, then slowly shook his head. "No hero," he said. "Merely one doing Allah's will."

"My friend Ali says that the buildings falling was Allah's will," Mohamud said. "But papa says Ali is wrong."

The man smiled. "Your friend sounds wise beyond his years."

Aliya frowned. "Ali is but an orphan child who lives on the streets. His parents were executed by . . ." He hesitated, and then said once more. "He is an orphan."

"There is wisdom in orphans—and strength," the bearded man said. "Strife strengthens our people; loss makes us wise in the true ways of the world. It allows us to see our enemies more clearly."

"I do not think so," Aliya replied. "I think it only makes us sad."

"Are there orphans in America where the buildings fell, mama?" Sarifa asked. "Is that why there's fighting, because the buildings falling made the Americans strong?"

Aliya began to reply, but the bearded man cut her off. "They are fearful cowards," he said, almost spitting the words. "They make war on the innocents of Allah."

"Are you afraid, too?" Jamal asked. "Is that why you're not fighting in the streets with the rest?"

The bearded stranger's face grew red, his dark eyes blazed. Then he mastered himself and said calmly, "I do not fight. Allah fights for me."

Mohamud's dark eyes went wide. "Will we see him fighting for us? Will he send the angel of death, as in the stories?"

"Perhaps," the stranger said, nodding. "And perhaps, when you are older, you could fight at his side."

"No," Aliya said sternly. "I will not permit it. There's been enough fighting. There's been enough death. We need not find glory and God's will in more killing. It is enough, now."

The stranger's eyes narrowed. "A good woman should know her place," he scolded. "Return to your cooking. When my people arrive, I will show your children the might of our Lord. The streets will run red with the blood of the infidels."

"I forbid it," Aliya said. "I will not have soldiers in my house."

"Your husband is not here, woman," the bearded man said. "In his absence, you will defer to me. Woman defers to man. It is the will of Allah."

Aliya started to reply, but something in the stranger's manner made her stop. Perhaps it was the way he glanced from her to her children, now sitting around the skirts of his robe. Could this man be mad? Could he be dangerous? Would he harm the children? Warily, not wanting to excite the stranger further, she returned to the stove.

"Do you have many warriors working for you?" Mohamud asked.

"A thousand and a thousand times a thousand more," the bearded stranger said. "My followers are as numerous as the drops of water in the sea—and just as difficult to capture or destroy."

"You must be very rich to afford all those servants," Jamal said.

The bearded man chuckled. "I was once rich with possessions, but poor of the soul. I gave those things up. I've devoted my life and my fortune to our cause. Now I use my wealth to bring strife to our enemies."

"When your warriors come, will the Americans leave?" Mohamud asked.

"Will the fighting stop?" Sarifa added.

The man shook his head. "Never. Not while one infidel is left alive."

"Do infidels have children?" Sarifa asked.

"Only devil children," the stranger replied.

As he spoke the sounds of fighting outside intensified. Gunfire echoed in the streets and shouts filled the air. The voices were foreign—American. They were coming nearer.

"Will the 'Mericans kill us?" Jamal asked.

The stranger glanced around nervously, like a wolf caught in a trap. "No," he hissed. "The Lord is our shield and sword. Come, and I will show you. I will take you to my warriors. They wait outside. They will see us safely to my cynosure." He turned to Aliya as she nervously chopped her vegetables. "Come, woman. You will lead your children before me. I will tell you where to go."

Slowly, Aliya nodded, but she did not put down the knife.

"But, the soldiers. . . !" Mohamud said.

The stranger turned his blazing eyes on the child. "Those who die in the service of the Lord are taken directly to heaven," he said. "We have nothing to fear." He put his arms around the children and pushed them before him. The children protested with frightened bleats, but the man's arms were strong and hard beneath his simple robes.

Aliya crossed the dirt floor noiselessly and plunged her knife into the terrorist's back.

The man spun, wide-eyed, reaching for the gun concealed within his robes. Desperately, Aliya leaned forward, putting all her weight behind the blade. The children clung frantically to the man's robes, trying to keep him from harming their mother.

The stranger's fingers tightened around the butt of the gun. The children clawed at his arms. The terrorist gasped once, a burbling, strangled cry escaping his throat. His eyes rolled back in his head. He toppled to the floor, dead.

Aliya and the children stood around the terrorist in awed silence.

"You will not take my children," Aliya said quietly. "You will not use us to shield you from judgment for your crimes. You've killed enough innocents."

"Was he an American?" Sarifa asked.

Aliya shook her head. "No," she said. "He was the devil."

As she spoke, the door thumped with the sound of a heavy fist. Startled, Aliya and the children jumped. "Open up!" a coarse, almost unintelligible voice called through the door.

The small family retreated to the corner by the stove and hid behind the battered dining table. As the door burst inward, Aliya realized that she'd left her knife—their only protection—in the terrorist's back. The battered door landed on the dirt floor, beside the body of the dead stranger.

Through the open doorway strode three tall, muscular figures, dressed in the fatigues of foreign warriors. Smoke blew through the door and billowed around them, making them strange, shadowy figures. They paused in the doorway, their automatic weapons leveled.

Then one stepped forward into the small room. In the dim light he looked as black as the pits of hell. He was bearded and grim-faced, a huge devil of a man. Solemnly, he surveyed the body on the floor, nudged it with his gun, and then turned it over with his boot.

He made an excited noise and spoke to his companions in a language that Aliya and the children did not understand. The two warriors with the huge devil stepped forward and dragged the carcass of the terrorist across the dirt floor and out of the doorway.

The huge devil-man turned toward Aliya and the children. She stood, and took the pot of water—not yet boiling—in her shaking hands.

The black faced man smiled, a broad, white, beatific smile. "Friend," he said in a thick, awkward accent. "Thank you." He reached into a pocket of his uniform vest and withdrew two small, foil-wrapped packages.

Aliya held tight to her steaming pot of water.

The man unwrapped both of the foils to reveal a dark, sweet-smelling substance within. He took a bite of one.

Chocolate. It was chocolate.

The children started forward, but Aliya hissed at them and they froze.

The big man chuckled. Gently, he set the chocolate bars down on the table before them. He backed to the doorway of the tiny house. He bowed politely and then picked up the battered door. He shrugged and said "Sorry," in his terrible accent. Then he backed out the doorway, replacing the door in its frame as he went.

Aliya ran forward and pressed her frail body against the scarred wood. Her hands and arms trembled, and some of the hot water spilled from the pot she still held clutched tight. The door seemed to tremble with her.

All that remained of the stranger's passing was a long bloodstain on the floor. The crimson streak passed between Aliya' s feet, crossed under the door, and vanished into the smoky darkness outside.

As their mother quaked and gasped for breath, the children ran forward and seized the chocolate, eating it greedily. The smoke, which had invaded the house along with the Americans, began to dissipate. Aliya's legs gave way. She set the pot down, slumped against the door, and wept.

The children ran to comfort her. They hugged her and kissed her and smeared her face with chocolate from their small hands. They cried as well, more because she cried than because they knew why she cried.

Eventually, the tears stopped. Aliya broke the eggs, put the chopped vegetables into the pot, and made supper. She avoided looking at the stain that marked the terrorist's passing.

Outside, the shouts and gunfire gradually died away. As Aliya sat exhausted, not looking, the children cautiously opened the broken door. The battered wood fell into the dust outside. Aliya cried out; she raced to close the portal, to block out the nightmares. She stopped.

Sunlight streamed in from beyond the doorway. A fresh breeze blew from the west, chasing the last wraiths of smoke away. Stillness had replaced gunfire and chaos. The silence seemed like the music of heaven.

Aliya leaned against the door frame, astonished, looking into the golden light of the setting sun. She blinked back the tears that had settled on her long, dark lashes.

As her eyes cleared, she saw a familiar figure approaching through the muddy streets. Aliya sank to her knees and praised Allah for his mercy. On this terrible day, the angel of death had passed them by.

The children cried with joy.

"Papa!"

GHOSTS OF SEPTEMBER ELEVENTH

The wind howled across the barren steppes, churning the fine sand into dusty specters writhing in the night. The shining sickle of the moon caught the whirling forms and cast dancing shadows across the camp settled in the valley below. Nearly one hundred tents huddled in the shelter of the hills, safe from the prying eyes of enemies or pursuers. Still, the few brave souls who ventured out of their tents that night gazed at the stars above, wondering if— even then, even there—they were being watched from afar.

The people in the tents did not fear their enemies. Rather they despised them and all their decadent trappings. The enemy was to be assaulted quickly and secretly, fleeing before there could be any reprisal. The people's agents had wounded the Great Beast badly, and now their foes came screaming across the rugged countryside, crying for blood and vengeance. Blood and vengeance were something the people in the tents understood—practically *all* they understood.

But the enemy would not find them, not today. Not tomorrow, either, nor the next day after that. They had dodged all the enemy's attempts to pin them down. They had melted into the shadows and hidden in a countryside they knew well. They had fought here for twenty years, some of them, and the enemy could not match their knowledge of these lands.

Still, the enemy was powerful, and relentless, and some in the camp feared that, even now, the enemy was gazing down upon them from the stars.

The zealot leader spit the dust from his lips, shook his fist at the night sky and laughed. How he had hurt them! A wound from which they would never fully recover, even if the damage was not in itself fatal. He had left his mark on history. He had struck the first blow in a holy war which would sweep the infidels from the Holy Land and, one day, from the face of the earth itself.

He laughed again and gazed over the windswept hills, seeing in each shadow a dance of blood and destruction. The zealot was the lord of this obscene dance. He would dance and dance until the world itself caught fire from his gyrations. Then all would be made anew again, according to a better plan, God's plan—*his* plan.

He walked to the top of the nearest hill and spun in a circle, his white robe billowing in the wind. He was master of all he surveyed; master of the entire world. Even as they sought his blood, he controlled them. Their infidel god was no match for his God of blood and fire.

One by one, the lights in the camp below winked out—like stars being swallowed by dark clouds. The enemy could not find what it could not see. Tomorrow, they would move again.

And the day after that as well.

The enemy might look down from above, but by the time the infidel could find them, they would be gone once more.

The zealot smiled again and licked the dust from his parched lips.

Out of the darkness below, a figure resolved itself. The shape of a man struggled up the hill from camp. The wind tugged at the man's black robes and caked his bearded face with dust. Even in the darkness, even in this shabby condition, the zealot easily recognized his lieutenant.

"Yes?" the zealot said. "Why do you disturb me?"

"Master," the lieutenant replied, kneeling on the coarse sand of the hilltop, "your people do not like this place. They say the valley is accursed. The say the wind speaks with the voices of demons."

"Tell them *we* are the demons," the zealot said, "and the cries they hear are those of our foes, begging for a mercy that will never come."

The lieutenant bowed slightly. "Yes, master," he said. "But, even though we are masters of the world, your faithful are scared."

"What have the faithful to be afraid of?" the zealot asked. "An impotent foe who shouts at us from half a world away? A country grown fat and decadent on the black blood of the Holy Land? No, my friend. We have no need to fear our enemy; far better that they should continue to fear us."

"But, master, perhaps—to appease the faithful—we could just move camp tonight."

"We will move the camp tomorrow!" the zealot spat. "I will not run from ghosts like a child afraid of the darkness."

The lieutenant bowed again. "Yes, master," he said.

"Leave me."

"Yes . . . master." With a last, fearful glance, the lieutenant scrambled back down the hillside. His cloaked form soon disappeared amid the dancing shadows.

The zealot chuckled to himself.

Even his people were foolish children. Only *he* had the vision to lead. Only he had the inspiration to strike at the heart of the enemy—to topple their blasphemous temples. When the war was won, only *he* would be responsible. Only *he* could claim the glory of victory.

The night breeze tugged at the sleeves of the terrorist's robe, and sand crept inside the crevasses, making him itch. The howling of the wind grew louder, and the air more chill. The dust devils dancing across the steppes multiplied. The shadows lengthened.

The zealot peered into the gathering darkness beyond the edge of camp. Was that voices he heard? Was there some town or settlement nearby that he had overlooked? It was impossible that his enemies had found the camp so soon. Still, the zealot clutched his robe tighter around his body to ward off the encroaching chill—or so he told himself.

He looked harder, straining his eyes in the dim light of the crescent moon.

Yes, he could see them now—sweeping over the hills toward him. There were shapes in the darkness, human shapes bobbing in the flickering light of the thin moon, people he had overlooked. Perhaps he should move camp tonight, after all.

No. There was a better way. These people, whoever they might be, would never tell what they saw this night. They would join the long ranks of the dead who had once opposed him. He would rouse the camp and slay them, every man, woman, and child. A smile cracked the zealot's weathered face.

He turned to call for his army, but the words died on his lips. Pale spectral figures filled the valley below. They surged around the darkened tents like a tide of shrouds, pulsing, tugging at the tent flaps, their distant voices echoing the wailing of the wind. Somehow, the enemy had crept over the hills and caught the faithful unaware.

Frantically, the terrorist turned away from the camp to the line of wraiths advancing across the hills toward him. He raised the machine gun hidden beneath his robes and fired it into the advancing crowd. The weapon's chatter shattered the night stillness. Hot metal tore across the dunes, shredding the sea of his enemies.

Yet, not a one of them fell. Not a one stopped. They swept ever nearer, even as the last of the terrorist's bullets lay spent in the dust among the enemy's feet.

Sweat poured down the terrorist's thin frame. Who were these people?

The face of the figure nearest him resolved itself out of the darkness. The zealot tried to cry out, but his lips moved noiselessly, gaping at the wind.

The face before him was as pale as the moonlight. Once it might have been lovely, but now a long gash traced across the woman's forehead, and a twisted piece of metal projected from the pit of her neck. Boundless sorrow filled her dark eyes, and tears of blood ran down her pallid cheeks. The dead woman moved toward the terrorist.

Behind her—through her insubstantial body—the zealot saw a sea of sad corpses watching, waiting, drawing relentlessly closer.

The fanatic tried to run, but tripped over the hem of his robe. He landed on his seat in the coarse sand and dust billowed up, stinging his eyes. He tried to scrabble away backward, but the ghostly woman reached out and seized his left hand. Her grip was like iron and her fingers cold as ice.

She gazed into the terrorist's horrified eyes with her dead orbs and whispered, "Seven years, three months, fourteen days more, if not for you."

As the dead woman finished speaking, pain shot through the zealot's body. He felt weak. His joints ached. Confusion clouded his mind. He tried to muster his courage, tried to sputter a reply, but could form no intelligible words.

With a final, heartbreaking wail, the woman faded into the shadowy darkness. Before the zealot could rise, though, a horribly burned man in a three-piece suit stepped forward to take the woman's place. He, too, seized the zealot's left hand and held it tight.

"Twenty one years, nine months, eleven days more, if not for you," he said before fading away.

From the valley below, the cries of the terrorist's people rose to join the howling of the wind. The zealot, though, could not scream, could not escape, could only tremble in fear as, one after another, the ghostly parade accosted him.

A legless old woman dragged herself across the sand toward him and took his hand. "Seven more months," she said, "and I would have seen the birth of my first grandchild, if not for you."

With each word, the zealot felt the aches in his body grow and the fear in his heart swell. The legless woman wailed and vanished into the night.

"Ten years more," said a fat man whose intestines spilled out of his yellow coveralls. He released the zealot's withered, aged hand and faded into the swirling dust.

The terrorist gazed at his fingers, now spotted with age and wracked with arthritis. He blinked his eyes, barely able to see through the cataracts that clouded his vision. He tried to rise but his hips broke under the weight of his body.

A child in a scout uniform stepped forward and took the fanatic's hand. "Seventy years, eleven months, thirty one days, if not for you," the child said.

Finally, the terrorist found the voice to scream, but the sound died in his throat as his larynx withered with age and his skin crumbled like paper.

The next ghost took the remains of the monster's hand and counted the years, days, and months left of a life snuffed out prematurely by unspeakable violence. With each word spoken on the moonlit hill and in the dark camp below, the terrorist and all his fellows aged. Day for day, hour for hour, minute for minute, they repaid the lives of those they had murdered.

By the time the sun rose the next morning all that remained in the valley was blowing dust, and the quiet weeping of the wind.

I'm always interested in knowing where stories come from and why they were written. I'm the type of guy who plays the commentaries on my DVDs, especially if there's a writer or creator commentary. (Joss Whedon is always a hoot!)

So, in this anthology I'm including notes about what I've written and why.

You are not obligated to read these ruminations, but maybe they'll tell you some interesting fact or tidbit, or enhance your enjoyment of some of the stories.

— Steve Sullivan, July 2007

*

Buried Secrets — A MARTIAN KNIGHTS Story
February - March 2001

I'd been writing and sometimes illustrating *The Twilight Empire* in *Dragon* magazine for about four years. The initial TE story was coming to its end, and the magazine's editors were pondering what to do next. Should we continue the TE serial? Should we start something new? I wanted to keep my options open.

Since I'd just spent so long doing a fantasy epic, I thought it might be a good idea to change genres. At the time, *Dragon* dealt with aspects of Sci-Fi gaming as well as fantasy RPGs. I wanted to keep working for *Dragon* (The monthly paycheck was nice.), so I thought I'd give them another option, in case they'd grown tired of fantasy epics. *Martian Knights* was what I came up with, creating a post-war Mars populated with human settlers, strange alien creatures, and deadly cybos.

MK never made it into the magazine, but I still had a bible, story ideas, and even some page samples kicking around my office.

And there all that material lay until Jean Rabe called and asked if I'd like to contribute a Sci-Fi story for *Sol's Children*—an anthology for DAW Books dealing with all the planets in our solar system.

"Can I do Mars?" I asked.

Luckily, no one had spoken for Mars at that point. So, I hauled out my MK material and wrote a new story. Time-wise, "Buried Secrets" would have been a prologue to the magazine series—had the series ever happened.

"Buried Secrets" is a story I'm very pleased with, though it ended up having to be trimmed (just a bit) for the anthology. That's okay, though. Jean's a great editor and the story still worked well. It's nice, however, to finally have it published at its original length—with all of its Martian atmosphere intact.

I hope some day to return to Mars and tell more stories about Sigourney and Wolfgang—including the tale of how they met. Feel free to visit my web site—www.stephendsullivan.com—or my Yahoo Group and encourage me.

A reasonable amount of research went into the story, including a lot of cutting-edge science ideas (at least, they seemed cutting edge to me). The hardest part turned out to be finding a decent map of Mars. You'd think with all the science going on there in the last few decades, someone would have put out a decent globe of the Red Planet. No such luck. Hopefully, Google Mars will shape up and give me something better to work with for the next story.

There are some playful names in this tale. (Authors love playful names.) Sigourney is from Sigourney Weaver, to give my heroine a suggestion of the actress' *Alien* persona. For Sy's last name I wanted something martial sounding, something suggesting armor and strength. I stumbled across "Saxon" while looking for a replacement name. Sy's original surname, "Shields," just wasn't working for me any longer. Tough guy actor and martial artist John Saxon came to my literary rescue. Podkayne's Dune is an obvious reference to SF great Robert Heinlein—one of my favorite authors. General Toth has a tough-sounding name derived from artist Alex Toth.

*

THE COILS OF THE PYTHON
June - July 2000

This story is a bit of an amalgam, combining my love of horror, ancient history and archaeology, and a bit of Indiana Jones. It's written in a pulp style, reminiscent of Robert E. Howard and (my hero) H.P. Lovecraft. The heroine of the tale, Fallon Shana O'Gale, is the sister of my *Luck o' the Irish* hero, Farrell Shawn O'Gale. (And, according to Shawn, his more competent and reliable sister.) Like Shawn, she continues the family tradition of going by her middle name. Maybe I'll do a story with both of them together one day.

I think the idea originated with the image of walking down a snake's back, thinking the serpent was a roadway. That eerie trek into the dark past remains vivid in my imagination to this day. The story may have been suggested, though, by my studies into the Delphic Oracle. Greek mythology has always fascinated me, and this was a great opportunity to delve into it. I even got myself a tour book showing the temple and its grounds as they are now.

The story also features another in a long line of sexy, smart heroines. Adventurous, competent women have played major roles in my stories for most of my career—long before Lara Croft and Buffy the Vampire Slayer took the concept mainstream. And Shana O'Gale is not the last of the tough chicks you'll be seeing in this volume.

Not by a long shot.

And, in genres still dominated by male action heroes, it only seems right that women get their chance.

*

FOREVER CRIMSON
January - February 2000

Dragon magazine (Yes, them again.) was looking for short stories. They weren't looking really hard, but fellow Alliterate Dave Gross had let it be known that they had some slots open in the upcoming months, if I was interested. At the time, I was hoping to expand my short story career and let the *Dragon* audience know I could do more than just comics.

I don't remember if I put together this story specifically in response to Dave's message, or if the call just happened to coincide with me writing the story. The idea of an "eternal hero" who died repeatedly only to be reborn in the bodies of those who died less worthy deaths really grabbed hold of me. I also liked the idea of starting a story with the hero's death.

But the thing that really rang my chimes about this was the conversation between Crimson and the god Chronalos. I wanted to write that scene from the moment I thought of it. It was my favorite part of the story to write, and I still think it's a hoot.

Once again in this story, my heroine is a redhead. Maybe I'm fascinated by women with red hair (and green eyes) because I've never actually known one. Or maybe it's some latent attraction in my Irish genes. Or maybe I'm some kind of premature reincarnation of Robert Heinlein—who was also famous for redheaded heroines. I can't be sure.

In any case, "Forever Crimson" was a strong concept and a fun story to write, even if it never made it into the magazine. Really, the idea is enough to write a whole book about. And maybe some day I'll do that.

The name Orlak is inspired by an old Peter Lorre film, though the god's motif is pure Lovecraft. There's little I write that isn't influenced in some way by either Lovecraft, or Heinlein, or both.

Illion is my original fantasy game world, invented in 1977 when I started playing D&D. It also served as the backdrop for

The Twilight Empire™ comic series. Perhaps I'll get back to telling stories in that world someday. For now, though, I'm wrapped up in the Blue Kingdoms universe I've created with my friend Jean Rabe. The first Blue Kingdoms book, the *Pirates of the Blue Kingdoms* anthology, is out now, and we expect to be doing two or more books in the series every year from here until we're tired of it.

And maybe it's time Orlak put in an appearance in the Azure Sea. Keep your eyes peeled. And watch out for the manticore's tail.

*

THE GIFT OF THE DRAGONS
December 2004 - January 2005

The inspiration for this story should be obvious: the terrible Indian Ocean Christmas Tsunami of 2004. "What would it be like to be caught in such an event?" I wondered, hoping never to actually find out. "And what should people not caught in the destruction do in the aftermath of such a disaster?"

This story is my attempt to answer those questions.

The *Starcutter* and her crew are some of my main characters in the Blue Kingdoms, the world I've co-created with my friend Jean Rabe. Ali is inspired by Sinbad, and may even be the fabled captain's descendent.

My love of water—especially the ocean—is apparent in much of my work. Hardy a story goes by—either fantasy, or sci-fi, or detective, or horror—without some water reference. Growing up with our house on a pond and my grandmother's house on the ocean, I feel a keen affinity for all things aquatic. One of the most obvious manifestations of this in my work is the book *The Dragon Isles*, now sadly out of print. Another is the recently released *Pirates of the Blue Kingdoms*.

Chances are I'll continue writing about rocks and trees and water for the rest of my life.

*

RENAISSANCE FEAR
March 2003

Interestingly, I've written this story twice; once for my *A Season of Fear* project (2007-8), and then, a second time for the *Renaissance Faire* anthology. When Jean called me up for that project (do you see a Rabe-related pattern developing here), I decided to use the story idea I'd developed earlier. But, rather than reworking the original, I recomposed it from scratch. As I recall, I didn't even look at the first version while writing this one.

It'll be interesting to compare it to the other as I finish *A Season of Fear*.

I'm not sure why I didn't review the earlier effort, though I seem to remember I didn't have it easily available. Or maybe I just wanted to make a fresh start. They say that J.R.R. Tolkien wrote the Hobbit at least three separate times, each time putting away the old manuscript and starting anew.

Clearly that worked for him. Did it work for me? When *A Season of Fear* comes out, you'll be able to judge for yourselves.

The impetus of this story comes from the loving "recreations" of history that appear in Ren Faires throughout this country. The fairs are a fun concept, but more of a recreation of movie history than real history. This story was my little jibe on what it would *really* be like if you held a historically accurate Ren Faire. It has an appropriately *Twilight Zone* feel to it, I think.

Speaking of TZ, I was lucky enough to meet Rod Serling when I was a boy. *Night Gallery* was on the air at the time, and I'd been very impressed with "Pickman's Model"—which had a great intro painting and a great monster costume, or so my pre-teen eyes judged. (This was well before I read the works H.P. Lovecraft and discovered where the story had come from and how much scarier the original was.)

I got Serling's autograph in that meeting, but what I'll always remember most is him telling the story of a convict who is hypnotized to believe he's an airplane, which works really well for the con until he crashes. (That story later turned up as a *Night Gallery* episode.)

Serling was a nice guy, and very kind to this budding artist and author. I'm proud to help carry on his storytelling tradition with tales like this one. Look for more in this vein in *A Season of Fear*.

Finally, this story was the one time I got to work with the late, great Andre Norton (through co-editor Jean Rabe). It was an honor to do such a project with one of the pillars of fantasy fiction. Andre said she loved my story, and that she considered it the most disturbing and moody in the entire anthology. I'm sorry we never got to meet in person. Godspeed, Andre.

*

DR. NARCISSUS' HOUSE OF MIRRORS
October - December 2001

The physical decrepitude that creeps up on many of us during middle age became the springboard for this tale of longing and revenge. How many of us haven't looked into the mirror and wished that we couldn't be more like our younger selves?

The creepiness of a carnival midway also inspired this tale. Going to a carny now, rides always seem more decayed than when we were kids—though I doubt they've actually changed at all. As we get older, we also become aware of the seamy underside of the whole carnival life. Traditionally, the carny was a haven for outcasts and misfits. People attended the carnival to see those people—to be scared, thrilled, or just make fun of the less fortunate.

But how different are those carny workers from the people gawking at them? How different are they from the rest of us? I think of these things every time I visit the county fair.

Joe Ordog, mentioned briefly, is named for an old college buddy—whom I've sadly lost track of. As I recall, his last name "Ordog" means something like "devil hound." A very cool name for a character in a horror story, even if it is just a toss-off line.

As with other yarns in this volume, this tale was spurred by a call for stories from anthology editor supreme Jean Rabe. And, again, I was honored to work with her.

The story was published in electronic form in the *Carnival* collection and appears in print for the first time here.

In the years since writing it, I'd forgotten that I'd set this tale in Frosthaven—which makes it the earliest Frost story published, aside from the original e-books. It's also the first Frosthaven-based tale in this collection.

I struggled with the ending of this story quite a bit, trying to get the tone just right. Hopefully, this time, I've nailed it.

*

INTO THE FIRE
October - November 2002

This story was originally published in *Circus*, the companion volume to *Carnival*, in CD format. When the call came for submissions, I just let my mind run through the experiences I'd had at circuses over the years.

I came up with the human cannonball idea, and I wondered, "What *really* happens during an act like that?" What does it take to load yourself into a dark tube with the expectation that an explosion will soon catapult you across the arena where—if you're skilled enough and more than a little lucky—you'll land safely in a net on the other side?

And, who's really beneath those colorful cannonball costumes, anyway? We can't see the performer's faces. The 'who' could be anybody.

It takes a special kind of courage to do such a foolish thing. But it takes an even more special kind of courage to be a Faustino. (Do I need to make the literary origins of that name clear?)

The sinister ringmaster was a given of the assignment, as I recall, but one needn't have read the other stories from the *Circus* collection to understand what kind of devilment he's up to.

The show must go on.

*

TRICKS & TREATS — A FROST HARROW Story
October 2006 - April 2007

It had been a long time since I'd written a story set in my Frost Harrow universe. The original Frost stories were five novels I wrote during 1996 and 1997. They'd been revised for online publication in 1999, but I hadn't really done anything with them since. Since *Frost Harrow* will likely be released as a series of novels in 2007-8, now seemed a good time to revisit the milieu.

I'd almost forgotten how much I like the FH world, which is a contemporary horror setting inspired by the horror movies and TV shows that I've loved since childhood.

The books are an ongoing series of stand-alone horror stories connected by characters, background, and setting. Each book is fairly short and should take only a few days to read. (As a reader, I've grown tired of plowing through 500-page shockers.)

According to my original plan, there would have been a new Frost book every month for as long as I could keep the series going. I had about three years of material planned, and I actually completed five of the books. Back then, I couldn't find a publisher willing to chance such a "radical" idea.

But I haven't given up on the idea. So now I intend to release the *Frost Harrow* books from Walkabout Publishing as I have the time. "Tricks & Treats" is a tiny introduction to the larger milieu. Not quite a prequel; merely a taste.

"Tricks & Treats" was inspired by a program I saw on the History Channel about the origins of Halloween. The show said that the first Halloween treats were set out to ward off visits by the hungry dead.

Well, how cool is that?

And thus, I wrote this story on the 30th and 31st of October, 2006. Then, for a variety of reasons, I completely rewrote it at the end of February, 2007. (Much like I rewrote "Renaissance Fear.")

Play some music from *Dark Shadows* while you read it.

Happy Halloween.

*

THE GHOSTS OF 9/11

In the aftermath of the tragedy, we all did what we could to survive and stay sane. For some of us, the thing to do was write.

The dates given at the start of the story are the dates the tales were written.

THE LAST TERRORIST (9/11/01)

Reading this story again for the first time in years, I'm struck by how prescient it is. It's apparent that even from the first day, I had a good idea of who was behind the attack and what was going on—and what our country's response would be. I don't remember that realization settling in on the rest of the country for a long time. Some people *still* don't get it; they still blame a middle-eastern country for the work of one evil man.

The reason I wrote this story was to grapple with the necessity to end the life of a terrorist like this. Yet, at the same time, I recognized that killing a terrorist makes the executioner no better than he is.

Since that awful day in September, the leaders of the United States have told us that we must fight the enemy using the same tactics they use: fear, misinformation, espionage, violence, torture. Our leaders seem to somehow think that if we just kill enough people, if we just make the whole world frightened enough, the problem will go away.

But violence can't end violence. And fear can't end fear. As a country, I believe we must avoid descending to the level of our enemies.

This story—with its samurai-like commando—is a plea for that.

110 STORIES (9/12/01)

This collection of micro-stories is merely a contemplation of the awful cost of innocent lives lost in terrorist events.

Every person on every floor of the World Trade Center (and in the other targets) had their own hopes and worries, aspirations, and flaws. The terrible events of 9/11 ended many of those stories in an instant.

This tale is a plea to consider the lives lost and to think about the fact that we can *never* know what we've truly lost in such an event.

Fortunately, my projection of a 30-percent survival rate for those in the World Trade Center buildings proved far too bleak.

My hope in presenting the list of survivors in alphabetical order, at the end of the story, was that it would force readers to go back through the story to discover who survived. Those who knew people in the towers were conducting similar searches for their own loved ones. I wanted to invoke empathy with the victims and their friends and families.

My feeling is that if all the terrorists and war-mongers had empathy for their victims, we'd have a lot less trouble in the world.

Many of the names in these stories are friends I've known over the years. Using their names, if not their actual biographies, gave me an even more personal connection with the material. (Plus, it's hard to come up with 111 names just off the top of your head!) I later found out that one of my friends had witnessed the crash into the towers from the hospital room of his dying mother. And another friend barely avoided being trapped in the train terminal under the WTC during the attack.

STRUGGLE IN THE SKY (9/14/07)

This story is wish fulfillment, pure and simple. What if someone had been able to prevent the attacks? What if the people on those planes had overpowered the terrorists?

We know now that many of the doomed passengers fought against their hijackers. But wouldn't it have been nice if all the good guys could have lived?

God, I wish that had happened!

Jason Wu is an ongoing character of mine, though his other stories remain only in note form as of this writing. When you read about him, picture an Asian-American Jackie Chan.

The name Jason is one of my favorite mythological names; I'm a big fan of Jason and the Argonauts, both the story and the Harryhausen film. (Thanks, Ray!)

The woman in the seat next to Jason is similar to Mrs. Avila in *Luck o' the Irish*—a common enough type of air traveler. Like her, I, too, hate take-offs and landings. But, then, I'm not too keen on flying anyway.

FIGHT THE DARKNESS (9/18/01)

This tale is another plea to consider the innocents ravaged by war. It is also a plea that people stop following unjust leaders. If we throw the devil out of our homes, then he cannot take us hostage.

The story also forecasts war and worries about the innocent people who can be hurt in a quest for "justice," especially by a powerful nation like our own.

Again, as evinced here, I remain convinced that we should *not* descend to the level of our enemies—that we should *not* make war on children. Unfortunately, in the real world, our leaders see the deaths of innocents as just "collateral damage."

Looking back, I'm interested in the parable-like approach I used to tell this tale. It clearly shows the influences of Rod Serling and the Biblical movies I've seen over the years.

The story's message is its title, an exhortation to "Fight the Darkness" both within and without.

GHOSTS OF SEPTEMBER ELEVENTH (10/1/01)

A vengeful ghost story and another wish fulfillment tale finishes off the set. Lacking the confidence that our elected leaders could, or would, bring the perpetrators of the 9/11 disaster to justice (a fear that has, at least so far, proven correct), I looked to a less-fallible, supernatural agent to act on our behalf—the ghosts of the slain themselves.

If only we could expect such justice in the real world. But we can't. So, as in the previous stories in this cycle, we must look to ourselves to bring justice and to resist becoming the very thing we hate.

It's dismaying that, nearly six years later as I write this, many of the perpetrators of this crime still have not been caught.

The tale—like the others in this cycle—also contemplates the essential selfishness of terrorists and people who make war.

A "just" war is a very, very rare thing. Chances are that anyone calling *their* war a just one is merely working for their own selfish ends. We've seen this in both terrorists and in leaders who claim to be fighting terrorism while (at the same time) lining their pockets or those of their friends with defense contracts.

Let's do better than that. Let's hold people to a higher standard.

Finally, this story is another tip of the hat to my "weird tales" predecessors, HPL and the rest, and Rod Serling, too, of course. How can one write a short story without thinking of such people? I certainly can't. It also reflects the sensibility of the Fleisher/Aparo *Spectre* stories from the 1970s. I always loved those comics.

That was justice!

About Stephen D. Sullivan

Since 1980, as a writer, artist, and editor, I've worked on some of the best known and most influential properties in the world, including: *Dungeons & Dragons, Teenage Mutant Ninja Turtles, Star Wars, The Simpsons, Middle Earth, Fantastic 4, Speed Rac*er, *Thunderbirds, Dragonlance, Legend of the Five Rings, Iron Man, Darkwing Duck, Mage Knight,* and many others.

I've written (and published) more than 30 books and numerous short stories. I've won the Origins Award, gaming's highest honor, for my fantasy fiction twice: first for *The Lion* (the final book in the original *L5R* series), and then for my *Mage Knight* short story, "Podo & The Magic Shield."

I created, wrote, and colored *The Twilight Empire*™ comic strip, which ran in *Dragon* magazine for more than 4 years. I can't even count (or remember) the number of comics and game projects I've worked on.

All that is nice, but what really matters to me is that my readers enjoy my stories and art. I hope that you will give my work a try, and if you enjoy it—and I feel confident you will—please mention me to your friends.

If you have questions or suggestions, you can contact me by writing to fanmail@stephendsullivan.com.

Thanks!

www.stephendsullivan.com

WALKABOUT PUBLISHING
Great stories by great authors.

Robert E. Vardeman—Michael A. Stackpole—Marc Tassin—James M. Ward
Lorelei Shannon—Dean Leggett—Kathleen Watness—Paul Genesse
Jason Mical—Kelly Swails—Sabrina Klein—Kerrie Hughes—John Helfers
Brandie Tarvin—Donald J. Bingle—Tim Wagonner—Anton Strout
E. Readicker-Henderson—Wes Nicholson—Linda P. Baker—Steven Saus
J. Robert King—Chris Pierson—Daniel Meyers—Elizabeth A. Vaughan
Richard Lee Byers—Jennifer Brozek—Brad Beaulieu—Dylan Birtolo
Paul McComas—William F. Nolan—Annette Leggett—Donald J. Bingle
Stephen D. Sullivan—Jean Rabe—And More!

Pirates of the Blue Kingdoms • Blue Kingdoms: Buxom Buccaneers
Blue Kingdoms: Shades & Specters • Blue Kingdoms: Mages & Magic
Zombies, Werewolves, & Unicorns • Stalking the Wild Hare
Luck o' the Irish • Martian Knights & Other Tales
Stories from Desert Bob's Reptile Ranch • Unforgettable
This and That and Tales About Cats • Uncanny Encounters: Roswell
Under the Protection of the Cow Demon • *And More!*

Walkabout Publishing
P.O. Box 151 • Kansasville, WI 53139
www.walkaboutpublishing.com
Official Home of the Blue Kingdoms.